Rabai al-Madhoun is a Palestinian writer and journalist, born in al-Majdal in southern Palestine in 1945. His family went to Gaza during the Nakba in 1948 and he later studied at Cairo and Alexandria universities, before being expelled from Egypt in 1970 for his political activities. He is the author of the acclaimed *The Lady from Tel Aviv,* which was shortlisted for the International Prize for Arabic Fiction in 2010, and has worked for a number of Arabic newspapers and magazines, including *al-Quds al-Arabi*, *Al-Hayat*, and *Al-Sharq Al-Awsat*. He currently lives in London, in the UK.

Paul Starkey, professor emeritus of Arabic at Durham University, England, won the 2015 Saif Ghobash Banipal Prize for Arabic Literary Translation. He has translated a number of contemporary Arabic writers, including Edwar al-Kharrat, Youssef Rakha, and Mansoura Ez-Eldin.

Fractured Destinies

Rabai al-Madhoun

Translated by
Paul Starkey

First published in 2018 by
Hoopoe
113 Sharia Kasr el Aini, Cairo, Egypt
420 Fifth Avenue, New York, 10018
www.hoopoefiction.com

Hoopoe is an imprint of the American University in Cairo Press
www.aucpress.com

Exclusive distribution outside Egypt and North America by I.B.Tauris & Co Ltd., 6 Salem Road, London, W4 2BU

Dar el Kutub No. 11311/17
ISBN 978 977 416 862 8

Dar el Kutub Cataloging-in-Publication Data

al-Madhoun, Rabai
Fractured Destinies / Rabai al-Madhoun.—Cairo: The American University in Cairo Press, 2018.
p. cm.
ISBN 978 977 416 862 8
1. Arabic Fiction—Translation into English
2. Palestine—History—1948
892.73

1 2 3 4 5 22 21 20 19 18

Designed by Adam el-Sehemy
Printed in the United States of America

First Movement

1

Ivana Ardakian Littlehouse

As soon as Julie's foot touched the first step of the rusty iron staircase leading up to the door of the house—pale blue, like a sky hesitating between winter and summer—the bells of Acre's old churches began to peal, announcing a funeral for which a procession had already been held. The voices of the shopkeepers chasing customers in Acre's old bazaar fell silent. Widad Asfur looked out from the balcony suspended on four wooden columns on the second floor of the adjoining building. "Let's see who's died today!" She spilled her bosom out over the iron edge of the balcony and started to collect her dry washing from the dingy-colored lines strung between two old metal posts on either side, throwing it into a metal basket. She noticed Julie climbing the staircase with a porcelain statue in her hands, whose details she could not make out. "She must be a stranger. What's she doing in our part of town?" she muttered, and pursed her lips. She picked up the basket and turned around to go back inside with her washing. She shut the glass balcony door and murmured a short prayer for the deceased, whoever it might be.

Julie was trembling. Her feelings were confused. Today she was holding a third funeral for her mother, entirely on her own. She wasn't expecting anyone to offer her condolences. She had even refused an offer of participation from her husband, Walid Dahman, as she was getting ready to leave the Akkotel Hotel on Salah al-Din Street where they were staying. She had claimed at that moment that Ivana had secretly conveyed to her a wish that she should be alone when she put half the ashes saved from her body, which the porcelain statue contained, in the house that would be her last resting place. She had walked toward the hotel's front door, as Walid, who was standing in the small hallway, watched her. He had been nervous for and about her, and hurried to catch up. Before she could push open the heavy black metal door of the hotel, which retained some of its original decorations, Walid had put his right hand around her shoulders, and with his left hand had pushed the door open. "Might you need me?" he'd asked in English, in a final attempt to persuade her to change her mind.

Julie had shaken her head, said goodbye to him for a second time, and gone out. Fatima had been waiting for her in her silver Rover at the street corner. Walid had whispered to himself: "If you hadn't been an Englishwoman, with an English father, I'd have said you were stubborn, with a head more solid than the Khalils!" He'd turned to go back in. From somewhere outside had come peals of laughter, growing softer as they moved away toward the eastern gate of the city wall.

Now, Julie heard a song from a street nearby:

Calm, sea, calm.
We have been in exile too long.
I long, I long for peace.
Give my greetings
To the earth that reared us.

Julie stopped. She didn't understand the words. Suddenly, she shuddered. She brought the porcelain statue, cradled in both hands, close to her chest, and raised her head a little toward the sky. *Ten more steps, Julie!* she thought. She considered going back and contenting herself with placing the statue at the foot of the staircase, then hesitated: *But then Ivana's soul will be neglected and forgotten.* She was ashamed of the thought she had just had, and couldn't bear it. She pulled herself together and solemnly continued upward. When she reached the final step, her intermittent panting stopped, and she began to calm down, and breathed normally again. She made the sign of the cross over her breast with feeling. The pealing of the church bells stopped, and Abbud Square surrendered to the noonday siesta that visitors to the city never noticed. In the old bazaar, the shopkeepers' cries resumed, echoing weakly and breaking on the edges of the quarter like exhausted waves reaching the shore.

Julie turned around to look behind her, and saw Fatima al-Nasrawi where she had left her a few minutes ago at the bottom of the staircase near the corner of the house. She had clenched the fingers of both hands together over her belly, below the belt of her slightly too large jeans, from which dangled her car keys.

Fatima looked back at her, sensing that she was torn between her wish to complete her task and her fears. She started to say something, then hesitated. She was relieved to have done so, for it spared her the need to say what she was going to say (though if she had said it, the account that Julie later gave to Walid when she got back to the Akkotel Hotel would certainly have been different). In the end, which came quickly enough, Fatima merely gestured to Julie to knock on the door, then turned around the corner of the house and walked away, without waiting to find out what happened after that.

It was Fatima who had shown Julie the building that had been the house of her mother's father, Manuel Ardakian, and had taken her to it. In Acre, they knew her as 'Fatima the Know-all' and sometimes called her 'Sitt Maarif.' People referred to her in her absence as 'Lady Information' and correctly described her profession as 'popular guide.' Some said she knew all the features and details of Acre better than any history or geography book. Others praised her philosophy of distributing historical facts to foreign tourists free of charge, and kept on the tips of their tongues her saying (as well known as she was herself): "We give them accurate information free of charge, it's better than them buying lies from the Jews for a price!" The people of Acre would make use of this quotation of hers when they needed to.

What a rare resident of Acre she was! She had passed through Julie and Walid's life like a gentle breeze, although a raging storm could not have borne her away. Walid had got to know her just a day before Julie visited her grandfather's house. He had introduced her to Julie on the advice of Jamil Hamdan, his old friend from a period with a leftist flavor, when they had been students in a school that trained Communist Party cadres in Moscow, where they had shared a passion for the Russian Jewess Ludmilla Pavlova—Luda, now Jamil's wife.

"My dear Walid, there's no one who can help you except 'Sitt Maarif.' Here's her telephone number, keep it on your cellphone!" Jamil had said as he drove them—Julie, Luda, and Walid—to Haifa.

He went on: "You'll love Fatima, Walid. A woman from Acre, dark as coffee roasted over coals. She drives you crazy and blows your mind! True, she's round as a truck tire, but she's an encyclopedia, my friend! And her tongue's quicker than a Ferrari!"

Everyone in the car had laughed.

When Walid and Julie reached the Akkotel Hotel in Acre, after a night spent at Jamil's house in the Kababir district of Haifa, Walid phoned Fatima, then took a taxi to Rashadiya in New Acre, where Fatima lived in an apartment in a building outside the city walls. When he got out of the taxi, he found Fatima waiting for him at the bottom of the building. It wasn't difficult for him to recognize her. Jamil's description of Fatima was enough. Her friendly smile fitted the description perfectly.

With no hesitation, she kissed him on both cheeks, and before withdrawing her lips—slender as plucked eyebrows—whispered in his ear: "A kiss from a girl in your city will keep you in Acre for the rest of your life!"

He was astonished. "Do you want to lock me up in the Old Acre prison?" he asked her. She laughed.

Most of the men of Acre left the city in '48 and are in exile, he thought. *What use for them were all the kisses they received before they left, or even all the wild parties?* He smiled with a sadness as wide as the distance that was later to separate them.

Walid outlined to Fatima the reason for his and his wife's visit to Acre. He explained that Julie was half English, and that her other half was from Acre.

"And is the Acre half on top or underneath?" she asked him.

Walid laughed. "You must have been watching *The School for Scandal*! In any case what I see is the genuine half!"

"Very diplomatic," she commented, and rolled her eyes.

He talked to her a bit about his late mother-in-law, the British-Palestinian-Acre-Armenian, Ivana Ardakian Littlehouse, and about her will, which was why Julie would be visiting her grandfather's house. They quickly arranged the details of the visit in the street, Walid politely refusing the cup of Acre coffee that Fatima invited him to take in her apartment.

Walid learned from Fatima that after Manuel and his wife Alice had left the city on 16 May 1948—two days, that is, before the city had fallen into the hands of Jewish forces—the Ardakian house stayed closed up for several years. The house was one of around 1,125 houses that had remained in good condition after the end of the war. Half of them were by now in need of repair, and a few of them were in danger of collapse. One of them had fallen in on the occupants the previous year, and five people had been killed. He also learned from her that a Jewish family by the name of Laor, comprising five people, had taken the house from the Israeli housing company Amidar, which together with the Acre Development Company had responsibility for managing eighty-five percent of the houses in the city that the state counted as 'absentees' property.' It still controlled 600 properties, and was keeping another 250 properties closed up to prevent Palestinians from living there.

The Laor family was one of several Jewish families, refugees from the Nazi genocide, who were living in the Old City—the previous occupants having fled under the pressure of the Jewish artillery bombardments that had preceded the occupation. The family included two sons and a daughter, all three of whom had been raised in the Ardakian house. They had all left the house and the city, one after the other, after completion of their compulsory military service and their transfer to the reserves, which usually continued without interruption until the age of forty-five. So the young Laors—or ha-La'orim ha-tas'irim, as Fatima called them in Hebrew—disappeared from the register of information circulating orally in Acre. 'Sitt Maarif' thought that their elderly parents had stayed in the Ardakian house until the end of the 1980s, after which she had not seen them. None of the Palestinian residents of the Old City remembered anything about them. No one claimed to have seen either of them, alone or together, in the city or outside it, for years.

Walid asked Fatima who was living in the house now. She gave a laugh to hide her slight embarrassment, and replied, "I know that the house has been lived in for about a year, but to tell the truth no one I know has any information on who's living there." She said nothing more. Walid, too, was silent, in the hope that she might add something useful to what she had already said. Fatima took advantage of their conspiracy of silence to change the subject.

"By the way, Mr. Walid, I'd like to apologize to you, and I ask you to apologize for me to your wife as well about tomorrow—I shall have to take Julie to the Ardakians' house and then come back. I have a Swedish tourist group that I want to take around the town before they fall into the hands of Jewish guides."

Walid made no comment. But when she noticed the sudden look of surprise on his face, she quickly suggested to him that he postpone the visit for three hours, after which she would have finished her tour with the Swedish delegation. Walid told her that time might not allow it. Fatima expressed her regrets and renewed her apologies. Walid thanked her.

"The Swedes, and Scandinavians more generally, like the Palestinians a lot," he said. He asked her not to worry about Julie and to take good care of the Swedish group. Then he said goodbye to her with a few light-hearted expressions, asking her to bring her information on Old Acre up to date "so that they don't strip you of your title 'Sitt Maarif.'"

He watched as she went back inside.

Julie took a single step forward. The house door, garbed in heavy mystery, stared at her. She raised her gaze up to the sky, and took in a bright blue expanse full of quiet summer clouds, and a sun that had been enjoying the sea breezes since the morning. She considered what 'Sitt Maarif' had said to her as they had made their way toward the house, and recalled her own comment in response: "You love Acre a lot, Sitt Maarif!"

And she remembered Fatima's reply: "Who doesn't love Acre? God willing, anyone who hates it will go blind in both eyes! Acre is this world and the next, my dear! An Acre man who goes outside the wall becomes a stranger, darling ("stranger, darling, stranger," she repeated in English), and an exile as well, I swear."

Julie was touched by Fatima's words. And although she hadn't understood the expression 'go blind in both eyes,' she had felt the exile of the people of Acre. Then in a whisper she had sighed for her mother: "Poor Mama Ivana, she was another resident of Acre who died a stranger."

Later, she recalled how Fatima had picked up what she had whispered between her lips and found it strange, "What, my dear? Your mother died in London a stranger from Acre? Well, just look at us here, strangers and refugees in our own country. So there's no difference between the dead and the living where we're concerned, praise God and thank Him."

2

ONE LATE, LAZY MORNING, INCHING its way toward noon, Ivana called her daughter Julie, and asked her to come with Walid to her home in the Earls Court area of London that evening to have a home-cooked supper, for an occasion that she said would be extremely private. She would be saying something that neither of them should hear without the other being there.

The couple reached Ivana's house just before seven. Walid parked his Peugeot behind Ivana's old black Mercedes, and they both got out. As they turned toward the entrance to the house, Julie noticed a silver Jaguar beside Ivana's car.

"It seems Mr. Byer has beaten us here, Walid!" she said.

"I suppose he must have been invited like us," he replied.

"I thought this was supposed to be a private affair."

"I guess we'll know what it's all about soon," replied Walid, as he pressed the bell by the front door.

"I've a feeling that Mama has decided to sell her house and move to a smaller apartment. It can't be a coincidence, Byer being here. Perhaps Ivana has really started to feel lonely. Her housekeeper is really important to her. She emailed me last week to say, as a joke, that the house—which is so warm that it doesn't need central heating—had started to shiver with cold. I told her off for letting Amanda take a holiday without telling me. If she'd done that, I could have arranged a stand-in for her, or at least visited her myself."

"Don't forget that we . . . "

Ivana opened the door before he could finish the sentence. She spread her arms, embraced her daughter, and kissed her with an intensity that exceeded her usual compassion. Then she embraced Walid, kissing him in a way that confirmed that her pleasure in him was a little more than he would have liked. She invited them both to come in and meet the others.

First, Mr. Byer, whose car had shown he was there, and his wife Lynn. Walid recalled Julie's wondering why they had been invited to a meeting that Ivana herself had said was private and confidential.

William Byer was renowned as a lawyer representing a large number of well-known middle-class people who perched at the top of their class and breathed its exclusive air. He had been a close friend of Julie's father, the late John Littlehouse. The two men had served in their younger days in the British armed forces in Palestine, and they had both reached the rank of major. They had been brought together by both their military rank and the death they had escaped at the same moment: when the Jewish Irgun organization, under its leader Menachem Begin, blew up the King David Hotel in Jerusalem—used as headquarters by the British Mandate authorities—on 22 July 1946. Forty-one Palestinians had been killed, as well as twenty-eight British, seventeen Jews, and five people of other nationalities, and forty-five people had been injured in various ways. The two British officers had escaped from the incident, and new features of their relationship became apparent after the dust of death had settled. But fate, which had saved John from death during the great explosion, returned to frustrate his life's key ambition, for he died before his daughter could marry Walid. Ivana inherited John's possessions, including the house that she lived in, his black Mercedes, a sum of money, and the friendship of Byer, whom Ivana had gotten to know during one of her secret romantic meetings with John before she had left Palestine. He continued to remind her of the most beautiful days of her life, stolen from the period of the British Mandate, so she kept him beside her later, and entrusted him with her financial and legal affairs.

Walid and Julie shook hands in turn with the short man with the classic spectacles, then shook hands with his wife in a matter-of-fact way. Julie didn't like Lynn, and had never understood her relationship with Ivana, beyond the fact that she was Byer's wife. Lynn was mean, pretentious, and more grasping than a tabloid newspaper.

Julie hid her shock at Lynn being there and didn't give anything away to upset Ivana. She calculated that her mother might have done this on purpose to publicize whatever took place that evening to the whole of British society.

Then Walid moved on, followed by Julie, and shook hands with Leah Portman, Ivana's friend, the Jewish poetess to whom she had introduced them more than ten years previously. Although they were happy to know her, they were nervous at the presence of Kwaku, who had lived with her for years. They were both wary of developing a close friendship with him, for reasons that had some logic to them. Kwaku was a strange character, though he was nice enough—despite often seeming as obscure as a password, and as puzzling as a riddle, raising unconventional questions. That sometimes made Walid uneasy, though Julie sensed some exaggeration in his attitude and was more inclined to think that Kwaku was just nice. She thought that sitting with him once or twice a year added some enjoyment to the events of their life.

Kwaku talked about himself in elegant language, in tones of royalty. From time to time, hints of aristocratic attitudes flitted across his face, even when he was confessing to others that he had no roots himself. Walid remembered how, during dinner together at the Suq Moroccan restaurant in Covent Garden, he had told him and Julie a murky story about his parents, the details of which were difficult to grasp. He said that he was the son of a Nigerian father—whose religion was unknown—and an Argentinian Christian mother. His father had divorced his mother when he was five years old, so she had taken him to her family in Buenos Aires. But she hadn't put up with being single for long; she had married a Mexican immigrant, who took them both with him to New York. His new stepfather didn't put up with Kwaku's presence for long, however, but threw him out of the house before he was ten. He had wandered for years before settling down as a worker in a fuel station.

Kwaku had a habit of giving away a lot of details about himself that he wasn't obliged to relate, as when he confessed in front of Walid and Julie on another occasion that he had been born with one testicle, saying that this fact hadn't worried Leah at all, because he didn't need a second testicle to make love, and as for having children, she didn't want them at all. At this point, Leah had laughed and praised his one testicle, saying that he was a rare man as a result. She had also confirmed what Kwaku had said about her not wanting children, claiming that if she'd really wanted children she would have had a whole battalion of them.

According to Kwaku's revelations on that occasion, he had already had six children with a former wife, though he could no longer remember when he'd married her, or where and when he'd left her, or even his reasons for doing so. Or maybe he preferred to be evasive about a family that in practice no longer belonged to him, and perhaps had never really belonged to him at all.

But Leah loved Kwaku a lot, with his mysteriousness and his ambiguities whose complications were difficult to unravel. In fact, their first chance meeting had been as ambiguous as his personality. They were standing in a queue in front of a young check-out girl in the Sainsbury's store in Holborn. She was in front of him, and he stared at her long, soft, blonde hair. His glances took in her shoulders, from which hung arms worthy of a dancer. Suddenly, as she stood there, Leah shuddered, and staggered backward a little. Kwaku instinctively put out his hands to catch her. In a few seconds, she was in a swoon in a pair of strong ebony arms. Her swoon didn't cause much of a commotion, but a whisper went around those standing nearby. Kwaku asked the girl on the till for some water and a bottle of perfume. The young girl left her place behind the computer, another employee in the store ran to fetch a plastic water bottle, and a lady standing in the queue got out a bottle of perfume. She opened it, shook it a little, and some drops fell into Kwaku's outstretched hand. He touched the perfume to Leah's face, and she began to recover from her short fainting spell. She opened her eyes in the man's arms, to see his face scrutinizing hers, with a smile all over it. When she was completely conscious again, and straightened up, his arms were still around her. Leah turned around as his arms dropped away from her, took a sip of water, and let out a sigh of satisfaction. The customers applauded the moving scene. Leah wished she had stayed longer in Kwaku's arms, even if it meant fainting for longer. She was embarrassed to be wishing it. She lifted her head to look at him.

"Thank you very much. You saved me from falling. I don't know what happened to me."

"The main thing is, how are you feeling now?"

"I'm fine, just a slight headache."

"An earthquake of emotions usually leaves behind an aftershock, because of its internal laws," replied Kwaku.

Leah smiled, and trembled slightly. As Kwaku took her back into his arms, she apologized to him for her aftershock, and then gently withdrew toward the check-out girl.

They both made their purchases, put them in plastic bags, and paid. Leah reached the door before him, and paused. She turned around and looked at him over her shoulder. She saw him smile, and his smile awoke her whole life, cleansing it of the suspicious thoughts that had surrounded her since childhood, when her mother Jennifer had impressed upon her: "Don't mix with strangers, Leah. Keep away from black men, Arabs, and Muslims, my dear."

He stretched out his hand, and Leah did not hesitate to take it. She was consciously taking him back, reproducing the moments she had lost when she'd fainted in his arms. At that moment, she felt her wall of fears collapse.

"My name's Kwaku. Kwaku Wol."

"I'm Leah, Leah Portman. An expressionist poet."

"Wow, that's exciting! I'm a guitar player. We could work together, then. We'd make a fabulous artistic duo."

She invited him for a cup of coffee in the Café Rouge near the supermarket. He accepted, and they walked together, carrying their plastic shopping bags to the café like old friends. When he had finished his drink, she took his cup, turned it over, and said, "If there was Arabic coffee in your cup, I could read your fortune in it."

Kwaku laughed and asked her, "Have you really learned to do that?"

"Yes. I was taught it by an old Palestinian woman I met during my visit to Jerusalem two years ago. It's just an amusing way of uncovering what is in people's hearts."

Since that first meeting, Leah had opened up to Kwaku a long corridor that she strewed with her emotions, which Kwaku walked through contentedly to her heart. Every time they met, the corridor became wider, until it became a way of life that effaced all the hatred that Jennifer had inflicted on Leah's childhood.

Leah really surprised herself. She had never imagined, it had never occurred to her, that she would make friends with a British man like Walid, who had sown Palestine in the cells of his body and made them into pools of mint, or that she would live a real love story, the only real one in her life, with a black man like Kwaku, whom she really loved. She never asked him about his origins or his religion, or about his one testicle (which didn't bother her), or about any of the other details she had heard from him which were the subject of gossip but never quite added up. At least, that is what she several times said in front of Walid and Julie.

The guests didn't stay long in the sitting room before the hostess invited everyone to make their way into the dining room. The six guests sat around the rectangular table in the middle of the room, three on each side of the table facing each other, while Ivana, as was her habit, sat at the head of the table, beside the window that looked out over the street, opposite John's seat, which had remained empty since he died. She gazed at it for some time.

"Where are the wine glasses, Mother?" asked Julie. Ivana apologized for her unintentional lapse, and asked Julie to fetch seven glasses. Julie excused herself and went off into the kitchen, with Walid following her, pretending to be wanting to help her.

In the kitchen, she whispered some thoughts to him that she had quickly put together.

"Mother is planning something big, Walid."

"What do you mean?" he asked in a whisper.

"It seems that it's more than just selling a house."

"Listen, darling, if it's to do with your mother's estate and her property, leave her to deal with them as she wishes," he said forcefully, though still in a whisper.

"I've never thought about that at all, Walid," she replied, then corrected herself with a measure of seriousness, as she put the seven ribbed glasses on a silver tray. "Oh, I remember . . ."

She hesitated a little before finishing her sentence, raising the tray between her hands and lifting her eyes toward him: "Mother is thinking of . . ."

Ivana's voice interrupted her: "Come on, guys!" she called.

Julie picked up the tray and went out, leaving the rest of her sentence between her lips. Walid took a bottle of wine from a shelf in the bar and followed her.

Ivana welcomed her guests formally, and asked them to listen to her without interrupting. The lawyer nodded to show he understood. His wife Lynn smiled at an anticipated feast of words sufficient for gossip to fill all the remaining months of the year. Kwaku lowered his chin onto his clenched palm, watching expectantly as he waited for what Ivana would say. Julie's green eyes were fixed on her mother's lips, ready to pick up her words the moment they were formed. Walid contented himself with following the expectation on their faces.

When she spoke, Ivana surprised everyone. She summoned up her distant past, relating her stories with her eyes fastened on her dead John's seat. She made them listen to a lot that they knew already, as well as some things that they had no knowledge of. She spoke about her early youth: she had been a teenager when she had fallen in love with the young medical officer John Littlehouse, who had given his daughter Julie his surname, together with the green color of her eyes and other details that anyone who had known him while he was alive could recognize in her features, even after she had turned sixty. She turned to Julie, as if to reassure herself that John's features were still there on her daughter's face. As if looking at the dead man in his seat opposite her, she said that he had been a handsome man, whom it was difficult for a girl of her age to resist at that time. Then she sighed, so deeply did she miss him, and started talking about her happy memories in detail. She said that a look from John's eyes was worth the whole blue sky of Acre, and that she had never for a moment thought about the madness of her relationship with him, in case her reason might make her lose the best love story she had ever lived. She said that from the moment she had fallen in love with John, he had no longer been for her a hated British colonizer or a medical officer, but rather the only young man who had knocked her down with his first smile. The young men of Abbud Square and the Sheikh Abdallah and Fakhura quarters, as well as her colleagues in the Terra Sancta School, would scatter their morning smiles at her feet as she walked along with the coquettishness of a teenager, showing off the power of her beauty over others, never turning to pick any of them up. She was ready to do anything to bind herself to John forever, even if a great war should break out between Great Britain and Abbud Square, engulfing all the Armenians of Acre.

She said all this and more, but was silent about the details of the real war that had flared up at the time in St. George's Church between the members of the Ardakian family and the residents of the quarter, which had inflamed their feelings and darkened their spirits. She didn't tell them about her last moments in Acre, the details of which some local residents still remembered and gossiped about decades later.

One calm July morning, the officer John Littlehouse arrived in Acre in a military jeep, which took him and a companion to Old Acre, where the driver stopped in Fakhura Street near al-Hadid Tower. John got out and walked toward the Fakhura quarter. He passed quickly through several narrow, winding lanes to the Maaliq quarter, and from there to Abbud Square. He walked to within a very short distance of the fountain in the middle of the square, and put his foot on the marble base.

Ivana was ready to leave the house of her parents, who had gone out to church in the morning. At that moment, she heard the sound of a heavy shop door being closed. She opened the front door of the house and heard Mitri, the shoe shop owner, shout: "I'd like to know who brought this Englishman here to us! What's he doing in our quarter?"

Ivana realized that John was early and had already arrived in the square, and that his arrival must have upset Mitri and the owners of the other shops that were open. She closed the front door and ran down the twenty steps of the staircase. She peeped around the corner of the house and surveyed the neighborhood. She saw Mitri standing in front of his shop with his face in turmoil, like someone emerging from a fight that was still unfinished. But she didn't see John in the square as she had expected. Instead, she saw little Ata, the son of Widad Asfur, kicking a small stone and chasing it. John had left the square quickly after hearing Mitri's shouts, sensing the man's anger. He was hiding in the alley that led to the Sheikh Abdallah quarter. Ivana left the house and walked past Mitri, who quickly displayed his emotions in front of her, and warned her: "Tell the man who brought you up at home, the residents of the Abbud quarter will not marry off their daughters to the British—they've been riding the country for thirty years, holding on to our shoulders and kicking their feet. And now they have to ride our women as well?"

Ivana hurried off without a word and soon spotted John, calling to him in English, "Hurry up, John! Let's go, darling!"

The young man grabbed Ivana's hand, and they left the quarter, hurrying through the quarters of Maaliq and Fakhura to the jeep that was waiting for them, leaving Abbud Square to continue its clash of tongues on its own.

John and Ivana were married a long way from Acre and its people. They had a small, untraditional party at a British base near Haifa, where the couple spent their wedding night amid the officers and men of the base.

Then Ivana became pregnant, and in due course was delivered of a beautiful girl who looked like her father and whom they named Julie. In March 1948, Ivana left the country with her two-month-old daughter in her arms. She disappeared from her parents' lives and from Abbud Square, where she had grown up. She became a mirage that visited the square on occasions to remind them of the scandal, a wind that blew somewhere else whose sound no one heard.

People said, "Ivana's in the custody of the English!" People also asked, "Wasn't Palestine enough for them? Did they have to take its daughters as well?" As for her father, Manuel, and her mother, Alice . . . they announced that they had disowned their only daughter the day after she left the quarter.

When 15 May 1948 came, Britain finished winding up its camps, leaving Palestine to Jewish military groups, who declared the establishment of the state of Israel. John went back to Britain, along with the other soldiers of the Empire who were withdrawing from most of the country.

On 18 May 1948, Acre fell into the hands of Jewish forces. Antranik Ardakian, Manuel's brother and Ivana's paternal uncle, was killed in the last battle to defend Acre, along with a number of volunteers armed with old rifles, who gathered in the police station under the command of Ahmad Shukri Manna.

Manuel and Alice fled to Lebanon by the coast road two days before the city fell. They stayed in a forest near the district of Furn al-Shubbak. The forest was later sold, and in 1952 the United Nations Relief and Works Agency (UNRWA) and the Lebanese government leased a piece of land in the region of Jisr al-Basha, where they established a camp, which bore the name of the locality. Manuel and Alice moved to the camp with more than three thousand other Palestinians, a mixture of Orthodox and Catholic Christians who had been forced to flee from Haifa, Acre, and Jaffa.

Manuel lived a wretched life in the Jisr al-Basha camp—a life that ended with his death two months before the outbreak of the Civil War in April 1975. He died in a state of grief for himself, for his brother Antranik, and for his daughter, all of whose attempts at a reconciliation he had refused. He didn't reply to her letters, which continued to reach him for the first five years after their elopement. Ivana implored him at least to accept and recognize his granddaughter, Julie, but she received no reply from him. On 29 June 1976, Alice was killed during a raid by the Lebanese Phalange on the Jisr al-Basha camp, the remaining inhabitants of which were forced to leave.

Ivana fell silent as she surrendered to an enormous wave of sadness that broke over her face. Her lips reacted with a tremor, and she clasped her hands tensely. Tears flowed from her eyes, as if stored up during the years of her loneliness since John had died. Everyone else—Byer and his wife, Leah and Kwaku, Walid and Julie—remained quiet as they contemplated her sadness, which had spilled over as her story had unfolded. She had never told it in such detail before, though it was still incomplete even now.

Eventually, Ivana dried her face with her hands, wiping from it the pain of her past, some of which she had recalled herself, and some of which had appeared despite herself. Then she spoke in a voice thick with suffering: "If I'd just said that my parents had died without my seeing them for more than fifty years, you wouldn't have believed me."

"Oh, Mama!" Julie let out a wail of sympathy for her mother. She got up from her chair, and moved behind Ivana. She took her head between her hands, then bent over it tenderly and kissed it. As she returned to her place, she said, "It's enough for me that my father and you were great lovers."

Ivana's lips parted in a smile that she hadn't displayed for a long time.

"Forgive me, my friends," she said. "I've upset us all. Perhaps my past has returned to bid me farewell."

She sat up straight and went on: "My friends, I invited you here today to say something else, which has nothing to do with my past or with my inheritance." Then she turned to Byer and addressed him in a business-like tone: "Mr. Byer, we will add some further details to my will together. I will come to your office for this purpose at a time that we will agree on later."

Byer nodded, as Ivana calmly continued:

"I may not live much longer. I want my body to be cremated after my death, and my funeral eulogy to be delivered to the John Lennon song 'Imagine.' I would like this song, which does not die as mortals die, to be the last thing my ears hear before the fire consumes them and they are turned to ash. Anyone who wants to deliver a eulogy shouldn't speak for too long, so as not to have to make up things that aren't among my attributes. Funeral eulogies, my dears, are usually nothing more than a recalling of the deceased, through advertised and prearranged parties, which the speakers use to wipe out the wrongs they did to the dead person during his or her lifetime. If I knew the exact time of my death, I would ask everyone who was going to mourn me to write down for me on a piece of paper what they were going to say, so that I could revise it before I passed away forever, with no questions afterward and no possibility of introducing amendments. After the end of the cremation formalities, you will scatter a handful of ashes from my body over the River Thames, which will carry them throughout the waters of the ocean. You, my dear Julie, and you, Walid, will be responsible for that."

Walid made no comment. Julie's fingers did it for him. They stretched out to Ivana's hand lying on the table and came to rest on top of it. Ivana put her other hand on top of Julie's, and they contented themselves with exchanging glances.

Ivana continued speaking, giving instructions that another handful of her body's ashes should be placed in a glass jar thirty centimeters high, the color of the sea in summer, and the shape of her own body in every season: a neck of haughtiness (she raised her head); a chest of pride (she pulled herself upright in her chair, revealing the elegance of her prominent, aristocratic nose); a waist encircled by a lover's hands (she put her two thumbs and her two forefingers together so that they formed a small circle); the belly of a virgin; and a Bedouin behind. She asked for the container to be taken to her parents' house in Abbud Square in Old Acre. "Take part of me and all of my spirit to Acre, so that they may apologize to it quarter by quarter. Take my remains and carry them in procession where I was born, just as London will carry me in procession where I die. My friends and loved ones, one day soon I shall die. I want to be buried here and to be buried there."

She fell silent for a minute and the whole company shared in her silence, before turning to Julie and Walid. "If it's too difficult a matter for some reason or other, I should be very happy for you to take half of my remains to Old Jerusalem. I know that Walid has friends there, and you may like to visit them and arrange to deposit the statue with them, or with any Palestinian family who will accept it."

Walid and Julie nodded their agreement. With a smile of satisfaction, Ivana added, "I want you to visit the Church of the Resurrection if you visit Jerusalem, which I think you certainly will. Pray for me, for that may purify my soul. And if things go smoothly, hold a small party with the mourners in the house that is to receive my remains. Burn sacred incense, and listen carefully to Fairuz raising the flower of cities to the highest heavens, and let her voice fill the city. I am sure I will hear it as well, because I shall be there in heaven."

Everyone understood Ivana's wishes. Each in their own way, they all showed a deep understanding of what she had said. Mr. Byer was thinking of his legal role in drawing up her will in relation to her wealth and the possessions that she still had; Lynn was preoccupied with finding the best way to remember the details of Ivana's instructions and to spread them around; Leah was thinking of the loss of a dear friend, which might happen at any moment; Kwaku was awaiting the next scene. And while Walid was thinking how careful his mother-in-law was being in arranging the rituals that would follow her death, Julie was hesitating between Ivana's two options; she had instinctively understood that her mother was afraid that Acre would curse her in death exactly as it had cursed her in life, so she had opened another window for her soul in Jerusalem, seeking mercy.

Walid poured out the wine. Before Ivana could raise her glass to signal the end of her instructions with regard to her funeral and the start of the party she had promised, Walid teased her: "Do you know, the Jews believe that anyone whose body is buried in Jerusalem will be the first to be resurrected, and will be at the head of the queue of people waiting at the door to paradise on the Day of Resurrection?"

"Then allow me the opportunity to reserve myself a place in the queue with a handful of ashes before the heavens are filled with settlers who have forced the Palestinians out in this world and want to appropriate their places in the next."

Everyone laughed and exchanged toasts amid the clink of glasses. With one voice they cried, "God bless Ivana!" They wished her a long life, then began attacking the food.

It didn't occur to any of them that the gathering that evening would be the last time they met with Ivana. She died just one week later.

3

Ivana passed away on a warm summer's day. Her body was laid out in a wooden coffin, in the wedding gown she had worn at her second wedding reception, held after she and John had returned to London in May 1948 from Palestine. Ivana had kept her dress all those years, just as she had kept all the dimensions of her body, so that she might depart this world as a bride for the third and last time.

The mourners cast their final glances on Ivana's face in turn. When they had finished, Julie came forward and contemplated her mother's face. Ivana's expression was relaxed; a slight smile remained on her lips, the smile of a child dreaming for the first time, the same smile that had lit up the last picture taken of her in Acre before she had left her parents' house. Julie closed her eyes on Ivana's final scene.

Soon after, the coffin was closed. As it began to move slowly down a mechanical metal conveyor belt, the voice of John Lennon rose up loud and clear. When Julie opened her eyes again, Ivana's body had disappeared behind thick, coffee-colored curtains.

In the evening, Walid and Julie went back home, weighed down by their emotions. He went straight into his study. He put his feelings to one side and gave himself up to writing—he had to finish a chapter of a new novel. He had promised his relative Jinin Dahman that he would let her see his progress when they met in Jaffa. Meanwhile, his wife carried on with arranging the first stages of the remainder of her mother's will.

Two days after the cremation, Julie collected Ivana's ashes in two small porcelain jars as she had been instructed. She took one of them to the Ashes Into Glass company in south London, and commissioned another container, also of porcelain, in the shape of a statue with the details that Ivana had specified.

Some days later, she went back to the same company, at a time already agreed. Peter Hopkins, the company's skilful designer, gave her the requested porcelain container. On the belly of the statue was inscribed the phrase: "She died here . . . she died there." Underneath, in smaller letters, was written: "London–Acre, 2012."

She raised her head toward Peter to thank him, tears in her eyes. The young man quickly presented her with a bracelet, which he had made himself from a mixture of Ivana's ashes and colored molten crystal. The two halves of the bracelet ended with the wings of a butterfly spotted with crimson dots. On the inside of the two wings had been etched the dates of Ivana's birth and death.

"This is for you," said Peter.

The young man took hold of Julie's right wrist and slipped the bracelet over it. Her hand trembled between his fingers, but she was calmed by a vague feeling that her mother would be there with her forever.

Julie went back home, conflicting emotions crowding her face. She put the statue on the make-up mirror stand in the bedroom. She opened the left-hand drawer of the dressing table, and took out a silver chain, hanging from which was a cross as small as her faith, which Ivana had given to her before she had died. She bent over the porcelain statue and twisted the chain several times around its neck, leaving the cross to hang over its breast. Around the statue's hips she twisted a fine strip of one of Ivana's colored silk scarves.

A week after Ivana's death, Julie took the second porcelain container and went with Walid to Waterloo Bridge in the center of London. A few meters before the middle of the bridge, they stopped, near a spot looking over the Royal National Theatre building. The evening was turning into night, undisturbed by rain, unruffled by wind. The South Bank area below the bridge, and all along the river as far as Westminster Bridge behind them, jostled with comings and goings of every kind, with men and women of different ages and nationalities sharing their happinesses and their griefs on the river's wide banks. Under the bridge, outside the theatre, a musical group played the *Concierto de Aranjuez* by the Spanish composer Joaquín Rodrigo.

Julie leaned a little over the bridge's black metal railing. She turned the container upside-down and shook it gently, and Ivana's ashes scattered down to the water below, as was her wish. As the strains of *Mon amour*, the second movement of the concerto, rose into the air, Julie and Walid quietly repeated, "Goodbye, Ivana, goodbye."

4

In Julie's absence, Walid decided to stroll around the streets of Old Acre. He left the Akkotel Hotel and walked along Salah al-Din Street. After about forty meters, he was brought to a halt by a white cloth sign, which had been hung on the corner of the Nazareth Sweets shop on the left side of the street. On it, he read in Arabic, English, and Hebrew: "We will not move out." He recalled what he had heard from the owner and manager of the hotel just a few minutes before:

"Now, sir, it's the French Jews who are attacking us. One group's coming after another, may God be your protector, and their pockets are stuffed with money. They go all around the houses outside the wall. They offer the owners high prices, far more than you can imagine. A house that's about to fall down is worth more than one that's standing. There are people, Mr. Walid, ground down by poverty, who have sold their houses. And there are others who've sold up because they've had so much trouble from the fundamentalist Jews who've occupied houses here and there. Then there are people who don't want to sell up, and never will. These are the *real* people of Acre, the people who hold onto their land, and their homes, and their identity, who will cling onto Acre's stones with their fingernails. These are the people who stood up to the French and the others, and threw them out. We can hear their shouting when we're in the hotel, coming up to us from the street: 'We don't have houses for sale!' But there are also people who dream of the homeland. What can we say? Okay, let the Arabs who are loaded with money buy them! No one will wake up and understand, Mr. Walid, that the Jews don't just want our houses, they want to buy them and sell off our history for nothing!"

The sign reminded him of another, which the Shona district committee had prepared and hung up on a wall in the Old City, in Hebrew and Arabic: 'My House Is Not For Sale.' But it also recalled a third sign, which had been hung on the bars of a window he had passed earlier with Julie, on which had been written, again in two languages:—'House For Sale.'

Walid continued on his way, his head full of signs challenging other signs, and slogans contradicting each other, while the houses of Old Acre, and the five and a half thousand residents who still occupied them, waited in a queue of victims of creeping Judaization—like the five buildings in the Maaliq quarter that had been restored for the Ayalim Society and had then been taken over by Orthodox Jewish university students.

The White Market, which no longer retained the color of its name, held little to detain him. There seemed to be nothing there except for an arched roof and the doors of shut-up stalls, so he walked past. He turned left, then branched to the right, and in less than four minutes was inside the Popular Market, standing in front of Hummus Saeed. There were some tourists gathered in front of the restaurant. They had taken over the four steps in front of the entrance, waiting their turn to get a table and blocking a third of the market path, while the boxes of vegetables and fruit belonging to the shop opposite had blocked another third, so that the shoppers and other tourists had only a slim central walkway to compete for.

He watched some of the waiting customers standing next to the closed blue door in the façade overlooking the market, gazing through the glass at the mouths lapping up their meals. He laughed, recalling that Julie had done just the same thing when they'd come to the restaurant yesterday. She had pressed her nose against the glass curiously during their half-hour wait, until she could almost eat from the plates of those inside. When the hummus they had ordered arrived, dressed in the traditional Palestinian manner with mint, green onions, and olives, they had both torn off a piece of bread and had quickly set to work. Even before swallowing his first whole mouthful, he had exclaimed, with his usual seriousness, "This is *real* hummus," while Julie had murmured her admiration: "Mmm!" As the meal progressed, they had opened up a channel on the plate for the oil to move along, like a river overflowing its banks. When they were finished, she had exclaimed, "Hummus Saeed is delicious. It's worth the wait!"

Following their lunch, Julie had taken Walid's arm in her own and they had walked to the al-Jazzar mosque. When they reached the thirteen marble steps that lead up to the entrance, they walked up to the yard. As they reached the water fountain on the right of the courtyard, Julie let go of Walid's arm and walked quickly toward the mosque, stopping by the door. From her bag she took out a colored silk scarf, with which she covered her head. She took off her shoes and left them outside, then crossed the threshold and went inside barefoot. As Walid approached the door, he saw her turning around, dancing like a Sufi carried by intoxication to a world beyond our own. He had watched her in silence, astonished. He heard her chanting. *Where has she got all this from?* he'd wondered. When she came out, she took the scarf off her head. Her face was glowing, like a flower whose petals had been opened by the first rays of the sun, and there were teardrops like dew running down her cheeks.

Now, having retraced their walk, Walid stood above the entrance steps, reflecting on what had happened yesterday without believing it. How had Julie done that? Julie, who hadn't inherited her parents' Christianity, and who hadn't converted to Islam when she'd married him—he hadn't asked her to—had come out of the mosque like a saint whose faith had soaked her in belief. And when he had asked her about what she had done, she had smiled and replied, "I liked what I did! I prayed in my own way, and I was happy with my prayers." Walid made no comment.

He headed toward the Greek Orthodox church and stood for a moment in the square in front of it. He looked at the coffee-colored building for some time, then wandered around the port for a while. Then he headed back to the Akkotel Hotel.

When Julie came back, Walid was standing near the semi-circular reception desk, next to a pillar built—like the hotel itself—from the remains of the old Crusader wall. He had rested his elbow on top of the shining wooden counter directly opposite the hotel entrance, listening to the hotel manager telling him the story of the hotel, which had opened ten years before and had been built on the remains of a building that had been a government headquarters in the Ottoman period and a boys' school under the British Palestine Mandate.

He raised his head to catch Julie's eye as she shut the door behind her and came down the three steps leading inside. He saw that her hands, which had been wrapped around the porcelain statue when she had left, were empty. A vague happiness spread inside him, producing an enigmatic smile. Had Fatima brought Julie back, or had she abandoned her in favor of that Swedish delegation she had spoken about? And what about the owners of the house? Had they put the porcelain statue where Ivana had instructed? Or had they just shut the door of her grandfather's house in her face?

Julie took his hands in hers and pulled him toward her. "Come on, Walid, come on, darling. I'm dying of hunger. Abu Christo is waiting for us. I'll fill you in later. Come on, come on!"

They left the hotel and hurried toward the harbor, which was no more than five minutes away on foot. In the

Abu Christo restaurant, which rested against the city wall, protruding from it like a tongue gossiping with the sea, Julie chose a table at the end of a row, next to the water. She greeted the waiter, and the young man, whose skin was tanned like that of an Acre fisherman, greeted her like a tourist.

When they were seated, Julie gestured at the wall, and said, "You know, Walid, your mother-in-law remembered everything about Acre."

Without pausing for him to speak, Julie went on: "Perhaps Ivana didn't tell you much about Acre or about her past here, perhaps she didn't tell you anything at all, but as her daughter she told me lots about her memories of the city. She told me a lot about that wall."

She sighed, and in her breath could be heard the sound of an ancient regret. "My mother used to say, 'Whether its men were weak or strong, only the wall protected and defended Acre.'"

She looked directly into his eyes like someone searching out old secrets, and the words she spoke to him were fragrant with hope: "I'd like that wall to protect our backs, Walid!" Walid made no comment. He sat in silence opposite her, as the sounds of Greek music reverberated, sending their rhythms along the shore.

As Julie spoke, Walid was listening to his own thoughts. He continued to mull over the questions he had brought with him from the Akkotel Hotel that he had not been able to voice until this moment. Finally, he decided to condense them into a single question: "How was your visit to your grandfather's house?"

"Oh, you won't believe it."

"Did everything go okay?"

"Better than I expected."

As she said it, she put her hand over his on the table, and then told him the story:

"After Fatima had dropped me at the house, I went up the steps, confused and scared. To be honest, I hadn't expected to be such a coward, especially after I'd refused to take you along with me. The important thing is that when I reached the top of the stairs, I was overcome by anxiety and fear of an unpleasant surprise. The porcelain statue was shaking in my hands. I looked for a bell, but couldn't find one. The door, which looked as if it hadn't been painted for decades, was old, and shabby, and full of cracks. I knocked at the door several times and waited. The door opened, and I found myself in front of a beautiful lady, who looked as if she was in her twenties, wearing a long black dress embroidered with silk, in which she looked like a work of art. Don't laugh at me, Walid, she was a real gem. The important thing is that she smiled at me, and I smiled at her, and then she introduced herself, saying, 'I'm Samiya!' Before I could tell her the reason for my visit to the house, she quickly greeted me by name and said, 'Fatima told me everything.' Then she invited me in.

"The house was decorated inside in traditional Arab style: some old red sofas of material like carpet, with embroidered cushions scattered over them. The lady, who spoke reasonable English, quickly apologized for the décor, explaining that in just a week she'd be undertaking a renovation of the house and changing all the furniture, as she'd decided to turn it into a small guest house for tourists. It would retain its Oriental flavor, though, which tourists liked, especially Europeans in love with the magic of the East, so she'd be keeping some of the acquisitions that were there before."

"You mean your grandfather's furnishings are still in the house?" Walid asked.

"Not only that, the woman surprised me with something that would never have occurred to any of us. I wish Ivana had known it before she died."

"What are you talking about?" he asked.

"Samiya will be naming the hotel after my mother, Walid. Can you believe it?"

"You're joking!"

"Not at all, she told me so. She'll be calling it 'Ivana's Guest House.' But listen, can we *please* eat?"

Walid called the waiter and ordered an assortment of traditional Greek and Syrian starters for both of them, and shrimps grilled with sesame, and garlic sauce. While he talked to the waiter, Julie looked at the sea, like a soul hovering over the the water. She gathered together inside herself the various emotions that her visit to her grandfather's house had left behind—all of which she was hiding from Walid behind this story that she had invented and was trying to believe in, so as not to shock her husband or collapse in front of him when she related it.

Julie dabbed at her eyes as the waiter went away, but Walid noticed the teardrops on her cheeks. She resumed her story, false happiness disguising her confusion.

"Samiya took my hand and led me to an iron staircase in the middle of the house. She gestured at it, saying, 'Since your mother has told you the layout, go on up. Turn left, then follow the directions that you know already.'

"At the top of the stairs, I turned left, and my eye fell on an old wooden grandfather clock standing against the wall. My grandfather's grandfather clock. I couldn't believe it, I almost collapsed weeping. I lifted the statue a little over my head and placed it on top of the clock. It was as if I were looking at my mother after she had put her make-up on just before leaving the house. That image made me think about my grandfather leaving the house for the last time, hurrying toward the sea with so many other residents of Acre, under threat of bombs, thirst, and hunger, to be either swallowed up by the sea or cast into exile. And while I was wallowing in contemplation, I imagined I was hearing the dawn call to prayer in the city's mosques, but there was no one left to pray."

5

At Terminal 3 in Ben Gurion Airport in Lydda, the four of them—Walid, Julie, Jamil, and Luda—paused to reflect on their visit. In a few moments, Walid and Julie would leave behind them their two friends, as well as several others they had met during their ten-day trip, and the cities they had fallen in love with as if they had both been born there. During the short silence, they all exchanged looks, preparing the way for their parting, until Julie broke the silence with a proposal that astonished Walid:

"Walid, darling, what do you think about selling our house in London and coming to live in Acre?"

Walid's face was colored by a sort of neutral surprise, to which Jamil and Luda added their own astonishment, without any of them breaking their silence. Julie took advantage of the other three's reactions to her proposal to explain that the time had come to go back to her roots—even though she had actually been born on a British military base rather than in Abbud Square. Somehow, though, she read what was going on in Walid's head, and quickly added that she would like to add a few new touches to the image she presented to others—the daughter of an Englishman who had been a colonizer in his youth, and of a disgraced Palestinian-Armenian mother, who had fallen in love in a moment of human weakness—that is, to rewrite her past in a way worthy of both of them.

As Julie spoke, she organized her emotions, gathered them together, and arranged them neatly in a hasty small celebration of joy. Her lips twitched with an equivalent optimism. With the movement of an adolescent turned sixty, she slipped her right arm under Walid's left, and gently pulled it toward her, just as she had done in the days when they were engaged, squeezing his hand.

Walid listened to Julie carefully. He was surprised that she had chosen that precise moment to present her proposal, letting the torrent of desires she had pent up behind a sturdy dam of silence gush out with no constraints at a moment loaded with such tension, just as they were about to leave.

While Walid was trying to disentangle what he had just heard, hemming and hawing as he searched for words to match his wife's happiness and eagerness to stay in the country, she hastened to refine some of what she had said, and this also surprised him: she said that she wouldn't be opposed to buying a piece of land in al-Majdal Asqalan, Walid's birthplace, where they could build a house if that was what he wanted. Her eyes searched his face as she spoke.

He asked her if her proposal and its subsequent correction were serious.

"Of course, darling, of course!" she replied confidently.

What was it that had made that ambition explode in Julie, a woman with an English father and Armenian mother, born in Palestine? What had made her suddenly think of returning to live in a country she didn't know, and which it had never occurred to Walid himself to return to permanently—even now that going back and living there had become somewhat possible—after the exile, banishment, and refugee camps that had dented his Palestinian identity since childhood? Or was it Julie's visit to her grandfather's house, which her mother had run away from some seventy years before? Had Ivana's will changed her daughter? Or perhaps Acre itself had affected Julie—Ivana's Acre, which she had abandoned in a moment of emotional rashness. Acre, with its special magic and its history, which was written in the streets, and which walked in the neighborhood alleys of its quarters and its ancient squares—its history etched in stone, which the sea thundered against day and night. Acre, with its churches, its Franciscan monastery, its mosques, its harbor, its ancient market, with Zahir al-Omar, Jazzar Ahmad Pasha, and Napoleon scorned and humiliated under its walls, Sitt Maarif its popular guide, Hummus Saeed, and the Pasha's baths . . . .

Thinking of the baths made him stop and sigh. *Oh, the baths of the Pasha, what have they done to Julie?*

Walid recalled that visit that had taken place on their first day in Acre. Julie had taken off her clothes in the 'summer room,' piling them up on the ground and looking at her body as she used to do when she was a teenager. Walid had watched her as she wrapped a cotton towel around her body under her armpits. She had put on wooden slippers, and walked pursued by their crunching, as if she was Ghawar al-Toshi, whom she'd never seen or gotten to know. Their echoing crunch had reverberated around the high-ceilinged room. Slipping them off, she had spread herself out face down on the wet tiles in the 'hot room' and had disappeared in the steam, murmuring, "Massage my whole body for me, Walid." He hadn't heard her because he was immersed in watching a video showing illustrated re-enacted scenes of what the baths and their rituals had been like until the nakba. It was accompanied by a commentary that talked about the periods before and after independence. In time, Julie had woken from her lovely, short-lived daydream and had started to look at the explanatory drawings that the authorities had put on light curtains to explain some facets of old-style life inside the baths. They were by the Israeli artist Tanya Slonsky.

This fact had made Walid recall Fatima al-Nasrawi's words: "We give them accurate information free of charge, it's better than them buying lies from the Jews for a price!"

Walid continued to turn ideas over in his head: Had Acre persuaded Julie to reclaim the half of her that had been lost as she grew up in exile? Had it convinced her to retrieve the Palestine she had inherited from her mother as pictures of a lost past? After all, they would soon be leaving the country as they had come to it, as British people who had completed a tour of Israel.

Julie hadn't been satisfied with their visit, Walid realized. She hadn't been satisfied with her return to the house of her grandfather. The handful of sand that Walid had scooped up with his hands on the shore two days before hadn't been enough for her, either. He had put it in a little nylon bag and given it to her, whispering, "The smell of the country!" She had taken it with the same reverence with which she had carried half of Ivana's ashes from London to their final resting place, but it hadn't been enough. Presumably she also hadn't been satisfied with the small piece of limestone she'd picked up from under a rock they'd sat on together near the Abu Christo restaurant after they'd eaten. Julie had been happy with the little piece of stone at the time; she had admired it and put it in her handbag, as the owners of several small boats moored in the harbor had watched the pair of them with typical local Israeli insouciance.

Julie had seemed sated by these little pieces of Acre, but now it appeared that she wanted more.

6

WALID WAS CONFUSED BY JULIE'S succession of emotions. He was several times brought to a standstill by the changes in his wife: a happiness that she had not displayed through the years of their long marriage; an increasing tendency to speak Arabic and use a varied vocabulary, having previously stuck to simple phrases; constantly touching the walls of houses, as well as those of public places and archaeological remains, which they visited like people visiting holy places. Julie was savoring the smells of anything in the country that was ancient, and filling her nostrils with it. Walid recalled how she had sniffed the walls of Acre the first morning they had gone from the Akkotel Hotel to the port via the eastern gate, and how she had stopped him in Jaffa to savor the salt of the sea. When they walked in the city, Julie revealed a surprising desire to smoke a joint, joking that it was like a pregnancy craving. She asked Walid to arrange for her to get high, to satisfy this postmenopausal child that would never be. They had laughed together. When he said to her, with a small touch of flirtatiousness that they implicitly both conspired in, that what she was looking for would require an adventure that might land both of them in jail, she replied, "If a piece of hashish would land us in jail, half the Arab inhabitants of Jaffa would be in prison. I've heard that hashish is all over the place here!"

Looking back, Walid realized that he had missed what was happening. For example, he had taken no notice of Julie's behavior on the second day of their visit, taking a stroll in the town and getting to know a lot of its details, when with Jamil and Luda they had met Roma al-Arusi in the only house remaining in the Dahman quarter of al-Majdal Asqalan.

But he recalled it now.

7

JAMIL STOPPED HIS SILVER SUBARU behind the remains of the old vegetable market in al-Majdal Asqalan. Once out of the car, the four of us—myself, Julie, Jamil, and Luda—dispersed in different directions. For myself, I started to search for a house with the flavor of the past, my parents' house that had seen and celebrated my birth—was it here, or there, or perhaps there? With tears in my eyes, I searched for my early childhood among the rubble of the city, but didn't find it. I cried for myself and my childhood, and for some time my emotions took over.

Finally, I took my cellphone out of my pocket and called my mother, tears still in my voice. I spoke to her with words washed in tears.

"Hello!"

"Greetings. Who's that speaking? You sound like Walid. Walid? Greetings, a thousand thanks to God for your safety, my dear! Where are you?"

"How are you? I'm in al-Majdal."

"Ah! Really? When did you get there? That means God is pleased with you, my dear. By God, going to al-Majdal is like a pilgrimage to Mecca ten times over! Where in al-Majdal, and what are you doing?"

"In the square in front of the mosque, beside the old market."

"Blessings on Muhammad, the best of messengers and prophets! If you are my son, Walid, and I am your mother, kiss the walls of the mosque for me, and if you don't find a wall, look for a stone—look for a stone and kiss that. And don't forget to go into the mosque if some of it still exists, and pray two rak'as. I know you don't pray. You don't want to pray, that's okay for you, you're free not to, it's between you and your Lord, only pray for your mother, it'll bring you a reward. One prayer in Palestine is worth a thousand at home, even in the camp mosque. What do you think?"

"Mother, do you remember where you lived before you emigrated? Do you remember our house?"

"How on earth could I forget it? Heaven forbid that I should forget the house I was married and conceived you in. Curse the Jews who took it away from us!"

"And where is our house?"

"If you're standing in front of the mosque, as you say you are, and are facing it, then our house will be straight behind you. Up, up a bit, in Ras al-Talaa. Turn around, turn behind you, you'll see it. God is your helper, the first house in Ras al-Talaa."

Behind me was some ground stripped of its features by American Caterpillar trucks. A few garbage bins had been placed at the edge near the old market. What my mother had described to me was now just barren land, and it was difficult to be sure that houses had ever stood on it.

I went back to looking bitterly at the remains of the great mosque built by the Mamluk emir Sayf al-Din Sallar in 1300. At its left corner, a minaret stood like an old lighthouse deserted by the ships; its domes looked like pale knitted skullcaps, their wool worn away with time. I crossed the street to the opposite sidewalk, and stood in front of an entrance, above which was a sign: Khan Asqalan Museum. On either side of it were some small shops and a restaurant, a mis'adah, in front of which was an area of thick green cloth awnings and some chairs. Oh my God! How could I pray two rak'as and dedicate them to my mother in a mosque that had turned into a museum and a bar?

Deep inside me, I gave a scream that no one else could hear, and turned around to wipe the whole scene away. My gaze wandered over a long street, which ended in some houses that had once had two stories; their lower parts still bore the traces of what had once been on top of them. To the left of the street, in the background, were three palm trees. Long ago, my aunt had stood there, waiting for me beside them, picking me up, taking my little hand in her own, and picking some dates.

The house had had an upper story, a second floor to which my mother took me once, carrying me on her shoulders when I was still small enough for her to do so. She took me up some marble stairs, which led into a tiled open area in front of two rooms. My head brushed against clusters of red dates. My aunt wasn't here. My aunt was there. My aunt wasn't there. My aunt had died in Khan Younis, in a house on the edge of a refugee camp. But I had found no trace of her when I'd visited the ancient graves in the town some years before; not even a letter of her name remained on the tombstones.

"There's a blue sign over there!" Luda shouted in broken Arabic. "Come on, *poshli*, let's go and see what's written on it."

Luda's call brought us all together in front of a house, the front of which resembled a tatty shoe. Luda stood looking at the sign as if she were looking at herself in an old dull mirror whose mercury had peeled off. She tried to translate for us the Hebrew written on it, but her Arabic deserted her. When she tried in English, Jamil wouldn't let her continue. He teasingly asked her to keep her tongue for some other speech. She did, apologizing in Arabic, English, and Russian.

Then Jamil went up to the sign, and we listened as he conveyed its meaning to us in his fluent Arabic:

Arusi's House

This house is the last major private house to be found in the Dahman quarter, which was named after a family that lived there. The house is an example of distinctive Arab houses. It was constructed with a square called a hawsh in the middle of it, which is a basic feature of Arab houses. It is usually surrounded by bedrooms, and most of the daily household chores are conducted there. The distinctive feature of this house is that it still preserves the simple, traditional methods that the Arab residents relied on in their lives.

At the beginning of the 1950s, the house was occupied by new immigrants from the Yemeni community. They included the Arusi family, who still live in the house, and use the equipment to be found there—such as the olive press, the grain and wheat mill, the bread oven, and the grain and wheat store situated on the ground floor—in their daily lives.

A whisper crept from the inside of the house, and I peered through a large crack in the door. I was embarrassed about looking into the house of a stranger and spying on the people who lived there. But it might be my parents' house, or the house of one of my relatives. I knocked on the door.

From the inside, I heard a voice saying, "Beseder, ima, ani bo . . . ," "Okay, mum, I'm coming."

"The house has got people in it, everyone!" I said. "There are Jews in our house!"

"Mi? Who's there?" a woman's voice asked apprehensively in Hebrew.

"Ani rotsah le-dabber im mi she-babayit," Luda replied, saying that we wanted to talk to whoever was in the house.

A woman opened the door with a smile, having lost her former hesitation. "Welcome, please come in," she said in Arabic with a slight accent. We didn't yet know her name, nor the reason for her smile, which to me felt like guilt hanging on the conscience of its owner. We accepted the invitation with pleasure and went into the house that had been my family's before al-Majdal Asqalan fell into the hands of the Israeli forces on 4 November 1948.

"My name is Roma," she said.

In the right-hand corner there were two rusty old gas canisters and a bright plastic water bucket. There was an old wooden door with several holes for locks and bolts that suggested it had been borrowed from the front of an old shop in the nearby market after the owners had been driven out, perhaps looted by the Jewish Agency, which had distributed our possessions to immigrant Jewish families after the city had been occupied. About two meters away from the door, there was a small window with a pale-green wooden frame. About half a meter from that was another wooden door beside a rectangular window, which was also painted green.

I stared at what I thought had been our bedroom. Had it really been our bedroom? I walked on a couple of steps. My small feet stumbled on the threshold, two low, narrow steps. My mother picked me up and exclaimed, "God's name be upon you, may God protect you!" I hid my tears, tears I was shedding secretly in my parents' house. Was this really my parents' house? Or was it a trick of memory weighed down by nostalgia, constructed out of stories piled up over the course of the years?

The woman excused herself for a few moments and disappeared into another room.

At the end of a yard, the floor of which was covered with small square tiles that had seen better days, there was a pair of black tattered men's shoes and a wheelchair.

Roma returned and invited us into a second room. In the room was an ancient woman, a heap of bones piled up by time in the middle of a bed. She must have been over ninety. She didn't register our presence, and she didn't understand anything of what we said. She muttered the whole time, but none of us could understand what she was saying.

Roma took us around the house. To the left was a kitchen with no door. "This is the oven," she said. "My mother used to use it." And she pointed to an old photo of herself and her mother in a wooden frame, propped up against an oven. She said that they used to bake their bread together in it. I wanted to tell her that it was *my* mother who used to use it, but I couldn't. "And this is the grain mill," she said, pointing to a round stone mill with damaged edges. She took a handful of oats from a bag nearby and threw them into the soft flour channel to show us how grain was milled. I almost laughed at Roma's ignorance, but I didn't want to embarrass her—the grain should have been put in the small circular opening in the middle of the upper part of the millstone. There was a piece of marble beside the millstone, part of an old olive press. That press had belonged to the house of my aunt Ruqaya, the wife of Abd al-Fattah Dahman. Abd al-Fattah had had a mule with a wooden yoke to drive the press. The blindfolded mule would go around and around on a path that ended only when its work was finished.

Abd al-Fattah and Ruqaya had perished in the Jibaliya camp in Gaza many years ago. They had left behind several boys who were no longer boys and girls who had become women. And these in turn had left behind girls and boys who had fought each other in order to defend their party allegiances. They had become Dahmani Fathis or Dahmani Hamasis.

As for the mule, they had left it behind more than sixty-five years ago, braying. No one had enjoyed its braying, so they didn't think of taking it with them as a means of conveying their possessions—they'd be coming back after a couple of months, so they'd been told. So they had carried away with them everything they could and went off, leaving the mule to meet a fate that the people themselves had not been strong enough to confront. Had he been here, walking around, blindfolded, unable to see anything around him? Was this my aunt Ruqaya's house, then? No, the press had been brought to this house, for there was no room here for a mule to turn, not even enough space for people to turn the millstone.

The Dahman house, which had become the Arusi house, was an example of an ordinary house, a memory of all the Dahman family's houses, and perhaps of the whole of al-Majdal. The Israelis had gathered together there our old implements like handed-down possessions from a past that would not return.

In the room of the silent old woman, who had retained her headscarf (which looked like a leftover from her Yemeni past), a large picture had been hung on the wall in front of the bed. In the middle of it was a large circular clock, whose hands pointed to 1:41. It was surrounded by photos, some black and white, some in color, which told the story of the Yemeni Arusi family. This was Roma's mother, and these were her relatives, in the days when she was just a Yemeni Jewish girl. This was a picture of a wedding; here were photos of family celebrations. At the far edge of this illustrated life story was a conscript carrying his weapon on his shoulders. I didn't ask Roma about her personal life, and in any event she didn't seem ready to say much beyond:

"I was four years old when I came here . . . I was only young."

I said goodbye to the house that had been our house. I said goodbye to a piece of my history that had been exchanged for a picture hanging on the wall. I gathered up my confusion and carried it with me as I left with the others, as if I were my father when he had left his birthplace to live as an exile, bequeathing me his exile until this day.

I turned back to Roma. In her sunken eyes, behind her thick glasses, there was a passing flicker of conscience, which flitted between her Majdal, which was not *her* Majdal, and the Yemen she had lost. I guess we were like an uneasy question that you want to ask though you are afraid of the answers.

We said goodbye and walked away. We didn't hear the sound of the door shutting behind us, but instead heard the sound of footsteps. Roma quickly caught us up. She suggested that she take us on a tour of whatever remained of al-Majdal Asqalan. We accepted.

I walked beside Roma. I compared everything I knew about Majdal from Khan Younis to the alleys we moved through. We were all walking in silence, accompanied by the sounds of our feet kicking the small pebbles that were strewn over the unpaved streets. Suddenly, Roma stopped.

"This is Zakhariya's Pharmacy," she said, and my heart lurched.

If I called my mother and said to her, "Mother, I'm at this moment standing in front of Zakhariya's Pharmacy," she would answer, "Good God! How often I talked to you about it. Who would ever have imagined that a day would come when you'd go to Majdal and see the pharmacy with your own eyes?" Then she would disappear into her past and forget that she was on the telephone: "We used to buy red mercurochrome there, and the English salt drink that cleans the stomach and draws the worms out. We also used to buy powder for the little children, and cough medicine. May God put an end to coughs! And don't forget the muslin either, and the ointments, and the liquid people soak their feet in. God put an end to aches in the feet . . . ."

Zakhariya's Pharmacy occupied the ground floor in a two-story building of limestone. The house was still beautiful, as if it hadn't witnessed any disaster—unlike the remains of the small buildings around it. Over the front of the pharmacy was a sign on which was written 'Sh.R.M,' and underneath in Hebrew, 'Bayit Mirqahat,' and then in English 'Pharmacy Megdal.' Behind the pharmacy was a small beauty parlor for women, the Magdalenes of the Israeli period.

Soon enough, we said goodbye to Roma and she said goodbye to us.

"Ma'assalama," she said.

Luda quickly tried to slip a bank note into Roma's hand, but Roma was quicker than her and pulled her hand away. Luda insisted that she take it, but Roma refused again, and pushed away Luda's hand, which remained outstretched at a distance for several moments. When Luda continued to press her, Roma said, with an embarrassed sigh, "Seliha, gvirti, today's the Sabbath!" Despite Roma's obvious embarrassment, Luda tried again. I myself understood that the giving or receiving of money on the Sabbath day was regarded as a sin by Orthodox Jews. I didn't ask Luda afterward if Roma had taken the bank note in the end or not. So I never found out which won, Roma's need or the sanctity of the Sabbath.

As we walked away, I was conscious of Roma saying something far behind us. I turned back, and saw her waving her short arm in the air. I stopped for a few seconds, and watched her as she turned away under my watchful eyes. I don't know whether tears were actually falling from her eyes as she moved away, or whether I imagined it. But I wondered whether Roma was looking for her Yemeni childhood in us. Or maybe she was happy with her role as tourist guide for the likes of us, who would pay money to gaze on their past, and just wished that we had come some other day.

8

In al-Majdal Asqalan, Julie had empathized with Roma, from her 'Welcome, please come in' to her 'Ma'assalama.' She behaved as if she was on a visit to an old neighbor. For the whole time the four of them were in the house that had once belonged to the Dahman family, she had never stopped chatting to Roma with a certain obvious affection, until Luda's impatience made it clear that she was tired of translating the two women's chatter in both directions.

Now, in the airport, Walid thought it not unlikely that Julie had been trying to test, and get to know the feelings of, the woman she expected to be their nearest Jewish neighbor in al-Majdal Asqalan if he agreed to her proposal and they moved to live there. He told himself that his wife perhaps wanted to persuade herself that it would be possible to live in the country. Hadn't she spent several days in Jamil and Luda's house in Haifa, in a three-story building containing six apartments, five of which were lived in by Jews? There, Julie hadn't woken up in a disturbed state. On the contrary, she had seemed happy with Jamil's talk about friendly relations between neighbors he described as ordinary, and about joining a committee of residents of the block to deal with any disputes and day-to-day problems, and to organize any shared concerns.

Walid himself had never commented on what Jamil had said. Instead, he persuaded himself that Julie would finally discover that as soon as Jamil left the building, which was governed by the democracy of neighbors and the conventions of ordinary people, he would lose half his citizens' rights, while his Jewish neighbors would continue to enjoy their full rights as citizens, inside their homes and outside them, including the right to choose the graves for their dead. When they left the country, Julie would realize that they had been wandering around like tourists who had seen only the rare beauty and holiness that belonged to the land.

Walid had to say something in answer to Julie, who had been waiting while reality grappled with his memories. In the end, he said to her, "This isn't Gigi's return. I won't come back to this country to live in it as a stranger. When we get to London, we can discuss the issue away from the pressures of this moment of parting."

Then, to hide his emotions, he turned in the opposite direction and noticed a black girl, who looked Ethiopian, lazily sweeping the long corridor leading to the airport departure lounge with a broom. She was cleaning the floor slowly, at a rate proportionate to the shekels being paid to her. Their eyes met for a few seconds, during which they silently exchanged undefined feelings.

Luda emerged from her silence, speaking with a measured expression of emotion. "Fully understood, Walid. Why not? Every Palestinian should come back to his country, he has to come back. But arrive home safely, and you can discuss the subject together as you said. It's the step of a lifetime, and this isn't the best place to talk about it."

Still, she went on to recommend Haifa as their place of residence, where they could live as neighbors, and swore an oath, for which there was no need, that the city "drives you crazy and blows the mind." Jamil hurried to support his wife's invitation: "Come and live in our quarter—you'll lend light to Haifa and the whole district, including the villages destroyed by the Jews. You'll honor Carmel from its summit to the seashore. Is there anything nicer than sitting on top of the mountain and looking out over the waves washing its feet?"

Julie kissed Luda goodbye. "Of course! I love Haifa so much."

Meanwhile, Jamil implored Walid: "Listen to me and to your wife, my friend, and sell your house. You've nothing to lose but your exile and loneliness. There's nothing better than this country, either in this world or the next."

Walid hugged him and Luda goodbye, and then he and Julie took their cases and hurried toward the departure lounge.

Second Movement

Nine Days Earlier

1

A Stubborn Palestinian

JININ SAT AT HER DESK in the only room in her house that overlooked Jaffa's old port, and continued to revise the chapters in her new novel. Basim called her just before two in the afternoon about the reply of the Misrad Hapnim in Tel Aviv to the application to extend his residency and allow him to work. Jinin recalled her total failure, which was still fresh. She told him that the Israeli Ministry of the Interior had once again rejected his application. Basim hung up in shock.

Jinin placed her own phone to the side on her desk, and tried to imagine the progress of his reactions. She followed him in her mind as he returned to the house as usual by al-Bahr Street, dragging with him his share of failure. He took advantage of the contraction of his shadow at this time of the day to attack it, cursing it, then trampling it with his feet. He punched the air and cursed the year he had returned home, thinking it was a homeland, while his head argued with the walls of the al-Bahr mosque.

The iron outer door opened, then closed. Jinin stopped following Basim with her mind—he was home.

The inside door opened, and Basim's voice arrived before his footsteps.

"The bastards! If I were a homosexual, they'd hang a human rights placard around my neck and let me work!"

The front door and his mouth closed together, and tension spread through the house. Basim walked toward the middle of the room and stood there, furious. With his hands, he wiped beads of sweat from his forehead. With his fingers, he tried to clean his face of the unhappiness that had stuck to it. He let out a long breath. With what remained of his emotion—which was finally subsiding—he said, "Of course, if I were like . . . ," then hesitated.

"Calm down, Basim, my love! It's not the first time, and it won't be the last," Jinin said, and then used his continuing hesitation as an opportunity to enquire maliciously, "Like who?"

"Who do you think?"

"Fine, it's obviously Samir Badran. Can't you let it go?"

Samir Badran had lived for a time with an Israeli friend of his called Hayyim Anbari, who was a member of the singing band Tseva'Ehad (One Color), the best-known group among Tel Aviv's gay clubs. It was Jinin, alone among Palestinian authors, who had borrowed his story for a short story she had published on the *Qadita* website. She had been one of the first to surf the site on the day it was released. "This website has brought together the country's homosexuals," she had remarked to herself bitterly at the time (overheard by Basim), "but ordinary people can't find anyone to bring them together."

Basim muttered something in response, then turned around and walked toward the kitchen. Jinin reckoned he must have gone to the window and looked at their neighbor, for she could read the contentment on his face when he returned a few minutes later. She knew that Basim felt at peace when he stuck his head out of the window and saw their Jewish neighbor, Bat Tzion. He would go into a trance of contentment as if he were taking a siesta on a hot afternoon. He would watch Bat Tzion busily finishing a new painting, or progressing on a piece she had started on a previous occasion, as she sheltered beside the wall of her house, which was near the entrance to the cooperative in the small courtyard between the houses in the Old Citadel.

Basim had known Bat ever since he had married Jinin and moved to her small house in the Citadel. One calm summer's morning, Basim had stood at the same window, leaning on his elbows against the window sill. He had started to watch Bat, who had soon raised her head and caught him staring at her. It didn't disturb her; she simply said good morning to Basim, calling him a handsome young man:

"Boker tov, tas'ir yafeh!"

Then she had introduced herself: "I'm Bat Tzion!"

"Shalom, gvirti, ani Basim!" Basim had replied. Of the four words, three did not require any knowledge of Hebrew: one was his name; the second (ani) was shared with the Palestinian dialect; and the third (shalom) needed nothing to turn it into Arabic except to change the *shin* into *sin* and the *o* into an *a*. The fourth word, gvirti, Basim struggled to select from among the dozen or so Hebrew words that were all he knew of the language.

Basim called on Bat frequently. Every time, he bore her a bouquet of fine words as befitted her. He often expressed his sincere admiration for her ideas and paintings in Jinin's presence, saying that her lines had the language of a poet, and her colors had the shape of truth. But he never used the old lady's full name, Bat Tzion. He had never done that, not once since they had become friends despite their different ages. He contented himself with calling her Bat, in what the old lady thought was a sign of affection. Even Jinin thought that Basim was flirting with their neighbor. But it wasn't like that at all; Basim simply hated the other half of his neighbor's name. Even to hear it provoked him.

One evening, he whispered to Jinin, "Everything about our elderly neighbor is wonderful except for her name, which brings together all the unhappiness in the world and distributes it to us. I'd like to change it; no, I don't just want to change it, I want to change it whether she likes it or not. I'm just not prepared to call her Bat Tzion, as if I were addressing the Zionist Movement and its offspring. I want to call her Bat Shalom!"

"Mmm," said Jinin. Basim's impetuosity, affected by his emotions and the summer heat, made her laugh. As if to savor the effect of the new name, she said: "Bint Salam, uh-huh, why not? It's very nice, and it suits her."

So Basim started to call their neighbor Bat Shalom. The old lady liked the name so much that she started to wait for Basim to walk through the quarter or appear near the window. She would pretend to be busy, so that he would call her and she could hear her new name spoken either by him or else by Jinin, who had taken a fancy to it in turn, because, as she told her the first time she used it to address their neighbor, "It makes me feel that there are people in this country who love peace, even though looking for them is like looking for a black hole in the universe!"

When Bat didn't see Basim or Jinin for a couple of days, she would tease herself, saying: "Come on, Bat Shalom!," "Get your food ready, Bat Shalom!," "You must finish your latest picture, Bat Shalom!" It made her happy, and she came to believe it as if it were the truth.

Basim came back into the drawing room as if he hadn't been upset by the decision of the Ministry of the Interior or even heard it. Jinin smiled at him, saying, "You're right, Basim, my love, the officials in the Interior Ministry are sons of sixty-six prosti—"

She thumped her fist on the desk, using the blow to complete the word she had left unfinished.

Basim moved to the window that looked out over the harbor, and said with feeling, "Didn't I tell you that the flag of democracy in this country only flutters over the heads of Samir Badran and his like?"

She opened the drawer of her desk, took out the Arabic *Yafa al-Yawm* newspaper, opened it at the third page, and spoke in a measured tone: "No, my darling, even he isn't immune. The flag you speak of was just lowered over Samir Badran. Listen:

"'On the evening of the day before yesterday, a corpse belonging to a man in his twenties was discovered on the hills overlooking the Kazakhanah graveyard in Jaffa. Police sources in Tel Aviv and Jaffa said that the victim had been subjected to twenty blows from a sharp implement on various parts of his body. His face had also been mutilated. An identity card was discovered in the victim's pocket, issued by the Palestinian Authority in Ramallah, in the name of Samir Badran, a resident of Bethlehem in the West Bank. Preliminary investigations have revealed that he had most recently been residing illegally with Hayyim Anbari in his apartment in Tel Aviv. Ministry of the Interior records show that the dead man had submitted an application two months ago for the renewal of his residence permit, which was refused by the Ministry. For his part, Anbari, when questioned under police oath, stated that he had not seen his friend for several weeks, but that he had learned by chance from other friends that he had not left Tel Aviv, but had been working secretly, moving between different gay clubs and bars. The Palestinian security authorities have been informed of the incident. *Yafa al-Yawm* has learned from its own sources that Badran's family refused to accept their dead son's corpse, informing the Palestinian security authorities, who were supposed to receive the body from the Israelis, that they had disowned their son when he left home and no longer recognized him. Contacts between the Israelis and Palestinians are continuing, with a view to a decision being taken regarding the corpse, which no one wishes to accept.'"

Jinin closed the newspaper and threw it onto the desk. She turned to Basim, and noticed that tears were flowing down his cheeks. She didn't venture to ask him what aspect of the strange story had made him cry. She heard him whisper, sharp as a knife, "Poor Samir, no one wants him, alive or dead."

He went through to the bedroom, took off his shirt, and threw it on the bed. Jinin propped her chin on her hand, with her elbow resting on one knee, her legs crossed, and watched him through the doorway as he undid his leather belt, then unzipped his pants and pushed them down his thighs.

At least my husband is still healthy and strong, she thought. Her heart fluttered at the prospect of a quick 'take away,' as they called making love during the day; they sometimes did it before Jinin went out to work, or as they woke from an afternoon siesta during the summer. Basim extracted his legs from his pants one after the other, and threw the pants onto the bed. She looked with admiration at his legs, seeing in them the legs of an American cowboy, despite the fact that he had never in his life tended cattle. Watching his body was urging on her desire for a 'take away,' almost insisting on it.

Basim shaved, took a shower, and came out of the bathroom, stretching his arms wide. He sighed with exaggerated pleasure.

"Aaaaaah! How much I needed that shower!"

He seemed to himself to have washed away his troubles.

"God bless you," she said, biting back her frustration.

He began to dress. "God bless you, too!" he replied.

He combed his hair, then tossed the comb onto the edge of the dressing table. Then he went into the kitchen and heated some food, which he ate quickly. He made a cup of Nescafé for himself, drank half of it in the sitting room, and left the cup on the edge of her desk.

"I'm going to Ramla," he said in a neutral tone, as he headed for the door. "I may be late back."

She didn't ask him for details or demand any justification for his excursion. She knew he was looking for documents that he needed for something he was working on.

"God be with you, my darling. Be careful and look after yourself," she called.

Basim crossed the threshold in silence, closed the door behind him, and walked off, as Jinin quickly gulped down the half-cup of Nescafé he had left behind him. She then began nervously cleaning and tidying the other parts of the house. She broke two plates before she had finished her work.

Then she sat down again at her desk and carried on reviewing her novel. The night was already half gone.

As 'The Remainer'—this was his nickname, which everyone used, because it fitted him and his character—crept into the garden of the house, the garden surrendered to his footsteps. He stumbled with his secrets toward the wooden shed at the southern corner of the garden. He opened the door, which was dotted with holes, just as the geography of Palestine is dotted with Jewish settlements. He reached over and turned on the small electric light that hung from a nail that had been banged into the wooden wall facing the door. As he straightened up, the light falling on his face revealed the untidiness of his features. Light passed through the holes in the wooden door, shining outside. The clank of small keys could be heard, the ringing of a metal chain, and the grating of wooden drawers.

Some of those in the house turned in their beds, and a nervous tremor awakened Filastin. The eldest son of The Remainer leaped tensely from his bed. He hurried toward the rear door leading to the garden, and found it open. He stuck his head outside, and inhaled the smell of summer, but paid it no attention. He heard the sound of a wooden drawer stuttering closed, and a little cough that told him that it was his father, not a thief. He remembered what his mother, Husniya, had kept repeating since his childhood: "If your father gets up in the night, he bangs around enough to wake up Lydda and Ramla, and if he shouts, he stops the waves in the middle of the sea!" Now he'd become like his mother, listening out for the sound of his father's footsteps, always on the alert for a clearing of the throat followed by a cough.

"What are you looking for, father?"

He was met by a silence in reply.

He calmly called again.

"What are you doing, father, in the middle of the night?"

Silence. He repeated his question as loud as he dared, hoping not to wake anyone sleeping.

"What are you doing, father, in the middle of the night?"

Silence.

He begged him: "We want to sleep, man!"

Silence.

"All right, don't answer. Just don't go on disturbing everyone!" muttered Filastin, abandoning his exhortations. He collected up his frustration and took it with him back to his bed. It's no use—my father's a goat, and an obstinate one at that, *he thought.* Even a devil doesn't do that sort of thing.

He tossed and turned for some time, then went back to sleep.

There was a nervous silence in the house. Husniya slipped out of her bedroom. The passage leading to the garden provoked a disturbed conversation between Husniya's light slippers and the floor. Once outside, her slippers made their peace and stopped the conversation. As she approached the shed, she was lined with streaks of light and darkness.

In a faltering tone, she begged her husband to desist from what he was intending to do.

"No, please don't go, Abu Filastin—the Jews don't have mercy on anyone. My heart is tormenting me, I'm not happy, I'm afraid for you."

No rejection, acceptance, comment, or murmur reached her from the wooden shed—not even a clearing of the throat. Suddenly, the tension between her silence and her expectation was shattered by a shrill cry from Aviva, the Jewish lady next door.

Afifa *(Husniya sometimes turned the name of their neighbor into Arabic, making it approximate to an actual Arabic word, not necessarily related to its meaning)* has been visited by a sudden German nightmare, which has scared her awake, *she thought.* May God grant us mercy, and grant her rest. The Germans burned the hearts of the Jews, and the Jews have burned ours in turn. What have we done that God burns both our hearts?

The Remainer had heard it, too. He gave a sigh of regret from inside the shed.

"Poor Rabia (he, too, would turn their neighbor's name into Arabic, though his version was a play on meaning), no one asks after her, not her husband, not her two kids, while the state sells her tragedy and the tragedy of others wholesale and retail!"

Husniya gazed into the darkness, which was lined with streaks of light. She called out to The Remainer provocatively, "What you're doing is stuff and nonsense, and it won't bring you anything except abuse, and insults, and a sore head. Do you think the Jews will give you a roof over your head, Abu Filastin? Do you think they'll sing and dance around you? Go and sleep, man—shut up and don't be so stupid. Tomorrow, if you carry on with your plan, the Jews will beat you up!"

2

Basim returned from his errand, just as the night was preparing to keep Jinin company. He seemed relaxed, like he had left a lot of his problems behind.

"I called in at the Dunya café in al-Malik Faysal Street," he announced, before Jinin could ask him. "I had an appointment with Dr. Ibrahim al-Zu'bi," he went on. "He's a social scientist. We talked for quite a bit—I had a splendid meeting with him, in fact, very informative. Afterward, I went to Ramla, and passed by the Jawarish quarter. I saw Nawal Isawi, the head of the organization Women Against Violence."

Jinin remained silent. He asked her if she knew Isawi.

"No. But I've sometimes read things about her in *Yafa al-Yawm*," she replied. "Did she tell you anything useful?"

"She talked about their organization's activities, and gave me information about the subject, with photocopies of some statements, articles, and analyses that she'd prepared for me. She told me things that I never imagined could happen in this country. What's going on in the Jawarish quarter doesn't bear thinking about. I thought people were exaggerating!"

"I know. The Jews are actually calling the quarter 'Mikhbeset ha-kavod shel ha-Aravim.'"

"What does that mean?"

"'The Arabs' shame laundry.'"

"Unfortunately, I haven't really obtained enough information yet about what they're saying," he muttered with regret.

"Do you want some food?" she asked.

"To be honest, I ate a cheese sandwich on the street as I was coming back. I bought two from the Abul Afiya bakery, and kept one for you."

He put the small paper bag he was carrying onto her desk. Beside it, he placed a file containing some papers that he had had under his arm. He said that he was tired from the long walk, his head was stuffed with too much information for him to retain, and he wanted to sleep. He bent down over Jinin, kissed her, and went to bed.

So this is the 'take away' I've been waiting for since noon, she thought, with regret.

Basim got undressed and stretched out on the bed. He turned off the lamp beside him, and was soon asleep.

Jinin, her physical disappointment stinging her, looked from the cheese sandwich to the file on her desk, which was tempting her to turn its pages.

3

JININ CLOSED HER EYES FOR a few minutes, listening to Basim's breathing, which swelled calmly around her from the bedroom. His breaths were like waves creeping lazily over the shore before withdrawing, folded in on themselves in a repeated rhythm that invited sleep. That relaxed her. Her attention wandered between the pages of the novel and Basim's breathing.

She tiptoed like a young ballet dancer to the window. Outside, two small fishing boats slept huddled together, like two lovers stretched out on the bed of their emotions. There were other boats bobbing about on waters of light and darkness. Further out at sea were pale lights in the distance, clinging to the edge of a horizon swallowed in darkness. Jinin thought that they must belong to merchant vessels or tourist boats heading toward the port of Ashdod to the south. And perhaps there were others—warships that had dispensed with their lights, edging their way toward Gaza, further to the south. Just thinking about the existence of warships gave her a fright—even moored in the open sea at Gaza, watching the fishermen and spying in every direction.

Jinin returned to her desk, pushed the laptop to one side, and took hold of Basim's file. The problems it contained had propelled him into a deep sleep. As she started to rummage through the papers in it, her eyes fell on both printed stories and others that Basim had handwritten. Flipping through them, she came across the story of a woman from Ramla, Nisreen al-Shawish, who had been washed in blood and kneaded in earth. Nisreen had been a young girl, happy in her femininity. She was about to turn twenty when she fell from the world into a hole in the road, leaving behind her a young child and her dream of a little house for the two of them.

Next, she observed Tannus's victory as she ran from her brother's pursuing Mitsubishi, until he put an end to her seventeen years at the Rama crossroads in Galilee.

Jinin pitied the simplicity of Ala, a girl from Haifa. The poor girl had believed that she was a first-class citizen in Israel. She was sure that the police would guarantee her protection from the threats of her parents, and cousins, and all her other relatives who had been entrusted with preserving her honor. Ala had made an official complaint, which she had left on the desk of Officer Avigdor—'Fatty,' as they called him in the Haifa police station. 'Fatty' Avigdor had left Ala to the family honor laundry, which had cleaned her stain away soon after.

"Faryal, Faryal . . . ," muttered Jinin with a regret that pained her heart, as she read the fourth story in the file.

Faryal al-Huzayyil. A Bedouin from the Negev. Eighteen years old. She had never known a tent, had never gathered wood to make a fire for her tribesmen's coffee. She had never herded cattle, had never hung a bell around the neck of a goat, or put a pair of golden or silver earrings in her ears like the Bedouin of long ago. Faryal was a child of the times: she usually decorated her ears with two small earpieces connected to an iPod. She had no one to spoil her, so she spoiled herself, calling herself 'Fufu.' Fufu danced with passion to the rhythm of songs that she loved. Her body swayed like an ear of corn set in motion by the winds of her desires. Her nose did not carry a ring, but she retained the pride of a young girl in love with her femininity. Fufu rebelled against the traditions of her tribe, her Bedouin identity. Fufu said goodbye to her town, Rahat, and traveled away. She lived alone, with no guardian or male protector, in a small apartment in Tel Aviv. Three men made an agreement to get rid of her. The first was her eldest brother, who couldn't find work, so threw himself into the ranks of the Israeli armed forces. He found no shame in cooperating with the army of occupation in its crimes against his own people and their Arab neighbors. Instead, he focused his shame on Faryal for living the life that she wanted. The second was her younger brother, who could not bear the fact that she had found work in Tel Aviv that would set her free from his supervision. And the third was her cousin, to whom the tribe had pledged her on the day of her birth. He helped to kill her so that a stranger would not take her virginity. Three 'heroes' in a tragedy that ended with Faryal's corpse being thrown into an old disused well near the town of Ramla.

Three men also came together against Abir al-Ladawiya: husband, brother-in-law, and nephew. The last of these, who was barely on the edge of manhood, and who even his mother called loathsome, became a man with Abir's death. The two brothers took him with them so that he could learn how to preserve his share of the family's honor. Together, the three men killed her.

As for Safa, her husband dealt with her on his own. He didn't seek help from any of his relatives, but set up a special court for her that quickly issued its verdict. He hanged her on a gallows that he had made himself, using the washing line on which Safa had hung his clothes after ridding them of his sweat and other filth. He killed her, and hung her corpse up like a piece of washing for everyone to see.

Poor Suheir was strangled by her husband. He took her four children, and no one asked him any questions. "She betrayed him," they said, "and a woman who betrays her husband doesn't deserve to bring up his children." They didn't specify how she had betrayed him, or offer any proof for it, and they didn't relate the children to the mother who had borne them.

The death of Hala, the virtuous nursery teacher from Nazareth whose killer remained unknown—no one even tried to look for him—woke the whole of Haifa, who marched in her funeral procession, with the children from her school at its head.

Jinin closed Basim's file with its terrifying stories. She sat with her eyes closed for a time before turning back to the pages of her novel.

One morning, later than usual, The Remainer returned to the garden shed. He took two large photos from a side shelf, and placed them on a small table in front of him. He took two delicate square wooden frames from among several other things in the corner to the right and put them beside the photos. Then he took a small square cardboard box from a shelf opposite, opened it, and took out a few yellow metal pins with small round heads. He put the first photograph on the first wooden square and fastened it with four pins, then fastened the second photo on the second wooden square in exactly the same way. He nailed the two pictures to the ends of long thin pieces of wood.

He now had two placards, which he carried over his shoulder. He shut the door of the shed and went back inside the house. He leaned the two placards against the wall in front of his office door. He pretended not to notice the presence of Husniya, who was absorbed in picking green mulukhiyeh leaves. She was aware of him, though she did not show it. He went into the office, sat down at his desk, and took a small key from his pocket, with which he opened a drawer on his right. He took out a file stuffed full of papers. He smiled. He grimaced. He laughed. He sighed. He let out a short groan of regret. He muttered. He turned the stories over in his head.

Husniya continued stripping the mulukhiyeh leaves from their brightly colored stalks. She gathered them together in an old brown sieve to her right—she would later wash them and dry them in the sunshine. She threw the slender stalks onto a page from the al-Ittihad *newspaper, the mouthpiece of the Israeli Communist party, Rakah. She peeled two onions, and threw the skins on it. She sliced the onions with a knife and chopped them finely. Then she peeled seven garlic cloves and threw the detritus on the paper as well. The newspaper articles, which brought together all of the Arabs and some of the Jews around her, acquired the smell of onions and garlic, to which was added the smell of green coriander, which Husniya chopped with the knife.*

She realized that The Remainer had been gone for a long time. She felt his absence deeply in his silence. "Abu Filastin! Abu Filastin!" she called. "Can't we hear your voice, man?"

The Remainer quickly shut the file and pushed it into the drawer. He shut the drawer and put his little key in his pocket. He was on the point of going out, but hesitated. He felt the key weighing down his pocket. He was afraid that he might one day take it with him to his grave. He thought for a moment, and changed his mind; he decided to leave the drawer open, to let its secrets breathe in the hearts of others. He returned the key to the drawer. His pocket now free of a heavy burden, he felt at peace. He got up from his seat and left the room, taking the two placards with him to the sitting room.

He walked past Husniya, who took in her husband's frame from bottom to top with suspicious eyes. She bunched her lips in the left corner of her mouth. He felt a desire to leave, and to let her dwell over her suspicions for the whole day.

Then her lips straightened and let out these words: "As God is my witness, the thing that's unhinged your mind, and will destroy us all with you, is that Jewish neighbor of ours that you're so friendly with."

Basim tossed and turned in bed, muttering words that made no sense at all. His prattling made Jinin sad. She left The Remainer there, getting ready to go out with the two placards in his hand, pursued by Husniya's words cursing the Jewess who had unhinged his mind, and thought about Basim, pondering their relationship since they had returned to the country together from Washington.

4

I CAME BACK INTO THE country as usual on my Israeli passport via Ben Gurion Airport in Lydda, while Basim arrived on his American passport via Amman Airport in Jordan. From there, he took a taxi to al-Malik Hussein Bridge. He spent three hours waiting there, after which he was allowed to enter the West Bank. He took a second taxi to Bethlehem, and spent two days in his parents' house before going to my parents' house in Ramla and asking for my hand. That return was the first real event in our troubled marriage, and would remain like a strange clause inserted into its text, since from that time on we've been required to travel separately every time we leave the country and to return separately, to be reunited as if we were a couple recovering back from a temporary divorce imposed on us.

A year after our marriage, Basim started to choke on the details of his daily life, which had turned into a programmed tedium. He had no right to work and no permission to do so, either. He enjoyed no form of health insurance or social security—in fact, he had none of the rights that other residents in the country enjoyed, including those immigrants who enlivened Tel Aviv and other big cities by night, while by day they invigorated the political life of the whole country. They injected into the state economy millions (some said billions) of dollars a year, all collected by the tax authorities.

But I didn't just leave him to his troubled thoughts, or to be squeezed by the laws of the land, because he might have decided to just leave. I continued to help him at every step, and to assure him that together we'd be able to overcome the harsh circumstances that we were living through here. All we needed was some determination and a lot of patience, until the Ministry of the Interior became tired of us and left us alone. I reminded Basim several times of the wonderful Emil Habibi. I knew that he loved 'Abu Salam' and everything he had said or written, right up to his last line, which he had never had a chance to give a full stop to before he'd died.

I said to him once: "Let us learn from the mu'allim (like many people in the country, we called Emil the mu'allim), who died content to have stayed in Haifa." On his instructions, his tomb was engraved 'Staying in Haifa.' This epitaph became a beacon for those who had emigrated, those who had not been able to bear the burdens of staying here for long, and those who wanted to return here in order to remain.

Just before we came back last time, I told him of the conversation I had had with Walid Dahman, my writer relative who lived in London, and whose words I much admired, and even quoted. I admired them so much that I didn't hide the fact that I had been influenced by his style, or deny the fingerprints that Walid had left on writings of mine that I'd asked him to review. "Listen, my darling Basim," I said, "I won't hide anything from you. I spoke to Walid frankly on the telephone more than once about our problems, and about the tragedy of Palestinians who hold an Israeli passport and have married outside the country, or even in the West Bank or Gaza. . . ."

Before I could finish what I was saying, he cut me off, saying, "Jinin, why don't you just leave the country to them, and escape? One day, the Jews will leave. And if they go, Israel will no longer be Israel. Israel is just a passing phase in the history of Palestine, Jinin."

I tried to explain what Walid had said to me, but suddenly he shouted provocatively, "My darling, Walid is living quite happily abroad! If he loves this country so much and is prepared to live as we do, let him honor us by coming to live here with his wife, and let them try it! Come on, forget about Walid. Listen to me, why don't we go and live in Bethlehem? Or isn't Bethlehem Palestine?"

"Go on, then, Basim, go! I won't be mad with you," I replied, with a sort of controlled fury. "You can have a contented life with your family in Bethlehem, but I'd lose my whole livelihood and with it everything I've gained through the sweat of my brow over the years—what about my healthcare, and all my social security? And on top of all that, I'd lose the perseverance of sixty years of my family's life, during which they've put up with more than most people could bear so as not to emigrate and leave the country to the Jews. And more importantly than all of that, I don't want to lose you and I don't want you to lose me!"

"We've gone back to the same old song—you don't want to lose me and I don't want to lose you, but one of us will have to give way. We either lose here or we lose there. Okay, why don't we go back to America? Wouldn't that be easier for us both? America means a nationality and rights that are broader and fuller than anywhere around here."

I didn't despair. I calmed myself, took a deep breath, and stood up to the first signs of his desire to retreat:

"No, Basim, no! Now that our homeland has called us back, and we've returned, why should we go back to America? I needed New York and you needed Washington when we were university students, but now we don't need either of them, my darling. Let's stay in Jaffa. I won't leave Jaffa again, it's where I was born. People dream of returning to Jaffa! Go and read what your friend Khaled Issa wrote on Facebook: the Palestinian who'll turn to stone is the one who has to spend the rest of his life in Sweden. His dream is to sit on the shore in Jaffa and drink a cup of coffee, even just once, slurping it as if he's actually drinking well-being, as he soaks his feet in the sea. We have Jaffa, its Citadel, its shore, its sea, its sky. We kick against the government, and poke our fingers in its eyes. We have a graveyard—when one of us dies, we bury him there. We have the whole country, Basim, and you want us to desert it and go back to America? Let's stay here, my darling. Look at the Jews; when one of them dies abroad, they bring his corpse and bury it in a country that he's never even seen. Let's stay here, Basim, it's better for us to live and die in our own country, one we know."

Basim listened to what I had to say till the end without comment. He was racked by two contradictory desires, though he calmed down slightly, even if only for a moment, when I again whispered in his ears those most beautiful of words, which I reserved for him alone: "Goodnight, Basim, may your morning be in Jaffa!"

The love of Jaffa cleansed him. I didn't realize at that moment that everything he had said was just a pool of emotions that he had been draining for some time. He smiled, expressing his delight in the expression. He used it to wash away his fears and nervousness whenever he needed. He whispered it back to me, still trying to convince himself of the necessity of staying. "Goodnight, my Jinin, may your morning be in Jaffa."

From that point on, I made Jaffa live in his dreams, from time to time taking him on a tour through the rest of the country. Despite that, he continued to be afraid of waking one morning and finding Jaffa swallowed up by waves of fundamentalist Jews, who were invading the city in their thousands every year, or finding that it was his exile that greeted him in the morning and accompanied him on his sometimes hesitant tours of the country, while he sought the right to reside in his own country from the strangers who had occupied it.

5

After that tense episode, which overshadowed our lives for some time, Basim tried to deal with his situation with greater flexibility. He tried in various ways to kill the enforced unemployment that the Israeli Ministry of the Interior had imposed on him. He occupied himself by preparing economic and sociological reports and studies, which he thought both useful and important, and which also provided us with some additional income. I encouraged him in that; I liked his work, and I thought it might persuade him to stay in the country and give up the idea of emigrating.

I much admired the study he had completed about family violence and the murder of women in the Lydda, Ramla, and Jaffa areas, even though I was frightened by the stories he discussed, which he had collected from houses that had purged their dishonor through crimes that were even more dishonorable. I'd told him that the Jews called the Jawarish quarter 'the Arabs' honor laundry,' but I just couldn't believe that a family from Ramla could kill thirteen of its young women in less than ten years. But I came to believe it when it was confirmed by the documents that Basim had assembled, and the testimony of dozens of men accused of these crimes, and even some female victims who had managed to escape the fates of the others. I started to fear for any Palestinian girl who I happened to meet on the road in the company of a boy. I started to dread the poor girl turning into a 'scandal' that they would need to cleanse their honor of. With the increase in the number of honor killings, and the inability of Basim's research to keep pace with the number of victims, I channeled my fears into my novel. I was afraid that my characters might join the nearest national honor laundry.

My lip pen slipped between my fingers, and a red line appeared in the mirror along my lower lip, twisting onto my left cheek. I wiped it with a tissue.

I gathered my thoughts and examined my reactions to the honor laundries scattered throughout the country. I finished my make-up, put my make-up implements back in my little handbag, and then slung it over my left shoulder, as usual.

I put my right hand, which was trembling, on the door handle, but I was pulled up short by a question that had been bothering me since the previous night, and decided to ask it so that it wouldn't nag me for the whole day.

I turned toward Basim. My hand was still on the door handle. I was waiting for it to stop shaking so that I could turn the handle. Basim noticed me. He put the screwdriver on the table in front of him, and pushed away the fan that he was busy repairing. But I didn't have the courage to put the question to him. Instead, to hide my confusion about myself and the characters in my novel, I asked, "Do you want anything from outside, Basim?"

He gave me a look of surprise, clearly having expected a different question.

"I want you to find out for me what's happened in the Ministry of the Interior."

"Oh yes," I said, "it's good you've reminded me. I've got an appointment with Ayala in two days' time."

I turned the door handle with a hand that was still shaking, opened the door, and went out.

6

Jinin arrived at the Misrad Hapnim (Israeli Ministry of the Interior) building in Tel Aviv, located at 125 Menachem Begin Street, at around nine in the morning. It had taken her more than twenty-five minutes, eight minutes more than she had expected, because of the heavy traffic. A number of Africans—most of them Sudanese—who were seeking asylum, or trying to renew work permits, were scattered over the steps of the building, which rose far higher than their hopes of staying in the country. These people usually arrived at the Ministry of the Interior at dawn to secure places for themselves among the waiting crowd outside, whose numbers continued to grow until the Ministry started work on security reviews and renewing residence and work permits. Between sixty and seventy temporary work permits were renewed each day, valid for just three months and capable of being canceled at any time with no reason being given.

Jinin put her foot on the first step. An officer in his twenties emerged from the building, his kippah clinging to the back of his head with difficulty. He was carrying a sheaf of documents like someone carrying a worry. He turned to one side, and a large section of the people scattered on the steps hurriedly gathered around him. He stopped at the bottom, and fiddled with the documents in his hands. A thin young man emerged from the crowd and stood behind the officer, his right hand clinging to the iron rail behind the space reserved for motorcycles, while he tried desperately to identify his own document among those the officer was flicking through. There was a general sense of expectation, like the announcement of secondary school examination results. Suddenly, the young man turned toward Jinin. He watched her approaching for some seconds, then greeted her with a wave of his free hand. She grinned at him encouragingly. This was Mawalu, a young man from South Sudan who had worked with his wife Tara for a short period as cleaners in the Harmony Cooperative (Ha-Havanah) where Jinin worked. She wished him success in his mission without speaking to him.

Jinin continued climbing the few steps in front of the building. She registered some of the reactions of those hovering around the officer and some of the unhappiness of their expectations. She stopped in front of the main entrance, and turned to look back. The officer was gathering up his papers. Some of the Sudanese were leaving happy, while others dragged their despair and frustration with them. They would be forced to endure another humiliating wait to renew their papers. They would wake up at dawn the following day for that purpose. Jinin didn't see Mawalu, and reckoned he must have renewed his residence permit successfully. If so, she was happy for him.

Inside, Jinin went up to the second floor. She immediately headed for the office for 'reunion' applications. She could hear Ayala's voice—this was the official to whom her application had been referred—ringing out tensely inside. It seemed to be lacking the element of shouting that had stuck in her memory from the first time she'd gone for a review and had asked to meet her to renew Basim's residence permit. The memory had never left her on subsequent visits, as the Israeli civil servant began to take an interest in the details of her married life, broadcasting them to the ears of the other officials in the section in her booming voice.

Suddenly, Ayala emerged from her office and noticed Jinin. She stopped, turned sharply toward her, and shouted, "Att Jin . . . ?"

"Ken, ani Jinin!" replied Jinin before she could finish the question, sparing her the need to articulate the two last letters of her name, which would raise her blood pressure even further.

"What are you doing here?"

"I've come for a review!"

"I gave you a phone number to call. Did you?"

"Slikha, sorry, madam, but the number was out of order."

Ayala made no comment but hurried away into the office opposite, leaving Jinin to fume with anger. A short time later, she came out again with a quiet smile on her face. She told Jinin to come into her office.

"You know that the new amendments to the 'reunion' laws don't allow us to grant your husband the right to work, but I'll renew his residence permit and try my best to secure an exemption so that he can work. Come back in three months."

Jinin could find nothing to say. She interpreted Ayala's promise as a sort of verbal contract, although she had no confidence in it.

She left the building.

The three months that Jinin had called 'Ayala's promise' went by, following which she returned to the Ministry of the Interior. She waited in front of the same office door with the same tension and anxiety as the last time, as the same echo of Ayala's shouting rang out, with disaster expected at any moment. She didn't dare knock on the door or go in to confront the woman she regularly described to Basim as having a face like the Israeli laws on the Occupied Territories. She temporarily suspended her hatred for Ayala, and resolved to pull herself together and be brave. She knocked on the door, opened it, and went in. Ayala greeted her with an unexpected smile, and gestured to her to sit down, before surprising her with an unexpected verbal assault to compensate:

"Yes, what's the problem? Do you have an appointment?"

"I came to arrange an appointment."

"What for, dear?"

As if she doesn't know! Jinin thought. "To renew the 'reunion' application, of course. My husband's permit is about to expire."

With a controlled irritation, Ayala took several papers from a file on her desk, proceeded to help Jinin to fill in the boxes, then returned them to the file.

"Come back with your husband in two weeks' time, with documents to confirm your place of residence," she said.

Two weeks later, Jinin went back to the Ministry of the Interior, with Basim this time, and the requested documents and papers: water and electricity bills, everything to prove that she actually lived in Jaffa. Ayala received them with uncharacteristic kindness. She didn't look at the papers and didn't ask Basim any questions. She spared Jinin the trouble of translating her questions for him, or translating his replies, and she spared him the suffering he would endure if he had to answer her questions himself in Hebrew. He would have spat out his words like someone expelling their last breath.

Jinin thought kindly of Ayala that day. In fact, she cursed herself for thinking badly of Ayala, and started to make excuses for her previous behavior. Jinin's visits to Ayala's office became more frequent, and the pair became like good, rational fellow citizens in a rational state that didn't discriminate between its citizens.

Then came a particularly fateful visit. Ayala confirmed Jinin's application for an extension of Basim's residence permit without hesitation. Jinin decided to call Basim as soon as she left Ayala's office to tell him the news. She took advantage of the sudden state of happiness that she found herself in, and the fleeting smile on Ayala's lips, to ask her, as she was on the point of leaving, "Can my husband now work legally?"

Ayala's expression changed, her smile disappearing in a sudden stroke of anger. She trembled like someone possessed by a blue ifreet (though those little devils were said to avoid possessing people in the country because it was holy). Ayala turned into a bundle of emotions sitting on a chair in an office. She screamed at Jinin, "Hamuda, ha-ishur ha-zeh hu lo ishur 'avoda!," "It's not a work permit, sweetie!"

Her shouting caught the ears of everyone in the office. Ayala threw the residence permit on the desk. Jinin took it and ran out, her ears still ringing with the shout that made a mockery of every yell she had previously heard, making them seem like whispered conversations between lovers.

On the way home, she recalled the exasperated roar that Basim let out when the insolence of the Israeli Ministry of the Interior officials became too much to bear. Now she did the same thing, repeating what he had said: "Really, these people are the sons of sixty-six prostitutes!"

And she continued on her way, still cursing and swearing.

7

JININ SAT IN THE HARMONY Cooperative snack bar during the midday break, eating a fateera she had brought with her. She was beset by fears that the Interior Ministry would continue to refuse Basim permission to work. Several times she had told Basim that her successful work in the Habna Institute, together with his studies and researches, would help them to counter the pressure of the Israeli authorities and the attempts of the Ministry of the Interior to drive them to despair and make him leave the country voluntarily.

It'll never happen, that'll never happen! she said to herself. She would be forced to leave with Basim if that happened, to preserve their marriage, and she would have to give up everything she had achieved since their return to the country. She would have to leave her job in the Institute that worked to encourage a common citizenship between the residents of the country, guaranteeing a psychological balance in confronting the current discrimination against the Arabs. The job helped her, with a large dose of imagination, to confront the complexities of life in the country. It guaranteed a reasonable income for her and Basim, which was enough for them to live comfortably.

She cried as she imagined herself separated from Basim or the house that had united them as though Palestine had reunited its ruptured geography. Their house resembled a splendid old royal yacht, decorated with waves and fishermen, boats, and the color of the dawn, all washed by the smells of the sea. It was still during their summer siestas, and lively in the evening breeze. Like them, it looked out over the remains of the day. It watched the lights of the ships drawing nearer, like pearls on a necklace against the sleeping bosom of the night. It confirmed to them the fact of their continuing presence in the country, since it was anchored in their local memories like the Great Mosque of Jaffa, guarding their past and their present.

For a few moments, she reflected on everything she had considered: the possibility of deserting the woman of Jaffa inside her, of going back and renewing her American exile, turning into a refugee. She was frightened, and muttered to herself, "I won't leave. If Basim decides to leave, let him travel alone. I won't leave what's mine, and what I've built, just to give it all up for immigrants from other countries to inherit from me while I'm still alive. I'll argue with Basim if he argues with me. I'll leave him if he leaves me. I'll divorce him if he divorces me."

A colleague of hers who was sitting at a neighboring table in the canteen laughed. Jinin noticed her putting her hand over her mouth so that no one else would notice, using her hand to wipe away any remaining emotion on her lips.

Jinin managed to calm herself down as she convinced herself that Basim wouldn't actually desert her. He wouldn't leave her and flee. He wouldn't divorce a country that he had returned to in order to settle there. Basim was a good man. Stubborn, like the hero of her novel, The Remainer, but a good man.

Both of them were like the Jaffa sea, stormy when touched by a strange wind, then suddenly calm again. But she thought it unlikely that Basim would calm down this time and take a rational position.

"Jinin, my life has become a computer game," he had said to her once, at the end of an argument between them. "Winning's no different from losing. I'm living in our country as if

I were a virtual citizen. I'm there in the official registers of the Ministry of the Interior and in police stations, filed under 'General Security,' maybe with Mossad, God knows. But I'm not represented in the legal institutions, or the health and social security programs. Even you, Jinin, are present though absent, like every Palestinian in the country, but I'm an absent absentee, my darling. I'm an invitation to punish the self. A bad advert for them to distribute free to every Palestinian who's thinking of returning home as I did. I'm like a website that can be wiped from the face of the earth with the jab of a single finger."

She had been hurt, and said nothing, exuding a sadness tinged with regret. Basim had taken advantage of her silence and began to deal with his personal regret under the cover of wishes: "Jinin, I wish our relationship had remained as it started off on the internet, when we first met one another. A virtual happiness that turned into reality. But today that reality has started to unravel. I'm afraid a day may come when I just disappear into the ether."

In the end, Basim had gathered his thoughts and had let out a sigh that summed up the pain of his whole life: "Aaaah, Jinin, aaaah, if only we could have carried on living a virtual life, like the first day we went on Messenger!"

Now, in the snack bar, Jinin took up her handbag. She smiled at the young employee who had sniggered at her, who returned the gesture lazily over the rim of the cup of juice that she was drinking.

Then Jinin left.

8

JININ HAD DREAMED OF DESIGNING websites for companies and individuals. Her dream grew as she studied multimedia, and came to fulfilment when she graduated, specializing in the field of computing, website content management, and electronic journal editing. She designed a personal website, which she called jininmultimedia.com, to attract people who wanted to take advantage of the services she was offering.

A long period elapsed before Jinin received anything useful that didn't revolve around the senders' wish to amuse themselves. One evening, her attention was caught by a message in which the sender asked her, in simple but elegant phrases, to design a website for him, for a company providing services in the field of economics, accounting, and business.

Jinin sent a brief reply, asking him to supply her with further information, and details about the company and the terms he wanted to highlight for search optimization purposes. She also asked him if he had a company logo or wanted one designed.

The information she had requested arrived in installments, much of it vague and in need of further detail. At first, she was irritated, then suspicious. But soon she was overtaken by a normal sort of curiosity, which led her to think that the person involved was someone who wanted to correspond with her rather than wanting her to design a website for him and his business (if indeed he had a business at all). She was aware that the elegance she observed in the wording of his messages could well disguise a personality with ill intentions. She found comfort in her suspicions, and enjoyed her curiosity. Both gave her a pleasurable feeling of suspense, together with a sense of expectation.

The exchange of emails between her and the unknown person, who used the name Basim, continued until they acquired a rhythm like a heartbeat, with set times that they awaited separately like lovers waiting at street corners, in cafés, clubs, gardens, and train stations. At the end of each virtual encounter, each of them would leave something of themselves for the other, which the other could call to mind between encounters.

Their relationship began to acquire an emotional flavor. They began to avoid the work for which her website had been designed, gradually exposing their inner feelings. Night after night, they would check their personal accounts, stripping off their inhibitions piece by piece, like clothes, and throwing them on the bed of their desires. One night, they shed their inhibitions completely and slept together on the Messenger 'chatter' page. They slept with a deep happiness on a bed of passion, covering themselves in words, and waking in the morning to a joy that blessed them as a 'virtual couple.'

On the first morning of their virtual marriage, Jinin sent Basim an original present: the address of a website that she had set up, called Honeymoon Paradise. She gave it a slogan, 'Love starts virtually,' and wrote on it the details of their relationship. In one corner, she subtitled it 'Tales of a virtual romance.' And she laid down conditions for subscribing to, and participating in, the site.

Basim replied to Jinin by inviting her to an urgent meeting in Washington, which ended in an agreement to return to the country together, in the first instance for each of them to visit their own relatives—he to Bethlehem in the West Bank, and she to Ramla. Afterward, Basim went to Ramla and asked

Jinin's parents for her hand in marriage. The moment they signed their contract, in an emotional display of warmth, Jinin realized that Basim was a young man who had surpassed all the white knights that had passed through her dreams. She had spent months drawing pictures of him from her imagination, but the reality of him was more beautiful than all her imagined pictures combined.

In the end, Jinin never actually designed the website that Basim had asked for. He no longer reminded her about it, and perhaps he no longer even remembered it. But she designed for both of them a timeline for living in Jaffa, beginning with a marriage that experienced minor family problems, and ending with them in a small yacht anchored on the shore of the city, at the foot of the Citadel.

9

After some years of marriage, supervised by the Ministry of the Interior, and with his residency extended from time to time by Ayala, Basim changed. He was no longer the virtual man Jinin had gotten to know through the internet. And he was no longer the real man she had married.

He talked all the time about the impossibility of staying in the country. He started to recall and feel nostalgic for his places of exile—as if he had never tired of America, from which his romance with Jinin had freed him and brought him back home. Sometimes Jinin screamed within herself: *God Almighty, what is this fate? My husband's gone stubborn as a mule again! Don't I have enough of it with the stubbornness of the hero of my novel and the rest of my family?*

One evening, she teased him affectionately. They were sitting at the table for a supper of green salad with mint, and chicken breasts roasted in the oven with sliced potatoes and onions. They were eating by the window, looking out over a Jaffa evening that could not take sides with either of them.

"You seem stubborn, Bassuma, my darling. Isn't the stubbornness and obstinacy of The Remainer enough for me?"

He stopped cutting his chicken breast, and rested his knife and fork on the sides of his plate. Then he spoke with feeling:

"It's not a question of obstinacy, Jinin. Tomorrow you'll finish your novel, and The Remainer will become just a character like any other in a novel. You'll be free of his obstinacy and pigheadedness, while I'll still be as I am, suspended between heaven and earth. I'm not stubborn or pigheaded. The position we've gotten into has left me without an ounce of sense. Tell me what I should do!"

He was silent for a moment. She made no comment, but waited for him to go on, which he soon did.

"Do you want me to sell hummus and falafel? Who'll give me a permit? And if we got one, could I compete with Abu Shakir in Jerusalem, or Abu Hasan? Or Saeed al-Akkawi? Or even Abu Khalil in Lydda? Do you want me to sweep the streets of Jaffa so I can stay in the country? But even working as a sweeper is forbidden to me! Even if the whole of Jaffa was buried under a mountain of trash, and they couldn't find anyone to clean it up, they'd never employ me. They employ Ethiopian and Eritrean women, and women from Darfur, to clean the streets. There's no medical provision, there's no treatment as there is for the rest of humanity. If I get sick, I have to bear my illness till I die. It's forbidden to travel from the airport. Whenever I want to travel abroad, I have to cross the West Bank, cross the bridge, which is steeped in people's blood, and travel from Amman. Even driving a car is forbidden to me. Your car that's parked outside—if you're sick and can't drive, we have to call a taxi to take you to the doctor, or look for one of your brothers to take you. The only thing the authorities in this country haven't said to me is that it's forbidden to sleep with Jinin, or if you sleep with her it's forbidden to have children. Should I say to them, 'Beseder, okay!'? Should I say to every Israeli—gvarim ve-nashim, man or woman alike—'Fine, okay, thanks!'?"

"I have many years ahead of me, Jinin," Basim went on, letting out a sad laugh. "You, my darling, will go on working, go on writing, while I pile up loathing, unemployment, and boredom, making of them a heap of pickles which I'll stuff into jars."

She chuckled, and tried to stir Basim from his dejected animation. "So what, my darling?" she said. "It'll give you the best headline in the best newspaper in Arabic and Hebrew: 'Palestinian with Masters in economics and accountancy sells pickles and a pile of unemployment and laziness.'"

"Very good, and add underneath it in smaller letters: 'Housework'!"

Basim and Jinin's quarrels grew more intense as they abandoned their normal pattern: they turned into verbal battles leading them into dangerous territory, as when Basim hinted to her of his desire for a civilized separation, since it would enable him to go back on his own to Washington or New York, and would preserve Jinin's right to choose between a suspended divorce or joining him. The hint turned into a threat, stirring a nervousness in Jinin that was steeped in unhappiness and obstinacy. Jinin herself said that stubbornness was a gene inherited from Grandfather Dahman, her family ancestor, and that it was something she in turn had passed on to the hero of her novel, The Remainer; Basim's stubbornness was different.

Recently, Basim had once again been recalling his American exile, flirting with it and pining for it. Jinin responded impetuously to the feelings he expressed by challenging him.

"Do you really want that, my darling? Get up and go, then, and leave me alone!"

Then she felt sorry for him, and made up to him in an original way; she didn't want to try to make it up with him as she had done before. So she knelt in front of him to beg forgiveness, and presented her apology to him clothed in Japanese ritual. She turned herself into a geisha for him, like those in Tokyo.

She tried to amuse him with a story or two from her novel about Aviva, The Remainer's Jewish neighbor. Jinin told her husband some amusing stories and others that were less amusing, as well as jokes that didn't make one laugh. Basim looked at her, as he listened to his heart beating louder than the rhythm of the jokes. "Once it occurred to Aviva not to receive anyone, or let anyone visit her, not even her children. She didn't want to see Ilan or Guy, let alone Yuri. She wrote on a piece of paper: 'Aviva lo rotsa li-ra'ot et ehad ha-yom,' 'Aviva doesn't want to see anyone today.' But instead of hanging it on her front door, she hung it on The Remainer's door. Her visitors that day didn't stop banging on her front door. When The Remainer came back from work in the afternoon and saw the piece of paper and read it, he tore it off the door, ripped it up, and threw it away." Basim didn't laugh. Jinin went on, paying no attention to his reaction. "Do you know, Basim, that The Remainer once went to check on Aviva before he went home? He knocked on her door, and she answered from inside, telling him that she wasn't there: 'Aviva lo ba-bayit.'"

Basim had a grimace on his face like that on the face of a peasant whose land had not seen rain in the sowing season, a frown of misery. His face turned into furrows like those of land stricken with drought. Jinin took refuge in a deep silence, and they contented themselves with a temporary annoyance that was like a suspension of everyday relations between them. They both began to let their eyes wander over the bright stone walls that the house had been built from, counting the number of stones, before being stopped by a moment of love held in reserve, which returned them to the warmth of their realities.

Finally, a night came when Jinin realized that she had started to hate herself.

10

Jinin didn't sleep that night. The sea matched her wakefulness, the waves tossing noisily beyond the window like heavy breathing while she lay on the bed. Basim had gone to bed before her, rolling himself up in an envelope of despair and sleeping. She had stretched out beside him, watching him breathe.

Earlier, Basim had asked her to move to Bethlehem with him. "Bethlehem is worth the whole world," he had said. "Come with me. My family, my sisters, and anyone left from my parents' days . . . they're all in Bethlehem or nearby. Soon we'll have a state, we'll have children there, and bring them up as proper Palestinians, not half and half . . . ."

Jinin had told him to understand that she wouldn't leave Jaffa and that it wouldn't let her leave. She'd reminded him of what had happened to her father when he'd left Jaffa. Basim knew the story well; he knew that what had drawn her father to emigrate was the stubbornness of others. Mahmoud Dahman, who hadn't yet turned into The Remainer, hadn't been able to put up with his exile for any more than two months and had come back. He'd returned to marry the woman who would become Jinin's mother. In Ramla, where he was forced to move and live, he started a branch of the Dahman family after the Israeli bulldozers had wiped out all that remained of the family in al-Majdal Asqalan. He had returned to become The Remainer in both fact and her novel.

Jinin had reminded Basim that her mother had had her in Jaffa, although he already knew it (he always laughed whenever she recalled her father's comments on her mother: "Your mother used to pop girls and boys out one after the other, you all came out from between her legs like rabbits!" "Is it true," Basim would ask her, "that when God gave your parents a new child, your father would exclaim, 'One in the eye of the Jews,' and carry on shouting until the neighbors looked out from their doors and windows and threatened him with the police?" And Jinin would laugh and reply, "True!" And her father would reply to anyone who asked him, "We produced a Palestinian in exchange for every one who emigrated and didn't return!").

"Bethlehem is a paradise," he had told her.

"I'm not budging from here," she had told him. "Jaffa belongs to me. It's my Jaffa, just as Bethlehem is your Bethlehem. Just as you can't bear Jaffa, I can't stand it there, either. It's like you came back here in a different way from me. I came back committed. Stay beside me and forget any idea of leaving. If you stay with me, nothing will drive us apart, not Ayala and not the government that's employed her and others to make life hard for us and the other Palestinians who've stayed in the country!"

She'd said all that to him in a state of shock.

When they'd returned from the US, she'd been certain that Basim really wanted to come back home. Where had this certainty come from? She didn't know, but she'd been sure that he wanted to live by her side. She'd been ready to support him, to dig together with their nails to bring Palestine out to the surface of their lives. They would seek shade in the shadow of a Palestinian city. They would give it an injection of new life so that it wouldn't be infected by the Jewish immigrants, old and new, who were changing its appearance before their eyes. Jinin had wanted them to be two palm trees on the shores of Jaffa, dropping fresh dates;

two stones in its ancient Citadel, to compensate for what had been destroyed; two waves that would never tire of racing toward its shores. Fish would dance for them, and the fishermen would trill for them.

Basim was never really a refugee, Jinin thought. The idea shook her certainties. Basim was from over there, from Bethlehem, which was content to look at Jaffa from a distance. It said quite openly that it was content for them to be neighbors. Two neighbors living side by side, divided only by a nine-meter wall that fed on their land here and their land there. Sucking their waters dry and giving the settlers perfect security. Dividing what was left of the land. Bethlehem, like Ramallah, was not ashamed to repeat, "What's past is dead and gone; we are the children of today!"

Basim wasn't a refugee, and Jinin hadn't reckoned on his returning there. She didn't understand things the same way that he did. She didn't feel as he did—returning to the country that seven million Palestinians dreamed of going back to didn't concern him as it concerned others.

"We'll go back to Jaffa, to live and die there," she had decided for herself and for him. "Come with me to Bethlehem, for God's sake, come!" he had implored her, and had used every means at his disposal to persuade her.

Now she cried for him and for herself. For their love, which had opened a path to return to the homeland, only to separate them when they'd arrived. *My God, it's ridiculous that exile should bring us together and the homeland should drive us apart!* She cried alone, her tears wetting the sheets. She cried because Basim was no longer hers. Because she soon wouldn't need a bed big enough for two. Basim was no longer on Jaffa's side—Jaffa, which they had loved together, intertwining their lives with its features for years. She realized that this had been a dry run for Basim, a rehearsal of his return to Bethlehem, the capital of his dreams! "Come with me to Bethlehem, our house is there, and my family, and our land. . . ."

He had evidently forgotten his last visit to his birthplace, when he'd come back to her angry, cursing at his parents and all his family, telling her that they'd argued among themselves even about distributing shares in their disagreements. He'd forgotten what his brother Mahmoud had said—Mahmoud, who hadn't called him even once since he'd returned to the country; Mahmoud, who considered his marriage to Jinin to be the mistake of a lifetime.

As for his youngest sister, Nawal, she'd never stopped being angry with her brothers, who had insisted on grabbing her share of the family's land and house. Whenever she chided one of them, he would quote the popular song: "Nawal, my sister, my darling, today or tomorrow you'll be married, and everything you own will go to a stranger!" As if the person she married would remain a stranger—this person, who would be their brother-in-law, and to whose children they would be uncles, would remain a stranger?

Basim, like the rest of his brothers, had forgotten the family disputes, and had remembered only that he would get an apartment in the building his father had finished putting up at the start of this year, and his share of the land that his father had decided to distribute while still alive, so that his sons would not solve their quarrels with bullets after he had gone. Basim was content with the division, which had no guarantee attached to it.

He had told Jinin, "It's fine, now we've got a guarantee for the present and the future!"

"Okay, but *my* present and *my* future—who can guarantee them, my darling?" Jinin had replied, and had reminded him, in an imploring tone, that she worked day and night for both of them. "It's for your sake, Basim. I don't have a present or a future without you."

"The Jews won't let me work," he'd replied. "And I can't live on your labors forever, Jinin."

Now she screamed to herself, *My God, how cruel Jaffa has become to us! Can't it stand two Palestinians born in different places living together here?*

She cried to and for herself.

She cried so much that her tears raised the overall level of sadness in the country.

11

Eventually, Jinin went back to continue with her novel. Dawn had broken through the window that looked out over the little harbor. The boats were still snoozing on the surface of the water, and the waves showed no inclination to disturb them. Jinin stretched her arms out in the air, drawing in her exhaustion and the whole pressure of the night.

"I have to make some progress before I go to bed!" she whispered, then pushed her back firmly against the chair and left it there. She picked up where she had left off, with Husniya castigating The Remainer, who was standing in the doorway, about the Jewish woman who was going to destroy them.

The Remainer looked back without saying anything. He was on the point of going out. Husniya stopped him for a second time, his left foot already across the threshold. "May God preserve you, Abu Filastin, and grant you long life, you keep on going out, but not this time, man! No more of this going out and messing up your face!"

He stepped out. "I'm going to Tel Aviv," he replied from outside. "I'm going! We're in a democratic country, and I'm free to do what I like. If they don't like it, I'll go and stand in the middle of Kings of Israel Square, and turn it upside-down!"

"Oh, do whatever you like," he heard her say. "But don't be stupid. I've said what I've got to say, and you're a free man."

"Take care of the children!"

The Remainer closed the door behind him and departed, leaving Husniya's heart trembling like the stalks of mulukhiyeh that were still between her fingers.

Jinin's fingers started to shake. She was tired from her dealings with Basim. She stopped her revision, saving the part of the novel she had been working on in a file that she called 'Filastini Tays.'

She opened her email browser, and selected Walid Dahman's address.

She attached the file.

Then she wrote a message:

> Dear Walid,
> Attached is a file containing most of my new novel *Filastini Tays*. I'd be grateful if you could look through it and let me have any comments. I'll send you the rest later.
>
> Sea breezes and love from Jaffa,
> Jinin

She hit 'Send,' then turned off the computer, and went to bed. She lay down beside Basim, and went to sleep with a feeling of oppression as the new day began.

12

I WAS PLEASED BY JININ'S choice of *Filastini Tays* as the title of her novel, but I was vaguely shocked by the opening paragraph.

My father is stubborn. Even my mother said, "Your father is stubborn." We all laughed in our own way. My mother ignored our laughter and went on. "He left your sister with her mother in Gaza when she was two months old and went back to the country." She fell silent. Then she pursed her lips and pushed them forward a little. We heard a sound that put an end to our laughter; my mother held the index finger of her right hand upright over her pursed lips, like a school teacher: "Hsssss . . . ." Then we heard the sound of my father's footsteps and the noise of the key in his hand, struggling with the door lock.

I found Jinin's language transparent, open, and challenging, sometimes impetuous, a bit like her, in fact. As for her hero, The Remainer, he suggested several questions to me. Was The Remainer in Jinin's novel actually her father, Mahmoud Ibrahim Dahman? Did Jinin derive the character from him, or import his biography into her novel? Whatever the answer, I believed that Jinin was playing with The Remainer's secrets, just as she played with the character of Mahmoud Dahman, who had crept into my unconsciousness via other people's stories when I was a child.

"That's it, cousin! Mahmoud's become an Israeli!" my cousin said to my mother in my innocent presence. I hated her for saying it, and I hated Mahmoud as well. I wished I could take revenge on both of them. By boycotting my aunt, for example—by not visiting her; by not greeting her if I met her in a lane in the camp, even if she was coming back from the hajj; by not reciting the Fatiha over her soul when she died. And when I grew up, by joining my own freedom fighter, the Egyptian officer Mustafa Hafiz. I would sneak into Ramla, abduct Mahmoud, and persuade him to return with me to Gaza, telling him firmly, "Your place is here, cousin, not with the Jews!"

I remembered how annoyed my mother had been at the time. She grew angry, looked glum, and stuck her jaw out so that it looked like a duck's beak, because my aunt wouldn't stop repeating that Mahmoud had become an Israeli: "Mahmoud's staying there and doesn't want to come back!" Whenever his name was mentioned in my mother's presence, she would refer to him as 'The Remainer,' then throw her tightly knit fingers into the air, like someone chasing his life story away from her. I didn't find it strange that my mother should have become tense and insistently demanded that my aunt stop regarding The Remainer as a strange nickname or as some sort of defect. Then I remembered how—small eyes open, with a mischievous inquisitiveness—I had watched my mother when her taut nerves had relaxed a little and she had begun to berate my aunt with language that she did not often use:

"The whole family has begun to consider the name an insult, hajja! What have you done, cousin? Come on, isn't the person who stays in the country a thousand times better than the one who emigrates and deserts it?"

My aunt was shocked. She loosened her belt and used her hands to lift her breasts, which had begun to sag toward her belly and press down on it. Then she tightened her belt again in a double knot, in which she always put her money. She left her breasts hanging down comfortably instead of slinging them over her shoulders, as I used to say to her jokingly. But my aunt didn't say anything. What she had done with her belt must have released her from the burden of excessive emotion, or at least reassured her about the money she was hiding in the knot.

My mother took advantage of my aunt's temporary silence and said something about Mahmoud to put an end to her heartache—which made me think that my mother had been in love with Mahmoud in her teenage years, though she hadn't really had her fair share of adolescence, unlike other girls.

My mother had married my father 'before her eyes were open' in the view of her father (who would become my grandfather) and her younger brothers, all of whom I called khali ("my uncle"). They were all afraid of little Amina opening her eyes to the world. If she had been given an opportunity to do that, even for a fleeting period of adolescence, she would perhaps have picked up Mahmoud, the neighbors' son, and put him in her heart straightaway. She and Mahmoud were relatives and neighbors, like my own father Ahmad, whose family home was next door to hers. Like other girls of her time, she had no chance to love, or to imagine a young boy sneaking into her heart from another quarter in al-Majdal Asqalan. If my mother hadn't married my father—after a love journey that extended from the moment his father, Nimr Dahman, asked for her hand for him from her father, Khalil Dahman, until the moment she was told that the parents had agreed (a period no longer than a week)—I would have trusted my suspicions.

Finally, my mother said to my aunt: "There isn't a Palestinian in the world who'd accept becoming an Israeli, cousin, and if he did, it wouldn't be through his own actions, desire, or inclination. Mahmoud became an Israeli despite himself, hajja, he became one despite himself. I'll say to you quite frankly, in full view of witnesses, it's a good thing that Mahmoud stayed there. It's a good thing he didn't emigrate like us, to be treated with contempt. Being treated with contempt back home, hajja, even with the Jews, is a hundred times more noble than being treated with contempt and abused here in the camps."

My aunt was silent, because my mother had turned the nickname, which was supposed to represent a sort of defect, into something for which its owner could be envied.

Like many people, my mother had heard things said about Mahmoud Dahman, some of which could be believed and some not. She collected facts and rumors. She drew pictures of him, and of scenes that she loved, and which made her love him. She once told me that a short time after the occupation of al-Majdal Asqalan, Mahmoud had formed a union of weavers to protect their rights. He had persuaded many of the city's residents to stay and had prevented many from emigrating. When I asked her, "What's a workers' union?"—I was still a child in the camp, and didn't know anything about employment or workers, apart from cleaners and people who made concrete—she replied to me airily, "How should I know, Walid? They say that the people that worked in weaving clubbed together. They used to grimace as if they were giving up the ghost, write petitions, and defend each other. More than that, my dear, I don't know. I never asked."

She spoke with pride, though, about a violent confrontation that had taken place between Mahmoud and Ben Gurion at Israeli Government Headquarters after the nakba. And she praised Mahmoud's challenge to the head of the first Israeli government, which had proclaimed the establishment of Israel on 14 May 1948. "My cousin Mahmoud," she said, "was worth ten men, by God. He stood up to Ben Gurion and spat in his face." My mother believed everything she was told, and embraced all the stories that praised Mahmoud Dahman and talked about his character, which had raised the status of the Dahman family back home and in the refugee camps in the Gaza Strip.

I laughed as my thoughts turned to a tale in which Mahmoud Dahman appeared at an untimely moment. I remembered the morning that the circumciser chased away a pigeon my eyes were fixed on, as the razor appeared like lightning in his hand and in the twinkle of an eye descended on my fresh foreskin. The head of my little penis appeared, gazing at those present and proclaiming its eternal purity, while the foreskin became just a piece of skin of no value suspended between the fingers of the circumciser. The man, who combined the shaving of heads with cutting the redundant foreskins of young children, threw it onto a small square cloth handkerchief, which he had spread out beside him. I remember that a pretty woman leaned over to my mother and whispered to her, and they laughed quietly together. Amid my confusion, my mother wrapped the handkerchief around the foreskin, which was streaked with lines of blood, while the circumciser himself was occupied with wrapping white cloth around my actual penis. My mother then handed the handkerchief to the woman, who thanked her (though she didn't thank me, to whom both the foreskin and the penis belonged!). Then she turned around and disappeared. Subsequently, I would learn that the woman had fried my foreskin in olive oil and had eaten it that evening with half a loaf of warm bread. I reckon that she must have made love with her husband that night, before sleeping deeply, dreaming of a young boy who would come to her as a result of a pregnancy in which a foreskin had played a part.

Anyway, on the morning of my circumcision, they laid me out on my little bed, which was spread on the floor of our only bedroom in the camp, and hovered around me, gossiping and mulling over Mahmoud Dahman's life story. This was the first time I'd heard stories about him beyond my mother and aunt's gossip. A lot of people cursed and swore at Mahmoud, astonished at his ability to live among the Jews. Others envied him for his 'Israeliness,' for which they had no equivalent. Some of them said, "A thousand times better to be dead than to emigrate, be dragged around from place to place, and be given a hard time." With their traditional clannish attitudes, others said, "I'd swear (on pain of divorce!) that life under the Israelis is a thousand times better than life under the Egyptian military administration that made us see stars at noon. The Israelis are our enemy, and they occupied us, but the others just flogged at us nationalistic self-importance to no purpose at all!"

Everyone praised Mahmoud's bravery. As my mother passed around red juice to those congratulating me on a successful procedure (and the safe delivery of my penis, of course), she said, "Ben Gurion deserved the spit on his face. Mahmoud, cousin, if only you could have taken a shoe off and hit him in the face with it!" Those present muttered appreciation of what he had done, while my father, who was busily gathering up the presents, reinforced their mutterings: "Great, cousin! Ben Gurion really did deserve hitting with a shoe." The guests asked for more to drink.

On the evening of the circumcision day, which doesn't happen to a penis twice, the whole camp was happy when they heard what my mother had said in the morning. The residents celebrated a happy, nationalistic day, and spent their evening basking in the small victory that Mahmoud Dahman had scored. I was still lying on my back, more concerned about the fire that had been raging in my penis ever since it had lost a redundant part. That fire didn't subside all night.

That was how I inherited from my mother an initial impression of Mahmoud Dahman, a hero pulled from her imagination, which took the form of The Remainer, both in nickname and in the characteristics my aunt had given him. This was before his name became well known and recognized by others in his absence; many years before Jinin borrowed his nickname and gave some of his features to the hero of her novel; and even before Mahmoud himself heard about the moniker and recognized in it the self that others had created for him.

That happened several years later, when in June 1967 Israel completed the occupation of the remainder of Palestine that had been postponed since 1948. During these years, the character of The Remainer had crystallized in isolation from him, acquiring characteristics that were later to become his: he became a man who resembled a reality overwhelmed with emotions. His family fled from the city of al-Majdal Asqalan, pursued by bombs and bullets, fires following in their wake. The collapsing walls, the winds, and the October winter—harsh that year—roared after them, urging them to flee, while he desperately urged them to stay.

My mother told me that she had heard Mahmoud say that day, "Anyone who leaves, my friends, will not come back!" I believed what my mother said because she had heard it, and also because she was my mother. I was upset when I learned that Mahmoud had in the end been defeated. He had been carried along in the general exodus, which had poured out of every corner and every alley of al-Majdal Asqalan like a mighty river. Everyone was thrown into Gaza, and camps for the Palestinians were formed from its human silt. Next I was happy, because Mahmoud had come back. He hadn't stayed in Gaza long, though, before he'd gone away again. He'd crept back into al-Majdal Asqalan on foot, fleeing from the Egyptian intelligence service, which had begun to be active in the Gaza Strip and which caught up with him with a charge of inciting refugees to return to their homes. The Zionist organizations hadn't yet entered the city of al-Majdal, or divided it among their own refugees, whom they imported to be the new residents there. They hadn't closed the border with the Gaza Strip at this point, because it hadn't yet become a strip—there were no borders at all to close. Mahmoud had fled the nakba and those affected by it. He'd left his wife and young daughter in a camp that had been planted among the yellow, sandy hills behind a city that remained for a time quite ashamed of him, as if it were somehow carrying him on its back. It called Mahmoud and others like him 'emigrants.' So he had returned home, hoping that his small family would catch up to him later. Israel had then closed what had now become borders following the battle with Egyptian forces withdrawing from al-Majdal in

October 1948, and the Israeli authorities had refused to allow him to bring his wife and daughter into the country.

The whole Dahman family described Mahmoud as mad. Even his father, Sheikh Ibrahim Dahman, said, "My son is officially mad, my son, I know him, he's gone to live with the Jews, whom no one can stand!" But he subsequently came to like the nickname that had been given—and had stuck to—his son, and started using it to refer to him. He became even more admiring when someone told him the news (originally announced in a message that Mahmoud had recorded and broadcast via the Peace and Greeting program, put out in Arabic by Israeli Radio) that his eldest son had gotten married again to another woman, from Ramla, and had established an Israeli branch of the Dahman family, leaving Sheikh Ibrahim to take responsibility for his small Gazan branch. That message changed the father's attitude to his son, and softened both his and others' opinion of him.

"Now we've planted our feet in the country and have a branch there," he announced to a family gathering. "It's not just Mahmoud who has stayed—the sons and daughters he will have in the future will also remain there!"

At that point, the head of the Dahman family asked him, "Okay, Sheikh Ibrahim, but what if the Jews get hold of him?"

"They'll go pop," he replied. "Mahmoud is a thorn in the Jews' throats!" Sheikh Ibrahim's eyes filled with tears, for he wished he could have stayed in al-Majdal, or even in Lydda, Ramla, or somewhere else—they were all home in his view. He wished he could have been present at the births of his grandchildren there, one after the other, instead of those who had been born in the camp here, so that the family could get a bigger share of UNRWA rations.

What Sheikh Ibrahim had said became a proverb repeated by others in the family and their children for three generations, as part of their store of oral heritage. When Israel occupied the Gaza Strip in the 1967 War, many of the

Dahman family said, "The branch has been reunited with the stem." The fugitive refugees were the stem, and The Remainer and his children were the branch. Jinin was one of the daughters of the Dahman stem that had not extended southward toward Gaza, but rather in the opposite direction, toward Lydda and Ramla.

I summarized for Jinin in a few lines my impressions of that part of her novel I had read. I asked her not to leave me in suspense, but to send me the rest of it. I told her that I would soon be visiting the country with my wife. I explained that Julie wanted to get to know the Acre that the run-up to the war of 1948 had made it impossible for her to grow up in, when her parents had whisked her away to London at the age of two months. I added that she would be bringing with her some of the ashes of her mother, to place them inside what had been the house of her grandfather Manuel more than sixty years before, as instructed. I expected Jinin to be very pleased, and to be even more pleased at the news of our visit to her in Jaffa with which I concluded my short message.

Jinin soon emailed me a file containing the rest of her novel, except for the final chapter, which she proposed to give me when we met, either in printed form or else in the form of a verbal summary. She said my opinion of what I'd read had reassured her considerably, though it had also surprised her. She told me that from now on she would be preparing herself for possible confrontations with her readers.

I printed out as much of the novel as Jinin had sent, and put it in the small bag that usually stayed on my shoulder when I was traveling.

Then I wrote back to Jinin to thank her, expressing interest in The Remainer and his personality as an actual father, and also in her novel. I told her that I would follow his progress through her novel closely. Most likely that would be during my visit to the country, while Julie would be busy reading Ahdaf Soueif's novel *In the Eye of the Sun*, which she'd told me she would take with her, and which she'd started reading some days before. For my part, I might be able to read some more chapters of *Filastini Tays*. I left the subject of the final chapter of the novel to our anticipated meeting, as she had suggested.

At the end of my email, I suggested to Jinin that we should meet at eleven o'clock on the following Monday—four days later—in Dina's Café in Jaffa.

13

A Warm Day in Montreal

I HAD GOTTEN TO KNOW Jinin six years previously, during a short stopover she'd made in London on her way to New York. I entertained her for dinner at home on that occasion, in the absence of my wife Julie, who was abroad. News of Mahmoud had been interrupted when exile had cut me off from the homeland and torn me apart. During the evening, Jinin took me back to some of what I had been searching for during my childhood about The Remainer, although she wasn't able to give much detail to many of the stories.

We were next brought together at an evening gathering (to which Julie was unable to accompany me) at the wedding party of the beautiful Lara, the daughter of our relative Zakariya Dahman, in Montreal, Canada. I accepted Zakariya's invitation immediately, although I had never met him before and didn't know much about him, except that he was a relative of ours who had been in Kuwait, where we had a lot of family.

A few hours before leaving London, I received a message from Jinin conveying to me some good impressions of Zakariya and his family, though there was also some disturbing information.

Jinin informed me that Zakariya had worked as a teacher in Kuwait until the First Gulf War in 1991. In August of the same year, Kuwait had been liberated from the Iraqi occupation, which had lasted seven months. "Then," she wrote, "Kuwait liberated itself from Zakariya in a moment of strategic national impetuosity, in which it dispensed with his services, along with those of 300,000 other Palestinians who had upheld it as a second homeland for decades. Kuwait made them take responsibility for a tactical error that their political leaders had made, and expelled them." Zakariya took his wife, his two sons, Khalid and Husam, and his only daughter, Lara, and traveled as an outcast from his Kuwaiti past (which he had loved), weighed down with all the complexities of that stage of his life, to settle in Montreal, the capital of the province of Quebec.

Jinin stressed to me in her email that Zakariya, unlike many other migrants, refugees, and exiles, liked his choice a lot. He had never regretted the fifteen years he had so far spent in Montreal. He had never struck his cheeks, cursed his black times, or complained about his exile. Instead, he had hastened to build a new life for himself and for the members of his family.

Zakariya and his family had learned French, and with the money he had saved from his long years of working in Kuwait, he had opened a restaurant serving Palestinian food, which he called '*la cuisine palestinienne*'. With the help and expertise of his Palestinian wife, he'd brought to Montreal maqluba from Gaza, West Bank musakhkhan, Bedouin mansaf, and Palestinian maftul. For his speciality dish, the 'Zikodish', he singled out warm Montreal evenings. This was a dish of fish and rice, to which was added some seafood, in what some of his customers regarded as a sort of 'Palestinian paella', by analogy with its Spanish counterpart.

Abu Khalid, as he liked to be called, was content with his delicious meals and resisted the temptation to sell hummus and falafel, leaving that to his Palestinian neighbor, Saeed Darawisha. Saeed had come to Canada as a refugee from the Burj al-Barajneh refugee camp in Lebanon. For several years, Saeed's dishes graced Montreal's mornings, while

Zakariya's dishes enlivened its evenings, adorning its late-night parties every weekend.

Although Zakariya had abandoned the profession and practice of teaching, which was no longer of the same value in a city like Montreal as it was back home, he set aside two hours every week with his wife to give free Arabic lessons to people in the local Arab community, in a large room on the second floor above the restaurant, with a separate outside entrance.

On the evening of the wedding party, Jinin introduced me to Zakariya and his wife. I shook hands with the man, with an inexplicable feeling of familiarity. Perhaps it was the warmth and curiosity of that first meeting. Perhaps it was the tie of kinship, which—despite whatever social changes and distance had done to it—still retained its power to bring us together and give warmth to our meeting. Or perhaps it was Jinin's email and the way she had spoken of his life.

I looked at Zakariya for a time, trying to read the details of Jinin's message in him, trying to place him among her various words and expressions: tall, on the edge of being plump, skin the color of wheat, pleasing features that paved the way for anyone meeting him for the first time to penetrate his world freely and easily. Then I shook hands with his wife, who was at least ten years younger than him (or so I thought), with features that confirmed the wise choice Zakariya had made. I showed particular pleasure in being introduced to the mother of the bride, for whom the world would not be big enough this evening, during which she would turn into the bridegroom's mother-in-law. Then I shook hands with Husam, Zakariya's son, the father's hand resting on the son's left shoulder as he introduced him to me. "Husam's started university this year," he said, "and compensated me for everything that's gone before. Husam is the man of the house, ustaz Walid, and my right arm!"

Before I could enquire what he meant, or ask about his son Khalid—whom he hadn't mentioned in front of me, and who was strangely absent on a night like this—Zakariya quickly started to tell me about the happy couple, his daughter Lara and Dr. Salama al-Farra. He announced, with a pride bigger than the wedding palace we were standing in, that they would spend their honeymoon on one of the Caribbean islands, then fly to Dubai to settle in Salama's work place. Then he moved his hand from Husam's shoulder to mine. I thought he was going to reveal something, and watched his next movements carefully: he sighed a little; he smiled nervously, like someone washing away an old care inside him with the happiness of this unforgettable evening. "I wish we could have gotten to know each other before now, ustaz Walid," he said. "I would have introduced you to . . . ."

Jinin quickly moved to drown out what Zakariya was about to say with a decisive interruption. "The couple have arrived, Abu Khalid, they've arrived!"

Her hastily contrived eloquence drew everyone's eyes to the hall entrance. A storm of happiness and cheers broke out at that moment, as the beating of drums assailed our ears. Zakariya withdrew his hand from my shoulder, excusing himself. He took hold of his wife's hand, and together they made their way through the guests toward the entrance to the hall, followed by Husam. There, the three of them disappeared into a crowd of women, who were practicing their wedding songs. I watched joy spread over the other guests' faces.

I felt Jinin slip her right arm under my left arm. I liked that, for it gave me the warm feeling that I needed. She stopped a waiter, took a glass of red wine from the silver tray he was carrying, and passed it to me with an encouraging smile. I took it from her hand, and she took another glass.

"Excuse me, cousin," she said, pulling me into a nearby corner. "I had to interrupt Abu Khalid so that he wouldn't complete . . . tonight's his daughter's night, the joy of his whole life, and I don't want him to get carried away with stories . . . ."

"Get carried away?"

"Oh, I mean . . . listen, forget it. I'll tell you later. Come on, cheers! Let's enjoy ourselves!"

We clinked glasses. The mystery would have to wait.

Jinin leaned her head slightly toward me so that her hair touched my shoulders, and whispered, "I had an idea to invite you to breakfast tomorrow morning. I'll take you to the Van Houtte Café, so you can eat the best bagels in town, and drink the best coffee, too. What do you think? Shall I come by tomorrow and pick you up from the hotel, so we can go together?"

I muttered my agreement, although it would mean I'd miss the delicious breakfast served by the hotel.

Jinin put her glass down on the table beside her. She ruffled her thick, flowing hair with all ten fingers. I watched her rearrange her hair over her shoulders and change the image she'd arrived with only a few minutes before.

"You'll rival the bride tonight, Jinin!"

"Umm . . . should I be flirting with my cousin?" she mumbled, and moved away from me. She took all her youthfulness with her, and threw herself into a group of young people who were absorbed in dancing in the middle of the hall. I stood watching Jinin swinging her hips around with the lightness of an ear of wheat caught by a light breeze. I contented myself with a second glass of wine, as I watched the words of Stevie Wonder work on the bodies of the dancers: "*I just called to say I love you . . . .*"

In the Van Houtte Café, I sat with Jinin at a square cane table in the front left corner, flanked by a low wall of flowers that extended along the front of the café and enclosed three other similar tables, giving Van Houtte the feel of a high-class Parisian pavement café. The French hadn't just brought the elegance of their buildings to the cities of this province, they had brought their cafés with them and deposited them on their sidewalks. I let my eyes wander along the street in front of us for a few moments, enjoying the morning. Passersby and their conversations were scattered around us like the masses of flowers that surrounded the place.

I ate the piece of cake I had ordered, with a pleasure that rivaled Jinin's, who had started to umm and ahh as she ate her own. When she had finished, she wiped her hands and lips, and drank the rest of her cup of coffee. There were no grounds left at the bottom worth reading. Then she picked up the thread of what Zakariya had been saying when she'd interrupted him in a moment of caution made necessary by the situation the night before.

She explained that Khalid, the eldest son, had been born in Kuwait City, but since his childhood had dreamed of visiting Gaza and of getting to know the city and his family there. This was despite the fact that all he knew about Gaza came from the odd comment made by his father. Many years later, the opportunity came to him, when he received a letter from the Palestinian Khabar agency in Jerusalem, offering him a job as an English-language correspondent in Gaza. They stressed to him their need for someone who had lived in the West and had a foreign nationality that would help him travel anywhere freely.

Zakariya vigorously resisted the idea. Khalid was his eldest son, who had given him the name Abu Khalid, the name by which people usually called him. Zakariya was afraid of the tense situation in Gaza, which he described as confused. He never stopped saying that Gaza lived in the hand of a devil who was continually calling people out to fight. But the dispute ended in a compromise, namely that Khalid should work in the agency headquarters in Jerusalem and forget the subject of Gaza. Khalid accepted the compromise, which the agency also did not oppose, so he moved to Jerusalem, where he made the acquaintance of his colleagues in the Sheikh Jarrah office. They all welcomed him, and considered him an important key to cooperative relations with the Canadian media as well.

One day, three months after he had arrived in the country, the Khabar agency commissioned Khalid to cover a protest march against the racist Separation Wall, south of Bethlehem, in which a number of foreign activists were taking part. There was a clash between the protesters and the Occupation authorities, in which Khalid found himself caught up. He was arrested and jailed for two weeks, at the end of which he was released on condition that he left Jerusalem. Khalid's old dream awoke again: he asked for a transfer to Gaza, to work as a reporter for the agency there, and his request was accepted.

In Gaza, Khalid rediscovered his Dahmani roots. He became the Canadian son of the family, which welcomed him with great joy. But the family's happiness was short-lived. Khalid was killed in an Israeli air raid on the outskirts of Beit Hanun while he was doing his job, less than three months after his transfer to Gaza. Zakariya was grief-stricken, as was the rest of the family, which had lost nine martyrs in the Second Intifada. But Khalid's death was the most painful for everyone. The others had had proper funeral processions, even when these took place during Israeli aerial bombing raids. But Khalid's parents and siblings were not able to get to Gaza to oversee his funeral. The Canadian Embassy in Tel Aviv intervened with the Israelis to protest the death of their citizen Khalid Zakariya Dahman, and informed his father that they were prepared to transport his son's body to Montreal. When Zakariya received this communication from the authorities in Montreal, he wailed aloud, as if his son had been killed twice: "My son returned to Palestine and was martyred there, and now you want me to bury him in Canada as an exile!" He informed the relevant authorities that he had decided to bury his son in his own land among his own family. So Khalid was buried in the Jabalia graveyard in the absence of his parents.

I was saddened by the story, though I wasn't too surprised by what had happened. By virtue of my work in the press and other media, I had seen a number of young men vanish from the family's ranks one after the other as a result of Israeli raids that had taken place in recent months. They were relatives I had never known, for most of the victims had been born in the years of my exile after 1967. Some had died in the settling of internal political and party scores between Hamas and Fatah.

I decided that I would visit Zakariya and his family before I left the country, to present condolences that were several years overdue. I was sorry for that, and I knew that I would be bringing up a dark chapter during an otherwise happy time. But the meeting was necessary in any event, and I also wanted to get to know Abu Khalid, and the Canadian experience, better. Jinin indicated that she would like to accompany me, which I welcomed.

We left the Van Houtte Café at around 11 a.m. The streets passed by under our feet, as commercial establishments and restaurant signs flirted with our eyes. We were detained by the image of a charming bride in a shop selling wedding dresses. I turned toward Jinin, trying to extract her and myself from the shadow of the story of Khalid Dahman, and asked her what I should have asked her a long time ago:

"So, Jinin, why haven't you gotten married yet?"

"You've caught me by surprise!" she replied. Then, after a calculated silence, she went on: "I've had five proposals, if you can believe that!"

"Now you've caught *me* by surprise!" I replied. "As if you were Marie Munib, melting all five of their hearts!" I joked.

She laughed. "Ha, why not? I could be proposed to twenty times. In our country, getting engaged is just marriage with a stay of execution!"

We mulled this over for a few moments until Jinin broke the silence, saying that the first man she'd gotten to know had asked for her hand very quickly. He was in such a hurry; he must have thought she would fly away. As the day of the Quran ceremony approached, he had proposed to her parents that they should live in Nablus after the wedding. Her father, Mahmoud Dahman, had refused, and she had added her own refusal to his. So that marriage had failed before it could even begin.

Her second fiancé was from the city of Umm al-Fahm, in the northern triangle of Palestine. "Everything about him took my breath away," she said, but she added that immediately after the announcement of their engagement he had started to hum and buzz around her like a blue fly. He had piled it on and was far too demanding. "If you want to live with me in Umm al-Fahm," he'd announced, "you'll have to wear the hijab. The hijab is chastity, Jinin. The hijab is the crown on a woman's head, preserving her honor!"

Jinin had continued to refuse, trying to convince her suitor to accept her as she was, but without success. In the end, she had taken advantage of a visit that he paid with his parents to her parents' house, and shouted in his face: "What do you think I am, a street girl with no honor or dignity? 'The hijab is chastity, the hijab is purity'! Leave me alone, you . . . ." She had pulled the engagement ring from her finger and had thrown it in his face, adding, "If you're so in love with the hijab, marry someone who already wears the hijab!"

We laughed together at the story, before Jinin moved on to her third experience. Suitor number three was an American of Syrian origin, from Homs. He had asked her to renounce her Israeli nationality and to live with him in America. He'd told her in no uncertain terms: "Look, I don't want anyone to say that I've married an Israeli girl and to accuse me of assimilating!"

She had cut him out of her life, but not before telling him, "I was born in Palestine and I shall die in Palestine. Israeli nationality, as far as I'm concerned, is a matter of citizenship and rights; it's true that it's incomplete, but it lets me stay in my country!" He just couldn't understand her position, so that was that.

Jinin had loved the fourth one as a lover ought, despite the fact that they had known each other only a short time. Sami was a handsome young man, loving and warm. He was from Nazareth.

His father had moved there from al-Khiyam village in the south of Lebanon a few years before the nakba. He'd worked as a shoemaker in Nazareth Market (which would later become the Old Market) for many years before the city was invaded by the commercial cooperatives and people gravitated to them in the search for new, ready-made shoes. He had had three sons, who had grown up and worked in various occupations. One day, the father had decided to leave Nazareth and go back to al-Khiyam. He'd said that he wanted to spend the rest of his life in his birthplace. So he and his wife had returned to settle in al-Khiyam. Two of their sons lived and worked in Beirut, after renouncing their Israeli citizenship and reclaiming their Lebanese nationality. But Sami, the youngest son, refused to return to Lebanon and insisted on staying in Nazareth. After the family left, however, he didn't stay in the city long, but moved to Jaffa to work as a civil servant in the Tel Aviv–Jaffa municipality, where Jinin got to know him on one of her visits to the town hall.

Jinin paused, and a sudden look of pain came over her face, from which she emerged a few moments later with a deep sigh, speaking with a vague regret. "If only it had been like that!"

"What's that?" I asked her.

She turned to me sharply. "The story."

Then she took me on to the Second Intifada, which had broken out on 28 September 2000. She reminded me of the notorious incident that had taken place on 12 October of the same year, when a group of angry young men had surrounded two civilians in a Ford car driving near the Friends' School in Ramallah, suspecting them of belonging to the Israeli special forces. A squad of Palestinian policemen had then intervened, arrested the two men, and transferred them to the nearby headquarters, but several groups of angry citizens had massed around the headquarters, attacked it, and killed the two youths.

I didn't understand the connection between the incident and her engagement to Sami from Nazareth, so I asked her. She stared me in the face, and replied, "Sami was one of the two men who were killed by the mob at the police headquarters. My fiancé, I mean . . . can you believe that he was . . . ?"

"What?"

"Sami turned out not to be 'Sami' at all. His real name was Samuel Samhun. He was an Israeli officer in an Arab infiltration unit, who had taken on the identity of Sami years before, and had lived as Sami—outside Nazareth, of course. That's how I got to know him, and that's how he asked for my hand."

I had read of Arab impersonators and members of Mossad marrying Palestinian girls after adopting Palestinian identities, including some who had studied the Islamic religion in depth in order to perfect their roles. One of them had had children by his wife, and had forced her to convert to Judaism and conceal her past from her children.

"And the original Sami?"

"All I know is that he disappeared from Nazareth some months after his family left."

"Okay, and what's the story of the fifth man?" I asked.

"The first four would have to be true for there to be a fifth. Haha, did you believe it, cousin? No, these four are the heroes of short stories that I intend to write, dealing with the problems of women in the country."

I liked Jinin's stories, and her deception plunged me into a sudden fit of laughter, which forced her to laugh as well. Finally, I repeated my last question, teasing her in a friendly way: "Okay, and the fifth, Jinin?"

"The fifth will really be the first, Walid. The fifth is the real one, different entirely, although my relationship with him has so far been a virtual one. We talk through email. We spend hours in conversation, getting to know one another better. I want him to be the one to lift the hijab of happiness from my face, the one hijab that every girl likes, because it can't conceal the happiness of the bride on her wedding night." And she pointed to a mannequin behind the display window, showing off a wedding dress that would tempt any young girl of marriageable age. "Look how beautiful she is, veiled in white lace!"

"What's his name?" I asked.

"Basim."

We walked on, then paused for some time in front of the entrance to the Ritz Carlton Hotel, as the late morning sunshine escorted the tourists, highlighting the details of the lovely city for them. I thanked Jinin for the delicious coffee and bagel, and for her umbrella of stories.

Then we parted.

Third Movement

1

Small Fires

THE PLANE TOOK OFF. MY neighbor in the seat to my right quickly introduced himself to me, before the fears I always feel when taking off had even subsided.

"Call me Edward. I'm an American from Dallas. You'll certainly have heard of it. I work in a tractor and bulldozer company in Jerusalem. In fact, I specialize in servicing the famous Caterpillar trucks, you must have heard of them!"

Ha, had I *heard* of them?

"Of course, of course," I muttered to him.

Enormous, efficient American bulldozers, capable of changing the geography of the West Bank and Gaza completely. They'd played a part in erecting the ethnic wall. They'd destroyed and swept away hundreds of Palestinian houses and other dwellings. And didn't your bulldozers, the Israelis' favorites, kill your fellow citizen, Rachel Corrie, on 16 March 2003?

What was a man like this really doing in Jerusalem? And what might he be sweeping away in addition to what we knew about?

My neighbor, who seemed relaxed, didn't disturb my musings as he waited for me to introduce myself. But I was under no compulsion to do so.

The man finally broke his silence, and started a rapid rhythmical chatter, like a barber in a Palestinian refugee camp. He wasted half an hour of the time I had set aside to read more of Jinin's novel, *Filastini Tays.* I was supposed to have finished reading the rest of what I had of it by the time we met in Jaffa. He chattered on without asking my permission or making any effort to find out whether I wanted to listen to him.

He plied me with unwelcome questions. He enquired in the most precise detail about my journey and my marriage. He was like a bulldozer which didn't pause between uprooting an olive tree and destroying a house somewhere else in Palestinian territory. In the end, I told him that my wife and I were on a short visit to the country, during which we would stay as guests in the house of a friend of ours.

Instead of shutting him up, my words encouraged him to continue his questions. With a burning curiosity that aroused my suspicion, he asked me if I was an Israeli. He asked me if I was a Jew. He asked me if I had Israeli friends. He asked me if I was visiting Israel for the first time. He asked me if I had visited Jerusalem before. He asked me if I would be visiting the holy places, and offered me platitudes about them. He asked me whether I had friends there. He asked me whether I had visited Haifa before. He asked me whether I had visited the house of my host in particular, or knew his address. Did the house have balconies for sitting out on summer evenings? Like someone divulging a secret, he said, "You Mediterraneans like balconies and sitting out after your siestas. I envy you your lazy afternoons!"

He fell silent, and I pointed out to him that he could learn the popular afternoon laziness prevalent in the country for free. He nodded, and then continued his enquiries: "Does your friend's house look out over Mount Carmel or over the sea?"

This strange American will tag along with us when we walk off the plane after landing, I said to myself. *Then we'll be forced to introduce him to our host as soon as we walk through the exit door where he's waiting for us in the airport.*

I might well have replied rudely, "And what's it got to do with you, man? Just leave me alone!" Instead, I said with a feigned English politeness, "I'm not sure, but that doesn't bother me too much. I'll walk around Haifa a bit, stroll on the shore for a little, visit the old Arab quarters, and climb Mount Carmel—Mount Carmel, in whose arms the city has slept since it first appeared, stretching its legs out to the sea and wetting its feet in the wa-a-ater!"

I yawned the last word with my eyes shut, before I closed my mouth over a curse that was trying to come out.

My neighbor made no comment and put no further questions to me after that, as if he had been struck by a sort of verbal paralysis. He didn't even yawn, suspecting he might pay the price.

I woke up from my pretend sleep after a few minutes. Out of the corner of my eye, I could see my neighbor looking at me, having now begun a pointless chat with a young Jew with two sidelocks dangling in front of his ears. From what I could hear of their conversation, I understood that the young man was a university student, American like him, and that he was visiting Jerusalem for purely religious reasons.

Julie was continuing to read Ahdaf Soueif's novel *In the Eye of the Sun*. She must by now be immersed in the details of Asya's relationship with Saif. She had told me about it two days before: since her marriage to Saif three years before, Asya had had no sexual relations with him, but had been in love with Gerald, who compensated for Saif's coldness in bed, leaving her with a thirsty spirit that she watered from time to time with what remained of her husband's love.

I took the pages of Jinin's novel from my small bag, wanting more than ever to get better acquainted with The Remainer. It would become clear to me that his wasn't an inherited stubbornness, despite the view expressed by Jinin that it was a gene passed on through the Dahmans. Indeed, after he had left his first wife and daughter in Gaza, a second incident occurred in his life that confirmed this belief in everyone who knew him.

This is what Jinin had written:

One ordinary afternoon, their Jewish neighbor Aviva took advantage of his absence and that of his family from the house, sprayed a bottle of kerosene on their wall, and set light to it. She then started shouting, "Shoah! Shoah!" until the al-Jamal quarter in Lydda was filled with her screams. Other neighbors rushed to the fire, and one of them called the fire brigade, who came immediately and managed to put it out before it could spread. The police also came and opened an investigation, for which there was no need, since The Remainer—who, on hearing the news, had arrived from the Dahman Clothes Washing and Ironing store, which he owned—chose not to press charges. Instead, he forgave his neighbor entirely, and rejected the idea of taking her to court. "Let's solve it the Arab way!" he said, despite the fact that the second party, the accused, was not an Arab. "Gveret Aviva is lonely and miserable," he told the police officer in charge of investigating the incident. "No one can blame her. What she's seen in her life, no human being should have seen, and it's driven her mad and ruined her nerves. God help her!"

The officer was pleased by what The Remainer had said. He appreciated his forgiveness of his fellow citizen and his sympathy with her past. "If all Arabs were like this guy, we'd have burned all those Arab homes and they'd have been quite happy!" he said in Hebrew, and everyone understood.

The Remainer was a Communist, whose leadership was acknowledged by Lydda and Ramla, and accepted by the Arab residents as well as some of the Jews. He saw in Marxism a way for mankind to escape from the hateful evils and greed of capitalism, and for the peoples of the East to escape from Western colonialism and the social classes that depended on and cooperated with it. He believed that the philosophy of materialism was a powerful one, deserving of his admiration and acceptance. He also believed that it didn't entail atheism, although its founders, Friedrich Engels and Karl Marx, had lost their way to God, introduced errors into their theory, and led their followers astray, bringing them close to the fires of hell. This was something that appealed to Husniya, The Remainer's wife, and led her to adopt the same beliefs and philosophy as her husband.

The Remainer believed that the materialist philosophy was deficient, and needed a real Remainer like himself—or at least someone similar—to connect it to God, as well as to mankind. So he turned to Sufism—as did Husniya later—and persuaded himself to undertake the reorientation of the philosophy in its path to God, at whose kingdom they (he and the philosophy, that is) would arrive together at the moment of revelation of a Sufism where he would be at one with the universe and its Creator.

The Remainer liked Emil Habibi a lot. When Emil won the Israeli State Prize for Literature in 1992, and accepted it from the Prime Minister of the time, Yitzhak Shamir, at a glittering official ceremony, The Remainer was happy, and said, "Comrade Abu Salam has surpassed their writers and raised the status of Arabic literature, sitting over their heads with his legs dangling, as if he were sitting on a rock with his legs hanging over the sea. And now, of course, he'll have some influence, after catching the biggest fish in the land, the Literature and Culture Fish. I swear by Almighty God (he was always swearing by Almighty God) that this man has raised our heads up high, higher than anything except the Israeli flag flying over all our heads."

Then he cried. The Remainer cried that day from too much happiness. He cried to and for Emil Habibi. Husniya saw him cry, she saw the tears of joy on his cheeks, which were the color of bereavement. She added her own tears, asking, "Do you want more, Abu Filastin?"

Finally, The Remainer wiped away the last tears from his eyes, and replied to her, "Don't be in too much of a hurry, Hassuna, my dear—keep your tears till the day they're needed. We might need a lot of tears tomorrow."

Like The Remainer, Husniya loved Emil Habibi and the Communists. She was invigorated by the lives of the comrades. She used to say that stories about a comrade smelled like the sweat of peasants in the harvest season. She could smell their scent in a statement, or a poster, or a news item in the al-Ittihad *newspaper. She used to say, "If it weren't for them, what happened to us in our country would have had neither color nor flavor!" She was constantly reading Abu Salam's writings, and never missed an opportunity to follow what 'Juhayna' wrote, but since the breakup of the Soviet Union and the dispersal of the local comrades she had used the newspaper after reading it for things that would soil it, like a believer going against her faith.*

One day, Husniya surprised The Remainer by saying, "Abu Filastin, after you stuffed my head with Abu Salam's ideas, I've used the al-Ittihad *newspaper to clean the windows!"*

At first, The Remainer was shocked by Husniya's words. If Husniya had said that in front of him only a few years ago, he would have ripped the windows from the walls and dashed them to pieces. Now, though, the matter really raised serious questions for him. Why is it that the pages of the *al-Ittihad* newspaper clean the windows when our comrades' ideas and essays have never cleaned the minds of the people in our country? *he wondered. Then he cried, "Clean the glass of your windows with the Communists' ideas! Marxism is a better cleaner!"*

He liked this outburst, which he considered an ideological plea for help. For the first and last time in his life, he wished that the sea would disappear and the country turn to desert, that a wind would arrive from every direction, laden with all sorts of dust—including both the local nuclear dust, which would probably come from the Dimona reactor in the Negev, as well as that imported from even more arid deserts—to deposit its load on the windows of all the houses, old and new, that the state had claimed as 'absentee properties.'

The Remainer smiled as he whispered to himself, "This is a wind that will raise the sales of our party's newspaper to the skies!"

Then he repeated, "Marxism is a better cleaner!"

The Remainer gave a loud laugh, then cursed the state of the Left in the country with tears in his eyes. Husniya repeated her previous question: "Can I help you with a tear or two, Abu Filastin? For God's sake, take two drops for yourself, man! I've got enough for any disaster. I've been collecting tears since 1948!"

2

Aviva Dies Twice

Aviva, our next-door neighbor, died. She died one night in our presence. She had a nervous attack, the second in a week. This time it caught her early: it came before dawn broke, like a warning, announcing to us that sleep was forbidden, and encouraging us to be on our guard. Most of us reacted to our neighbor's shouts and started awake. Some of us slept through it, then woke to an unexpected after-attack. We all tossed and turned to the interrupted rhythm of Aviva's shouts, then some of us, including me, went back to sleep.

The Remainer—who sometimes leads our awakening, and who always gives the call to wake while taking his breakfast—said that as the night went on he was half awake, half asleep, his anxiety divided between carefully balanced expressions: he would pity Aviva a little, and would curse her a little. He would blame himself for coming back to the country, then curse his luck and blame it for the choice he had made for himself and his family—a repressive, stifling neighborhood that made it difficult to breathe. On the one side, there was a Jewish woman inhabited by her past, the horrifying details of which she regularly doled out to us—as if the large share of the nakba we'd had to suffer wasn't enough, so she had to give us an extra portion of a past that had no connection with us. And on the other side, there was Hilmi Matar, our Palestinian neighbor from Lydda, an unpleasant and irritating hashish addict, whose proximity increased our misfortune.

That extraordinary night, the details of which were lost amid Aviva's cries, our neighbor heard the voices of soldiers whispering to one another. As subsequently related by my father on the basis of a subsidiary complaint of Aviva's husband, Shaul Shamir, our neighbor saw in her dreams a large placard before her eyes, which she proceeded to read, as follows: "To the people of the city of Kiev and neighboring regions. You must attend at eight o'clock in the morning on Monday 29 September, at Dorohozhytska Street near the Jewish Cemetery, with your money, documents, and all valuables and heavy clothing in your possession. The punishment for anyone who does not comply will be death."

The young Aviva raced along a side road, which led to Babi Yar, paved with human bones. The sky was raining down weightless, naked people, who fluttered like butterflies as soon as their feet touched the ground. She felt her body. Her fingers sank into her naked flesh. In vain, she tried to hide her private parts. She fell into a ditch. A lot of mud and bodies fell on top of her. She got up and ran again. She fell into another ditch, on top of bodies still warm. She lifted her head and saw four soldiers pointing the barrels of their rifles in her direction, ready to fire. Still asleep, she shouted deliriously, "My Shaul!," the name of her husband. Then she woke up, and continued her delirious prattle while awake. The soldiers she had seen were like the other soldiers who had climbed onto the wall that adjoined and ran parallel to our own house wall. This was the same wall that Aviva had previously sprayed with kerosene and set fire to. The soldiers, with their enormous frames, leaped into the courtyard of the house, took up position at the door of her bedroom, and shut it. Aviva let out a cry like never before. Shaul woke up, as did everyone in our house, to hear her shouting, "Germans, Shaul, Germans!" She continued to hallucinate for some time. She then started to hiss like a snake slithering over the sand on a hot summer's day, until she collapsed completely.

"There'll be no more attacks to disturb you after today, Shaul!" he murmured to himself. After a short silence, he went on: "Or will Aviva add her suffering to your suffering, for you to lament your fate together?"

Shaul gradually realized that Aviva's silence was something new, and that he hadn't experienced anything like it in the whole of their life together.

"Aviva has diiiiiied!" he screamed.

Shaul Shamir—who had taken part in four wars against the Arabs, and had completed his years in the reserve—turned his mind to arranging a funeral befitting his wife. He ignored, temporarily at least, his jealousy at the fact that his late wife had been one of the best-known survivors of the massacre of the Jews that had taken place in the Babi Yar valley, in Kiev, Ukraine, during the events of 29 and 30 September 1941.

Shaul put aside all his differences with Aviva and resolved at least to be loyal to her in her death. He thought of her funeral and what it would require. He thought of the kind of flowers he would bring to it. He thought of where Aviva should be buried, and of what he would say in the funeral address he'd deliver in front of the government officials, delegates from the Jewish Agency, and rabbis of her sect, who would all come to bid her farewell. Shaul thought it likely that the German Chancellor, whose country was eager to be at the forefront of those participating in all such occasions, would be there to offer condolences for those Jews who had died and for those who had lived on in torment.

Shaul took all of this into account in his musings. With considerable pride, he designed a splendid funeral worthy of the deceased, hoping that the local Arabs would not be denied the opportunity to participate in it—especially as it might well have an international dimension, and if that happened, it would not be right for their Arab neighbors to be absent. Shaul expected that the current President of the US would take part, though he doubted the participation of former Presidents who had changed their attitudes of support for Israel after leaving the seat of power. Shaul wasn't too worried about that, for he recalled that Israel would compensate for their absence by the presence of leaders of states that had signed peace agreements with Israel or had even secured some forms of agreement without the need for any signing. He was quite convinced—believing as he did that everyone was either a neighbor or a neighbor of a neighbor—that mourning was a duty, and that death did not distinguish between people.

Shaul had confidence in his own judgments. He decided to anticipate all the formalities, and to invite Mahmoud Dahman—he didn't know that the others called him The Remainer—to take part in the funeral. At the end of the day, *he told himself,* Mahmoud's our neighbor, he's one of us, he's our neighbor and an Israeli like us.

So he contacted Mahmoud and invited him.

The Remainer thanked Shaul profusely for even thinking of inviting him to take part in Aviva's funeral, because he was actually extremely sad about Aviva. The Remainer joked with him, "Do you know, Shaul, I shall miss Aviva (by God, she wasn't worthy of you!). As soon as I come back from the funeral, my children—especially Filastin—will ask me: 'Daddy, now who's going to keep us awake half the night and disturb our sleep, as Israel disturbs the sleep of the whole region?' Don't blame me for saying this, neighbor! As for Jinin, you know her, Jinin's my daughter, she'll ask questions out of turn, she'll say to me in complete surprise: 'Daddy, who's going to spray kerosene on the wall of our house and set it alight? I missed it last time!'"

The Remainer was silent for a few seconds, then quickly reassured his neighbor:

"Adon Shaul, don't take any notice of what I said. Put a watermelon in your stomach, as we say. No, don't do that, a watermelon will be too expensive for you. I sometimes say ridiculous things. Listen, I'll reassure my daughter Jinin and everyone at home. I'll tell them that I wish everyone was like Aviva; at least when she set fire to the house, she didn't burn us with it! You know that most people living in this country would sooner burn us today than tomorrow."

The Remainer thought to himself, though, something that he wouldn't say to any of his family—namely that Shaul's invitation, if it was genuine, would cause a tsunami of scandal the length and breadth of the land. This was despite the fact that the length of the land had increased in 1967, with the Golan Heights at the head in the north-east and the Gaza Strip and Sinai at the foot in the south, while its breadth had increased and its belly had become bloated with the West Bank in the east. It had then quickly become pregnant, time and again, giving birth every month or two to a new settlement with new residents, and sometimes even to twins. Even so, the invitation would shock everyone.

He also said to himself that Shaul's invitation would confirm his position on the Holocaust (Shoah), and his respect for its victims, and his desire to remember Aviva together with the other mourners as they lowered her body into her final resting place. This unusual and solemn event would give him a place in the Guinness Book of World Records as the first

Palestinian to take part in an occasion such as this, and The Remainer hoped that other people would not challenge him.

But what if Shaul were to ask The Remainer to say a word of condolence on this occasion, in the name of the Arabs of the country and neighboring Arabs as well? Or to recite the Kaddish prayer over the body of the departed? During her lifetime, he had been one of the closest to the departed of the likely mourners, and he had enjoyed friendly relations with her. He must have something he could say. Would he do it? Would he say words to Rabia, as he called her, for her soul to hear? Would she be comforted and thank him for them? And would she thank him for turning a blind eye to her being buried in a piece of land that used to belong to Palestinians like himself? Of course, *he thought,* Jews die here, and are buried here. But they also die elsewhere, and are still buried here. Can't they just be buried wherever they've lived for their whole lives? Why come and share the only 'here' we've got?

The Remainer recalled what he had read one evening in the Talmud: "The body of a Jew who has died outside Palestine, after being buried in the ground, will crawl until it reaches the Holy Land and is united with it."

"Good God!" he commented. "A Palestinian refugee can't get there dead or alive. Not crawling underground, not walking on their feet, not even falling from the sky. Palestinians crawl toward Sweden and Denmark instead."

He wondered whether he should accept all this, and cursed the Nazis, and their black history, and what they had done to the Jews, which was the reason for most of them being made to emigrate to the country.

So The Remainer's tongue lashed all the countries of Europe, as he cursed them one after the other, and sometimes collectively, because they had renounced the Jews at the time of their suffering and had committed a massive crime by helping them to emigrate to Palestine instead of absorbing them themselves. He singled out Britain for particular historical curses, then brought it all to a conclusion by asking for mercy on the soul of Aviva, his neighbor, whose life had been part and parcel of the struggle. God have mercy on you, Aviva. You took what's ours in this world, and tomorrow you'll ask for our share in the next.

Meanwhile, Aviva, stretched out on her bed, was struck by a sudden longing, like a cold wind, to return to the waking world. She hoped that her return would terrify Shaul, who had paid no attention to her fears and had disregarded the possibility of her being killed by the four soldiers and their rifles. He had never even thought of hugging her to his chest and protecting her during her ravings, or of hurrying her away to safety.

So the 'dead' Aviva conjured up her original shout—the one that had awakened The Remainer and the members of his family—and cried out again. This time, it had more impact on Shaul, as well as on The Remainer himself, who exclaimed from his own house, "You came back quickly, neighbor!" When she had fully returned to this world, Aviva suffered the effects of a new bout of raving, telling her husband—who was astounded by her awakening—that the pair of them had to flee immediately or else take refuge with their neighbor Adon Dahman, as they called him.

Shaul doubted whether Mahmoud Dahman would accede to their request and guarantee them protection together, for he recalled a conversation he had had with The Remainer on the eve of the outbreak of the June 1967 War. In broken Arabic, Shaul had asked him, "If you win the war, my friend, and occupy the country, will you hide me in your house, Adon Dahman, and protect me from the revenge of the Arabs?"

"Come on, neighbor . . . ," Mahmoud had replied, in a reassuring tone. "What's this talk? I'll divorce Husniya three times before I abandon you, and if anyone gets near you, I'll finish him off with these two hands of mine!" And he had clasped his thumbs and index fingers together, drawing the rest of his fingers around them like he was strangling someone.

The Remainer had recalled that the Arabs, even united, had not won the 1948 War or any war since, and that there was a considerable possibility that they would lose the war that was about to break out. He had turned to Shaul and asked him, "Okay, and what about you, Adon Shaul, what will you do with us if you win the war?"

Shaul had coughed, ignoring the polite response, and had exclaimed, "Congratulations to us!"

So now he turned to his wife, and rebuked her with feeling. "Adon Dahman won't hide us in his house!"

Aviva begged him. "Okay, Shaul, ask those four German soldiers to fire on you, my love. Try death for my sake, just once in your life. It's really essential for a German to kill you for you to gain a share in the Holocaust like me."

In his house, The Remainer heard Aviva's ravings, which continued faintly on the other side of the wall: "I don't want to die tonight. I don't want to die again. One death is enough. I don't want to . . . ."

Those members of our family who had not gone back to sleep heard the sound of a door being slammed just before dawn, and Shaul's voice cursing Aviva and her life, repeating that he wouldn't be coming back home again.

And indeed Shaul never returned to the house after that morning. Even when Aviva finally died for real several years later, and her death was reported to him by his sons, Ilan and Yuri, Shaul contented himself with simply asking for God's mercy on her. He then asked them if the government would continue to pay compensation for their deceased mother as a survivor of the Holocaust or not.

"I am her true legal heir. I own her past and all that has followed from it, good and bad," he said.

As for The Remainer, he sympathized with Aviva after Shaul left her and her two sons stopped visiting; after Ilan married and settled in Ramat Gan, he no longer came regularly to visit Aviva at home, while Yuri opened a lawyer's office in Jerusalem and was busy with his clients' cases.

The Remainer now went more often to Aviva's house, and started spending more time with her than previously. That annoyed Husniya, who was not enthusiastic about establishing relations with the Jews who lived in their quarter.

She once said in front of him, "Can it be right that these houses, equipped with a stand for a poker on the top of the stove, should be taken by people who've come from overseas, while their owners lie in camps among sandstorms and live their whole lives as refugees? Who could put up with such injustice, oh Lord?"

Then she burst out laughing and said to him, "Do you know, Abu Filastin, I was the first one to get to know Afifa? She was complaining to me, slagging off the Absentees' Property Administration, from whom she rented the house. She told me that when she'd first looked around the house, she hadn't seen much furniture in it. I said that the furniture had been stolen. She told me, with no shame or embarrassment, that the kerosene stove that the owners of the house had left behind was all messed up. It reminded her of the eyes of her husband, Shaul, each one looking in a different direction, because the flames came out of the top in two different directions. What's more, she hadn't found a poker to clean it out. She was hysterical. She went and sat on the bed in the bedroom, and found that it had rusted and become loose. She went out of her mind, and cursed the owners of the house who had fled before they could repair the bed on which they slept. She couldn't think how she and Shaul would be able to sleep on it. 'Curse them! Shame on them!' she shouted in Arabic—these two expressions being ones the old rascal had learned from me."

"Rabia's right, Umm Filastin," commented the Remainer. "The Palestinians are tramps, gypsies—only a few are genuine, they've no breeding or shame. They fled the country and left behind them a jumble of furniture, cookers with no kerosene in them—and no pokers, either!"

Since moving to Lydda, The Remainer had never stopped encouraging Husniya to establish relationships with the Jewish neighbors in the quarter. Whenever Husniya showed some hesitation, content to have warm relations with our Christian neighbor, Umm Jurj, who lived two doors away, he told her, "We can't live in a ghetto on our own, Husniya. In this country, we've always been open to the world, with hearts as wide as mankind. My dear, you don't have to like them or treat them like relatives, just let your relationship with them be normal."

And as the days and years passed, Husniya changed and began to make friends among her Jewish neighbors, the first of them being Afifa, as she called her.

3

Dahman in Gaza

MAHMOUD DAHMAN USUALLY WENT TO the Israeli Radio building in Jerusalem once or twice a year. He recorded a message to be broadcast to his relatives in the camps in the Gaza Strip. Tall as a palm tree, and with the girth of a mature mountain olive, he would stand in the queue for the Peace and Greetings program, to talk to his family, who could not be more than fifty kilometers away from him, via a microphone that conveyed his message but returned no reply.

"I am Mahmoud Ibrahim Dahman, nicknamed The Remainer. My peace and greetings to . . . ."

In the airplane, I put the pages of Jinin's novel into the pocket attached to the seat in front of me. I shut my eyes and thought.

The Remainer hadn't imagined his message going around camps he had never visited before, searching for a family that had been swallowed up by the Khan Younis camp—searching for one of them to come to one of the radio post offices, known as Abu Lisan, which used broadcasts instead of postage stamps. The Remainer hadn't expected that his message would be lost without arriving, even in a public road that opened into the camp. The carrier, a café radio of which there were only four (all made by the Dutch firm Phillips, and designed in the shape of a wooden chest), broadcast songs to refugees and non-refugees at no charge, together with the noble Quran recited by Abu al-Aynayn al-Shu'ayshi' or Abd al-Basit Abd al-Samad, the news, some Egyptian soaps, and Radio Israel programs.

Neither The Remainer nor Jinin knew that the owner of the first radio, Muhammad Abu Muslim, had been a refugee from Jaffa, who had been killed with his four children in the Khan Younis massacre on the morning of 31 October 1956. The man and three-quarters of his family had perished, leaving only his wife, his daughter, the café, and the radio, together with those café regulars who remained alive after the massacre.

The Remainer didn't know, either, that the second radio had been in the al-Balad Café in the middle of town, or that my father, Ahmad Nimr Dahman, was until the day of his death one of the most important customers in the same café, by virtue of a rumor that had injured his pride; or that the Egyptian military governor of the city of Khan Younis was his constant companion in the café, as a way of emphasizing his humility and expressing his desire to share in the troubles of the city's residents.

Neither The Remainer nor Jinin knew that a third radio was in the Dirgham Café. They might have been surprised if I had told them that the café was closed and lost its customers because a popular radio station carrying women's voices had broadcast that the owner's daughter Ratiba—sixteen years old, with a chubby face, coffee-colored eyes, a chest that rebelled against its supports, and the distinctive Jaffa physique—was pregnant, despite not being married. Or that the man who made her belly swell was actually her father, Salim, and that, according to Hanafi radio—the management and broadcasting of which was supervised by the women of the quarter, and which was in the middle of our quarter—he had secretly performed an abortion on his daughter, with the assistance of his wife. Thus they had removed a grandchild who would have been Salim's son, but they never escaped the scandal.

As for the fourth and final radio, it was in the Ottomans' Café, the best known of the cafés and the one most crowded with lazy or out-of-work men, who were brought together by cards, glasses of tea, and narghiles around small square card tables, until sleep caught up with them after it was past midnight, and their wives had gone to bed and stopped sending their sons with warnings repeated from previous nights: "Father, Mother says to come back home—and if you don't come, then go and fetch her from her father's house in the morning!"

The Ottomans' Café radio was the loudest of the radios. When Voice of the Arabs and the commentary on the news by Ahmad Saeed were being broadcast, it was the loudest voice in the camp. It would bid us farewell with a nationalist cry which would give us a sound night of sleep: "To a bright and glorious future! To a united Arab nation!"

But the radio also created a space for evening conversation, especially every Thursday evening, as we hovered outside, too young to go in. We would lean our arms on the edge of the low wall outside the café and prick up our small ears, like satellite dishes these days. Then we would listen to a new sequence from the Noah's Ark series. Each of us would assemble an amusing collection of jokes, which we would hide in our chests, ready to be taken home as soon as the gathering finished. There, we would rebroadcast the sequence in our own words to anyone still awake, or retell it at the breakfast table in the morning to make everyone else's whole day happy. The camps went to sleep at night happy and laughing. We continued to sail on the deck of Noah's Ark for several years, singing the songs left behind by its captains.

Abu Tafish took over the hearts of the refugees like love filling the hearts of virgins, as his chatter emerged from a ship of entertainment, borne on waves of imagination. This wonder ship contained a crew of sailors: Marun Ashqar, who knew by heart the Palestinian heritage of songs and poetry; and Abdullah al-Zu'bi, Ishaq Dawud, Musa Rizq, Bahgat Maqlasha, and Muris Shimali (Abu Farid).

The Remainer knew all of these, or had at least heard of them, and he well understood how the ignominy of history had compelled them to capture the jesting speech of the people and distribute it to the afflicted so they could reclaim a homeland of laughter and irony:

Radio Israel invites you, dear listener, to a voyage on the deck of Noah's Ark!
Trin-tin-tin-tin-tin . . . tary rat-tat-tat-ta!
Taaayib ooooh, taaayib ooooohiiiy!

"Shaalan, Shaalan."
"Yes, Dad!"
"Where are you, Qarut? Abu Khalil's coming with Andrea now. When they come, open the diwan and pretend to be busy! Always say hello, but don't be too generous, don't open packets of cigarettes all the time!"
"Ah!"
"Don't give a cigarette to either of them until he can't take it any more, and his moustache starts to quiver!"
"Ah!"
"Whenever Beijou stands up, tell him quickly that the coffee's on the fire. Two or three times, Andrea's been quick to get angry—he's left the place quickly, gone home, and not drunk the coffee."
"Ah, okay, Dad!"
"Only, hey, as I told you, say hello, hello, but don't say more than that!"
"Ah, okay. But Dad, every time you tell me that Abu Khalil and Andrea are coming, they take no notice of us and they don't eat here. Why do you think it'll be different this time?"
"Oh God, are you a son of Abu Tafish? By God, if I adopted a goat, it would be more of a man than you are! This is politics."
"So, are you going to start dabbling in politics?"
"No, I'm going to start dabbling in rat poison!"

The Peace and Greetings program had disappeared before any of The Remainer's messages arrived. No one enquired after him, or informed him of how the family had eventually fared. His father, Sheikh Ibrahim, died without fulfilling his wish to return to al-Majdal Asqalan, and without ever again sounding the call to prayer from the minaret of its mosque, as he used to do before the nakba. His brother Salih went mad and never recovered. He was sent by the Egyptian military governor in the Gaza Strip to al-Khankah in Qalyubiya. His sister Fathiya grew up and married Muhammad Sheikh. He was like the moon; the camp stayed awake by the light of his glances. But he died. He was one of two hundred and fifty young men killed by the Israeli forces after they occupied Khan Younis in the Suez War of 1956, when the Israelis reconnected the geography that they had cut in two and for the first time united the Palestinians in the Strip with those who had fled. But the reunion only lasted four months, ending with the Israeli withdrawal from the Gaza Strip. Still, it came back with the third occupation in 1967, and endured. It became stronger than Salah al-Din al-Ayyubi's unification of the Arab world, and far longer lasting than the Egyptian-Syrian union. Israel swallowed new Palestinian land and was unified, with the result that the Palestinians were able to wander the length and breadth of their land, which was no longer theirs, and enjoy themselves from Rafah to Ras Naqura, and from the River Jordan to the Mediterranean—or, as it used to be said, from land to land and from water to water—a unity that allowed The Remainer to finally visit his relatives in Khan Younis. He was the first Israeli to be carried into the Gaza Strip, to the joy of his relations and the amazement of the neighbors.

The Remainer arrived at the Khan Younis camp in the summer of 1967, the year in which Israel unified the land again. One person he never found there was his divorced wife, Nadia, the young woman who had filled al-Majdal Asqalan with her shouting as she had tried to persuade him to board the refugees' truck. Mahmoud Dahman had refused to budge, stubborn as a donkey fixing his legs to the ground, while the planes in the sky had screamed, the bombs had screamed, his daughter Ghazza had screamed in her mother's arms, the people in the truck had screamed, the engine of the truck—which was getting ready to leave—had screamed, and his father, Sheikh Ibrahim, had screamed, "Mahmoud, my son, get up here with us, otherwise everyone will end up in a different place. If we leave one another, we'll never meet again, my son. Tomorrow the Jews will beat you up if they find you. Listen to me, put the devil to shame and get up here with us!"

In the end, which marked the beginning of a collective regret that would last a lifetime, The Remainer had screamed himself, before they could leave: "Father, if you leave, you'll never come back!" Al-Majdal had reverberated with the sound of the echo, "Father, if you leave, you'll never . . . , Father, if you leave . . . , Father, if you l . . . ," until his voice was lost in the hubbub of voices that the truck had carried far away, taking with it the thousands who had left on that ill-omened day.

After her divorce from The Remainer, Nadia had married Ismail Muqbil Dahman. Ismail worked as a teacher in the city of Dammam, in Saudi Arabia. His first wife had died of a swift, incurable illness, leaving him with five children, the oldest of them being Munir, who had been ten years old, and the youngest Suad, who had taken her first steps—wobbling on her little legs, laughing, falling, trying again—on the day her mother had died. "She'd have loved to have seen this," Ismail said, making the mourners around him weep all the harder.

"Trust in the one God, man! He has fated it, and there is no escape from it," they consoled him; and praised Him, who alone may be praised for a disaster.

Nadia couldn't stay a divorced woman, gossiped about by the camp in Khan Younis and the popular news agencies. Nor could Ismail manage his own life with five children. The Dahman family brought together the widower and the divorcee. Nadia moved to Dammam with her daughter Ghazza, and took charge of bringing up Ismail's children, who acquired another sister. Nadia and Ghazza became distant from their original family branch in Ramla, and had disappeared from The Remainer's life forever.

More than sixteen years before going back to visit his family, The Remainer had recorded his voice message: "I am Mahmoud Ibrahim Dahman, nicknamed The Remainer. My peace and greetings to my dear father, Sheikh Ibrahim, my beloved mother, Imm Salih, my two brothers, Salih and Faruq, to my little sister, Fathiya, and to all the members of the Dahman family in the Gaza Strip and abroad. If you wonder about us, we are well. Be reassured!"

I opened my eyes. I collected the pages of Jinin's novel from the pocket in front of me, put them back in the little bag, then dozed off, and only woke when I felt Julie's hand shaking mine just before landing.

4

My wife and I were led into a wide hallway in Ben Gurion Airport in Lydda by a female security official, whose heavy backside slowed our carefully measured steps behind her and doubled the time it took to get to where she asked us to wait.

We sat together on a wide wooden bench, near a side room. The door of the room was half open, allowing us to overhear a conversation in English and Hebrew from inside, though it was difficult to make much sense of it.

"Will we have to wait here long, darling?" asked Julie.

"Only until we've been interrogated—'investigated,' I mean," I replied nervously, leaning back against the wall.

A man roughly my own age came down the hall. His face had an Arab appearance, with a dusting of troubles similar to those on my own face. He was of medium build, with a plain face. He was carrying a small black leather case, and was accompanied by a middle-aged woman, of average beauty but extreme elegance. The pair walked down the hall toward where Julie and I were waiting. The man put his case on the ground, then threw his backside onto the seat opposite us. The woman sat down beside him with more concern for her own behind. The man leaned back. Between us sat a silent tension of the sort that invites curiosity.

Suddenly, the man straightened up and his back left the wall. He started to read my face with something like recognition. As if he knew me. I'd never seen him before, nor had

I seen the elegant woman who was accompanying him. But perhaps he did know me. I thought of asking him, then hesitated, for he suddenly looked away. Then he put his hand into his bag and took out an Arabic newspaper. Perhaps he was also a Palestinian, summoned like me for an interrogation for that reason alone. His position would be worse if he was a real Palestinian.

The man opened the newspaper, and disappeared behind its pages. The face of Amjad Nasir peeped out at me from the photograph that hung over his weekly column, Fresh Air, on the back page. So it was *al-Quds al-Arabi*.

I still couldn't place the man's face, and started to ask Julie in a whisper if she had seen him on the plane, or even at some other time, but suddenly another female security officer appeared, slender where the last one had been heavy, putting an end to my whispering as it began.

She gestured to the man with the newspaper. He stood up and followed her, leaving his paper on the seat. The woman who was with him caught up, and the three of them disappeared inside the room. The officer then shut the door.

He'll doubtless now be interrogated with questions that will shortly be repeated to me, I thought. I turned over all the possibilities, and went through all the questions—old and new—that awaited me, including the questions that my American neighbor on the plane had put to me. He had constantly repeated the name of Israel, rather than using 'there': "Is this your first visit to Israel? Why are you visiting Israel? Do you have relations in Israel? Where will you stay in Israel? How long will you stay in Israel?" Then, and this was more important: "Will you visit the territories?" Which territories? The administered territories. The disputed territories. As if our 'territories' didn't have a name! "Do you have a Palestinian Authority identity card? A passport issued by them? Number of your identity card?" These were all personal effects that it was forbidden to smuggle into the country.

*

I had answered questions like these again after we'd landed, when Julie and I were lined up in a short queue, fed by passengers who rushed along in the hope of a speedy passage through passport inspection. I gave our two passports to a female security officer in her twenties, with a face that seemed slightly too small to contain all her features, so that they almost spilled out of it. The officer asked me the same questions that had been put to twenty other travelers. When I realized that she was bored with her questions, and perhaps with my answers, and was about to stamp the passports, I asked her not to, but to put the entry visas on separate pieces of paper instead.

She eyed me with obvious disgust, then let her tongue loose on me:

"Why don't you want an Israeli stamp in your passports?"

"Apologies, madam, but that would hinder our travel throughout the whole region."

"Wait there!" she said, waving us away from the window with her fist, which she used like a remote control. We moved away in silence.

The official with the backside arrived.

"Mr. and Mrs. Dahman, follow me, please," she said. So Julie and I had followed her to the 'Restriction of Entry Procedures' room, where we now were.

While we waited for the couple to emerge from the room—dignity in tatters from their questioning—I decided to leaf through *al-Quds al-Arabi*.

I took the newspaper from the seat opposite and returned to my place. Julie had paid no attention to any of this. Since we had sat down, she hadn't lifted her eyes from Ahdaf Soueif's novel.

I opened the newspaper surreptitiously, and flicked through its pages. On the second half of the second culture page, my attention was caught by an article titled, "Don't

Believe Them: After Forty Years They Haven't Forgotten Me." The name of the author gave me a jolt: Rabai al-Madhoun.

Oh my God! I thought to myself. The familiar name was sparking various dormant connections in my mind. I started to read the article:

> *"Wait for a bit," the officer at Cairo International Airport had said. We waited. He raised his head toward my wife, who was standing behind me, then handed her her passport. "Welcome, madam, have a good stay in Cairo!"*
>
> *Then, abandoning his politeness, he turned to me, and reverted to the traditional security service lexicon: "Okay, sir, please come with us for a moment."*
>
> *I swallowed my feelings. "It will be a pleasure."*
>
> *The officer asked an employee standing in front of him—a detective like him, of course—to do a computer search for me in the security files. Some minutes later (I was still standing and blocking the queue of passengers waiting their turn behind me), the employee concluded his search with a public confirmation:*
>
> *"Wanted, sir!"*
>
> *The word, which appeared before my eyes at the top of an extremely official piece of paper like a ten-meter-wide banner carried by an army of detectives, sounded more like "Waaaaanted!"*
>
> *Yes, I was wanted by State Security, the highest security authority in the land. I, who had come with my wife to lay our heads for five nights in the bosom of the Mother of the World, and to tour the country and its river . . . I was wanted by the highest authority in the land. Yes, indeed, O joy! O happiness! Forty years after being imprisoned and deported from Egypt for political reasons that had never bowed my head, the Egyptian security officials had still not forgotten me. Here they were, explaining to me how technological developments had enabled them to transfer my records—with the lists in their old records now covered in ancient national dust—to clean computer files. Now I was wanted digitally.*
>
> *As I breathed a reluctant sigh of admiration at the Egyptian security apparatus, which had remembered me after forty years, I*

reprimanded the fraternal Syrian security units, which quickly forgot their most important operations. I had been visited just before midnight on 10 August 1976 by a unit of 'Protectors of the Homeland' made up of fourteen armed security men led by an officer. The unit had raided my apartment, number 54 in building 6, Baghdad Street, in the 'Beating Heart of Arabism,' Damascus. They had killed my companion, Wajih, 19 years old, who was living with me, throwing his body from the fifth floor. They subjected me to torture that lasted for a full week. Then they forgot me, leaving me, for several weeks, with the shadow of Wajih falling from the window of my dark room to the foot of the building, until I left Syria altogether. I recorded all the details in my book The Taste of Separation: Three Palestinian Generations Remembered.

My wife left the airport for the center of Cairo, and it was decided to send me back to London on the first plane. A policeman led me to some side offices, then to a prison cell a little further inside, where he threw me into a group of young detainees. And what detainees!

During my happy stay in the cell, I was privileged to meet a Bahraini wanted by the international police; another, a Pakistani who had arrived at Cairo Airport without a passport; and a third, a hashish smuggler just like his prototypes in old Egyptian films. There was a fourth, a man who claimed to be Lebanese, and who spoke with the accent of a Sunni from the Basta quarter of Beirut—like the Beiruti Abul Abd, the well-known Lebanese popular character—though our friend spoke it with an Egyptian twang. This obvious undercover policeman behaved like someone renting the cell, and sometimes like the general manager, administering it by virtue of his long residence, or so it appeared. To emphasize that, he marked himself out by using a worn-out mattress, which stank of damp and which he spread out in the left-hand corner opposite the door. The others envied him for it. A fifth resident of this restroom for important personalities joined us at midnight—a Palestinian from Gaza, who had arrived from Libya with the intention of returning to the Strip via the Rafah crossing point. There were hundreds of people returning, and the Egyptian authorities had reduced the daily quota of buses permitted to transport people to Rafah. For some reason, which was never revealed, it wasn't permitted for the lucky returnee to stay in a hotel until he was able to travel, so he found himself a guest of the authorities, just like me.

That December night, I slept on a cold floor that was infused with the smell of decay. I was covered by a double layer of nervousness and tension, which gave me recurrent nightmares throughout the night—a night full of foreboding and anger. I gathered myself together in a mass of national humiliation and insult, in a plastic chair that had once been white. I shivered for a while and slept a little. I woke up from a nightmare, the voice of a policeman still humiliating me with a clumsy apology: "Excuse me, doctor . . . ."

During the twenty-four hours I spent in detention, I was subjected to two rounds of interrogation, in a room where an officer with the rank of colonel in the State Security apparatus sat behind a desk. If I had been in his place, I would have been embarrassed by the requirements of my job.

I was astonished at what I read in the newspaper, as if borders were just borders, ports were ports, and airports airports for a Palestinian. I would stop the owner of this paper as soon as he emerged from the interrogation room, and ask him about himself. What was his connection, if any, to the author of the article? I hesitated before doing so.

The door of the room opened, and the man appeared at the door with his wife, smiles on their faces. He turned toward me, then looked at the chair opposite, where he and his wife had been sitting a short time ago. When I offered him back the newspaper, he said, "Keep it, if you like!" then hurried toward the exit with his wife.

I was called by name from inside the room by what sounded like the voice of a woman, though it was hard to be sure. I got up from my seat and went into the room. Julie stayed where she was, for she hadn't been called, and might not be subject to any interrogation.

Inside the featureless room, a female officer from Internal Security—Shin Bet—in her midthirties was sitting at a low desk. She reminded me of my aunt in the 1950s, sitting behind an old hand-operated Singer sewing machine, creating underwear from a piece of spare cloth.

The officer waved her hand to indicate that I should sit down on a small chair beside her, which I did. Without turning toward me, she asked me the purpose of my visit, and I replied to her.

The woman with the heavy bottom returned and stood behind her colleague, who continued to interrogate me. I guess that she might be there to suggest questions additional to those that had been prepared for me.

"What's the name of your father, and where does he live?"

I told her that he had been a permanent resident in the old Khan Younis graveyard since I was thirteen, leaving her to calculate how many years had passed since his premature death.

"What's the name of your mother?"

I gave her her full name, and informed her that she lived in a house in the Khan Younis camp in the Gaza Strip, because I knew she would ask me that next. So as not to give her the chance to put the question that would certainly follow, I quickly added, "But I don't know the location of my mother's house."

"What's the number of her personal identity card?"

"I don't know."

"Your mother's full name again?"

I repeated the three parts of my mother's name, which I'd already provided, pronouncing the letters extra carefully this time so that she wouldn't have to ask a third time.

She turned the computer screen toward me, and there was my mother, staring out at me, as I surrendered quietly to my situation. I had known her for more than five decades, remembering her as being weak and helpless as a chick, scared of a sparrow standing on the edge of the tiled roof of our house and chirping at her—but here she glared like a hawk.

I imagined her shouting at the officer, "You'll turn into a monkey, God willing! What is this lack of shame, what is this meanness? My son's not a foreigner. This is his country, and he's coming back to stay for a few days. Why do you have to come down and question him like this? Is he a thief or a murderer? God damn you all and the day when you came to the country!"

Wiping away a tear, I imagined that we talked:

You come home, Walid, and you don't visit your mother?

I was embarrassed for my mother and for my country.

Not this time, mother. Leave it till next time.

I won't live for ever, Walid. Then she implored me: *It's only a little way, my son. Move your feet and come to Gaza!*

Are you inviting me to the blockade, mother?

May evil be far from you, my darling! Stay away, and spare yourself trouble until our Lord brings it to an end.

In my mind, I gave her some words to help her to sleep at night and to greet her in the morning. I told her to keep my words under her pillow. I asked her to carry on with this ritual until we met one day, when Gaza again became the Gaza I had known.

For a brief moment, I joked cheekily with the officer as I thanked her: "Toda, gvirti, thanks for the reunion!"

She made no comment, so I went on: "In the 1950s, you let us meet through a radio program called Peace and Greetings; after the 1967 War, through committees of the International Red Cross; and now by computer."

"Excuse me?" she asked in English.

"Sorry, I was just . . . talking to my mother."

"Beseder, okay, Mister Dahman."

So saying, she handed my passport to her colleague, who went out, dragging her backside, apparently reluctant to take it with her. Accompanied by Julie—who had by now shut her novel and put it in her handbag—I tagged along behind her to the other end of the hall, where she asked us to wait again.

This time, we did not have long to wait. The same officer came back a few minutes later, with a short-term professional smile on her lips.

"Mr. and Mrs. Dahman, have a good trip. Shalom!" she said, struggling to keep her smile until the end of her task.

I took the two passports from her hand, flipped through them, and found inside each one an entry visa on a separate piece of paper. I took Julie's hand, and we walked together happily to the baggage conveyor belt, where we collected our two cases and left.

Fourth Movement

Two Possibilities

To Haifa

Julie and I went out, each dragging our own suitcase. Our eyes were fixed on the people waiting at Exit Gate number 2. In the distance, which began to shrink as we smiled with happiness, our host, Jamil Hamdan, appeared with his wife Ludmilla, both waving at us. We waved back at them, with smiles that reached them before we did, while the leaves of a palm tree outside waved at us through the glass façade behind them, as if some breeze had told it we'd arrived.

To Jerusalem

Julie and I went out, each dragging our own suitcase. Our eyes were fixed on the people waiting at Exit Gate number 2. In the distance, which began to shrink as we smiled with happiness, our host, Salman Jabir, appeared, waving at us. We waved back at him, with smiles that reached him before we did, while the leaves of a palm tree outside waved at us through the glass façade behind him, as if some breeze had told it we'd arrived.

1

Jerusalem

SALMAN APOLOGIZED ON BEHALF OF his wife, Aida, who hadn't come with him to the airport to meet us. He said she was busy with an appointment with her supervisor for the Master's thesis she was preparing, but she'd promised to stop work at a suitable time and come to the Ramada Renaissance Hotel, where we would be staying, before we arrived. So she would definitely be waiting for us.

Salman's car started off, with me beside him, and Julie in the back seat. We took a mountain road that passed through pine and green cypress trees, while my eyes scanned the low hills and small forests, searching for villages that had remained in my memory.

We chatted the whole way, sometimes with a sense of wonder, and sometimes with bewilderment, like tourists visiting a country for the first time.

I talked with Salman about our plans for travel in the country, and about visiting Jerusalem, Acre, and Haifa, where he lived. About my mother-in-law, Ivana, and her instructions to place her ashes—which we had brought with us inside an elegant porcelain statue—in her family home in Acre, or else deposit them with a Palestinian family who lived in Jerusalem.

Salman looked over at me.

"You know, you're in real luck! Tonight we'll be spending the evening with Dr. Fahmy al-Khatib and his wife at the

Nafura Restaurant in Bab al-Khalil in Jerusalem. Fahmy was a friend of Omar, from an old Miqdasi family in Sheikh Jarrah. I studied with the doctor in the Hebrew University. But life led us in two different directions that had nothing to do with each other. He went into medicine, while I said goodbye to everything I'd studied and went into publishing. By the way, his wife Nada is also a doctor, a pediatrician, and she's opened a clinic at home. The important thing is that Fahmy and Nada are great fans of your writing, and when he heard that you were coming to the country, and I'd be bringing you to Jerusalem, he insisted on inviting us all to supper. Let me consult him on the subject of the late Ivana."

I was surprised by what Salman said, as well as by Dr. Fahmy's invitation. But before I could reply, he hurriedly asked, "By the way, how come they let you bring human ashes through the airport?"

I answered him with carefully chosen words: "The matter's not very complicated. It required Ivana's death certificate, and we got a health certificate from an institution that specializes in procedures of this sort, saying that the ashes were free of bacteria and the like."

Salman nodded his head, as I returned to his previous topic: "It will be a splendid evening. And any help would be appreciated enormously."

I summed up for Julie what Salman had said, and she exclaimed in English, "Wow, amazing. Salman, you're our new best friend!"

As the car made its way along the road, Julie fell quiet, her attention captured by the stunning scenery on either side of the car.

Salman broke the silence.

"Hey, guess what? A short time ago, I saw a man coming out of the airport with a woman who seemed to be his wife, and I thought he looked like the writer Rabai al-Madhoun. Do you know him?"

"No, though I've read things he's written."

"Well, back at the airport I saw the two of them appear with a pale, stocky young man with a black moustache. I saw them go off in the direction of the parking area."

"You know, you've reminded me of something that happened earlier. There was a man detained with us at the airport. He was reading a newspaper, *al-Quds al-Arabi*. When they called him and his wife for questioning, he left the paper on the seat. I picked it up, started leafing through it, and found an article by al-Madhoun, which I read. But it may be that the man was just someone reading the paper, nothing more, and al-Madhoun's article was just a coincidence."

"Or maybe the man *was* al-Madhoun . . . ," he said.

"Not impossible," I said. "But do you know al-Madhoun well, or do you just think it looked like him?"

"Like you, I don't know him personally, but I've read some things about him and I've seen photos of him in the papers."

Then he glanced in the car's mirror and spoke to Julie:

"What's up, Jolly, my dear? Why don't you say something?"

"Oh, I like this Jolly. I'll call you Sorry in return!"

I chuckled, and Salman laughed so loud that his voice verged on the edge of a roar, which he held for a few seconds. Julie met his eye in the mirror, saw the happiness on his face, and went on:

"I'm happy with what I'm seeing—mountains, greenery—even without al-Madhoun or his wife."

During the week that had preceded our visit to the country, Julie had changed. When I'd suggested to her the idea of traveling a couple of months earlier, she'd refused on principle: "I don't want to see Israelis and I don't want to meet them," she had said.

Now, she was simply ignoring the existence of Israelis and keeping them out of the picture. Instead, she loaded her memory with scenes of the country where she had been born but lived far away from.

"I can't believe I'm in Palestine. If it weren't for Mama's instructions, I'd never have seen this country. Thanks for having us, Salman."

"You're very welcome."

"I want to see Acre."

"Don't worry! You'll tour the whole country, have your fill of Acre, and take a little of it with you when you leave."

"I'll pick up plenty of souvenirs," she replied.

The car continued to climb up and down the forested hills. It took us into our past, which was still present here, where the ground was like the front of a peasant dress—decorated with thyme, tumble thistle, plums, the shepherd's staff, lilies, gazelle horn, wheat ears, every type of saffron, and mountain lupines. That's not to mention the holm oak, carob, all sorts of mastic, terebinth, Christ's thorn, willows, medlars, and plane trees that adorned the slopes. The fragrances of the plants were carried on the breeze, inviting wanderers and passersby to gather their leaves.

Trees rushed past, and the car sped on toward Jerusalem. History rushed past. At the edge of what had been the village of Deir Yassin, my senses froze, imposing on me a bitter silence. *Deir Yassin*, I thought, *the massacre that changed history, and sketched the harsh face of the nakba of 1948. It's the black hole that the Israelis don't know how to deal with, in the view of Eitan Bronstein.*

"Eitan Bronstein," I murmured to myself aloud. Salman heard me.

"Who's Bronstein?" he asked me.

"The leftist Israeli who founded the Zokhrot organization. You know, they try to tell the story that the Jews don't want people to hear. Bronstein thinks that the massacre of Deir Yassin defined the relationship between the Jews and the Arabs. When I read that, I recalled that the Holocaust Museum isn't far from Deir Yassin."

"You're determined to visit the Holocaust Museum, then, like you told me?" he asked.

"I'll try. I want to see Deir Yassin from there. I want to see how the victims see their victims."

We fell silent.

The car passed through the outskirts of West Jerusalem. We spotted the top half of the Ramada Renaissance Hotel above its lower neighbors. Salman turned the car, only to be stopped by a red light. When it changed to green, it gave Salman two choices: either to turn right and swing around the hotel to look for the main entrance—or so I assumed—or else to go past the light and turn in at the next street along. He waited too long, and the light turned red again. As Salman wondered aloud about the best way to go when the signal changed, I suggested turning right toward the hotel.

The light changed. Salman took my advice—the advice of someone who had never visited Jerusalem before. He was relying on my basic Hebrew to read the traffic sign at the crossroads we had left and translate it for him so that he could keep his eyes on the road. He turned to the right. The road led under a bridge, and gradually opened up. If the car had continued onward, we would most likely have ended up outside Jerusalem completely.

"You've made me get lost with your rotten advice!" Salman exclaimed, slightly irritated. "Your guesswork has ruined us."

He pulled over less than a hundred meters on to ask a man standing on the sidewalk for directions. The man started explaining. I couldn't follow most of what he said, but one word he said in Hebrew with a distinctive rhythm made me hide a laugh with my hands: '*istabakhta.*'

As he pulled out into traffic again, Salman explained to Julie that '*istabakhta*' meant 'you're in difficulties' or 'you're stuck.'

We would use this word a lot throughout the ten days we would spend in the country. I would repeatedly say, "*Istabakhta*, and everyone knows it!" "*Istabakhta*, but what's happened has happened!" or "*Istabakhta*, and you'd better remain nameless!"

When we finally got to the Ramada Renaissance Hotel in West Jerusalem, we were met by a girl in her twenties, with a smile like a balmy evening, enough to wipe out half the troubles of the journey. I stood there for some moments, then gave her my passport.

I was greatly relieved by the sight of this employee, who continued to smile as she started to record our personal details. She was the first Israeli I'd seen in Jerusalem who didn't have the professional worried look of the Israeli women in the airport. Meanwhile, Julie stood at a distance from the reception desk, contemplating the décor.

Salman came up to the desk and proceeded to engage the receptionist in a jokey conversation in Hebrew. They chattered together and exchanged smiles that sometimes turned into laughter. Suddenly, Salman put a question to the girl: "So, how is Ahmad related to you?"

This question, in Arabic, changed the whole scenario, and I felt reassured about my first impression. Her name was Ni'mat, and she was a Palestinian, like all the Ni'mats of this country. I was greatly relieved. I felt like I was in a Palestinian hotel (despite the fact that it wasn't Palestinian), and that this woman would smile at the next guest to the hotel as soon as he arrived. She'd ask him for his passport to record his details. She wouldn't pause at his nationality or ask him for his religion. She wouldn't change the shape of her smile according to the customer. This Ni'mat made me feel relaxed, for she confirmed to me that we were still spread through the country.

I would feel even more relaxed the following morning, when we had breakfast with Salman and Aida. The staff in the restaurant would welcome us with an extra greeting: "A hundred welcomes! You have honored us!" And we would smile because we were being honored by them in turn. On the morning after that, we would be welcomed by the restaurant manager, who would chat with us warmly, while one of the waiters surprised us with an extra act of kindness, offering to bring us a selection of the tastiest available food himself rather than making us queue up at the buffet. I personally thought he must be the owner of the restaurant, though he was only a waiter. The same thing would happen at the breakfasts we would take in the Dan Carmel Hotel in Haifa, when we visited the city some days later and stayed in the same place where the former Egyptian President, Muhammad Anwar Sadat, had stayed during his trip to Haifa in 1978. Salman would tell me the story of how Sadat had made him the first holder of an Israeli passport to secure an Egyptian entry visa, and how Salman had later become the 'King of the Arabic Book' and their biggest distributor in Egypt. In Beersheba, where we would spend a single night in the Leonardo Hotel, we would be welcomed by a Bedouin employee, and served an excellent breakfast by another Bedouin who supervised the restaurant staff, most of whom belonged to the Arab tribes in the region.

But that was all still to come. For now, I signed the papers for the hotel and the three of us went up to the twelfth floor, where we had adjacent rooms, to begin our journey of discovery in the country.

2
Haifa

ON THE INTERNATIONAL ROAD TO 'The Bride of Carmel,' Jamil took me away from my contemplation of a place that no longer looked like it did, back to our friendship in Moscow in the middle of the 1970s. At that time, he, Ludmilla, and I had formed a troika, more important to us than the one that dominated the Kremlin in the name of the dictatorship of the proletariat at the time of comrade Leonid Brezhnev.

Jamil made this comparison as we drove. Ludmilla had a smile on her lips, like a comma between phrases, inviting reflection. Jamil's comments forced me to reflect on our collective romantic partnership.

I was a student with Jamil in a school that graduated Communist Party cadres. We had come from different places to participate, with others, in trying to find a solution for our country, which we dreamed would one day reunite us. He had been born in Palestine, and had stayed there. He came to Moscow as part of a group attached to the Israeli Communist Party (Rakah), which included a number of Jews. I was born there, too, but I hadn't stayed. I became a Gazan who didn't even retain his Gazan identity, but fled in the course of the national struggle, dragged along by events wherever the men moved who carried guns and raised banners (sometimes light, sometimes heavy) to flutter in the breeze, settling down wherever they settled in the hopes of freedom and return—though I never returned and neither did they.

That is how I came to know Jamil, a Palestinian in Israel, a half-citizen in a democracy that had no relevance for him, and which didn't pay him any attention except at election times. And he came to know me, a Palestinian exiled in God's vast land. Some years later, I married Julie, a British citizen, half-English and half-Armenian, and Jamil married the Russian Luda, who left Moscow and moved with him to Haifa after he had completed his course at the Party school. After their marriage, she became an Israeli with full citizenship.

In the car, I turned to Jamil.

"Jamilov!"

He looked over. "Da, tovarishch, yes, comrade!"

"What did your family say when you returned to Haifa with Luda?"

The question didn't surprise him. It surprised Luda, though, who leaned forward and started to play with his bald pate, wondering what he would say.

"You've reminded me of that day," he replied, as he surrendered to the fingers sliding over his head. "My grandfather, God rest his soul, was still alive. When I told him about it, he looked at me, and teased me, his eyes worn out with suffering. He took the cigarette that was in his hand, stubbed it nervously in the ashtray, and said to me, "Look here, you should be ashamed of yourself. Does the country need Russians so much that you have to go and bring back a Russian girl, and a Jewish one at that?"

His grandfather's stance made me laugh. I was surprised that Luda was Jewish. It had never occurred to me, though I wouldn't really have attached any importance to it; in a secular society, officially at least, no one asks about anyone else's religion or attaches any importance to it. The last vestiges of Russian believers generally buried their God in their hearts and kept him hidden, fearful of government militia men. All three of us belonged to a group that didn't ask.

"I've never been a Jew in my life," Luda protested. Julie laughed, then addressed Luda in a whisper loud enough for us all to hear:

"I like what you say, Luda, because we both speak Arabic like Egyptian koshari."

We all chuckled, then Jamil proceeded to wind up his conversation with his grandfather.

"I said to my grandfather, 'Sir, God prolong your life, Luda isn't a Jew. Luda's a Communist, just like me! And you know we—' Then he interrupted me in a sarcastic, jokey way and said, 'Shame on you both. You're like the man who came to paint kohl on someone and blinded her. You needed an extra member for your Communist Party, so you went and added to the number of Jews in Haifa?!'"

Luda was the Party school librarian. Jamil and I used to call the library 'Ludi Malenki Grad'—'Luda's Little City,' that is. It was home to thousands of philosophical, historical, and economics books, and a lot of classical Russian novels, and other literary works. Luda spent some of her working hours wandering the streets of her 'city,' busily rearranging them after the school students had returned the books they had borrowed. Otherwise, she would be sitting at her desk. We both fell in love with Luda's city of culture at the same time, and allocated pet names to the different sections of the library: this was Karl Marx quarter, where his books lived; and this was the suburb of Vladimir Ilyich Lenin. I would sometimes jokingly advise a comrade who was looking for a book called *What is Political Economy?*, "Go to Rosa Luxemburg Alley in the Political Economy quarter!" To someone else, who couldn't find a book by Friedrich Engels, I might say, "Go to such-and-such a lane and you'll find it, it's not very far from Marx Street, just before Lenin Lane." Jamil would argue with me and protest: "Don't take advice from Walidov . . . he'll get you lost, comrade, and you'll end up in an ideological hell!"

We would laugh and make others laugh—a short-lived diversion from our normally dry diet of ideology.

Jamil and I would go to the library almost every day, to borrow the books needed for the academic and political papers we were required to write. We were nothing but a pair of lying hypocrites, both equally devoted to our lying, and loving it. Of all the comrades in our groups, we were the least concerned with expanding our knowledge of materialist and historical philosophies. We were each searching in Luda's world for the woman of our dreams, despite the fact that women were scattered like flowers in the restaurant and cafeteria. Their beauty defeated the ideology that had done away with the Russian Tsar, Nicholas II, in February 1917, and had removed the government of Alexander Kerensky in October of the same year. The doors of relations between the sexes were open to all desires, from a first look to sex in the food stores attached to the school restaurant, or anywhere where the secret could be kept, even if just till the next day. Despite that, Jamil and I pursued the same woman, who was beautiful and elegant, despite the poverty and backwardness of fashion in the country, which was governed by a boycott of everything that was a capitalist product. Luda, the object of our desire, distributed her feelings between us in installments. Each of us felt he received more looks from her than the other was getting, and that the meanings of her words were closer to his own desires than to the desires of the other. As a result, we loved her together in secret, disguised by a public friendship. As soon as we finished lunch, which began at one o'clock with the discipline of a military mess, we would slip along together or separately to Luda's Little City.

After some months of intense study, tiredness became an additional factor, imposed on us by the daily grind of pursuing sources for the studies we were preparing, as well as by the very monotony of life inside the school. We would take our exhaustion with us to the library. In Luda's office, there were two long, wide couches, which became temporary beds for secret siestas. I would sometimes go there, pretending to want to study, while in practice I would be watching Luda moving around the library stacks. I sacrificed a restful siesta in my room in the student accommodations for fear that Jamil might be alone with Luda.

One mild summer's afternoon, I went to the library as usual, and headed straight for Luda's office. I didn't find Jamil there, and was happy. *He didn't get here before me, then!* Luda, however, greeted me with her smile (a substitute for the kisses I didn't get), immediately excused herself, and went out to work among the books. I was left alone, so I went to sleep, hoping to meet her in a dream; but instead I dreamed that Jamil appeared, carrying a thick stick and pursuing me down strange streets.

The three of us carried on like that, until a day arrived when a field trip to Leningrad had been arranged, during which we were to visit an agricultural kolkhoz near the city. It so happened that the trip was a shared one between the Israeli and Palestinian groups, even though we went in separate buses.

Just before leaving, Jamil and Luda stood near the door of the bus that was to transport the Israeli group, whispering quietly to each other, until the time came to move off. Luda planted two kisses on Jamil's cheeks as he got onto the bus. Then she ran over to our bus, which had stopped behind the first one. I had already taken my seat. She came up to the bus window I was sitting beside. We whispered to each other for a time, until the noise of the engine got too loud, followed by the voice of our guide shouting, "We're going now, comrades!" Luda hurriedly gave me two kisses, the same as Jamil had got, through the glass of the window.

On our last day in Leningrad, gripped in the heat and humidity rising from the Neva River as it meandered along its channels, Jamil and I made a tour of the city that lasted several hours, ending up in a large gift store. "Let's take a look," we said together at the entrance, then parted. We were separated by hidden desires, which sent us in different directions among the articles in the store. None of them caught my fancy, but eventually I found some plastic roses of various colors, chose a white one, and paid for it.

At the end of our shopping expedition, I met Jamil at the store entrance and we walked out together. He was carrying something in a wrapper similar to mine. He didn't tell me what he had bought, and I didn't tell him. Neither of us asked the other about the lucky girl he would be giving his purchase to. Maybe we each feared defeat. In a voice like a whisper, we just said to each other, "I've bought a small thing that I liked."

Did Jamil have the same feelings that day as I did? Did he, like me, feel that the two gifts were to be given to one woman? I don't know. All I know is that we had divided up Luda without our knowing if she considered us equals in her affections.

The day after our return, we visited Luda in her office at different times. I went after Jamil. I was late because I had a lesson in political economy, as I recall. Luda was looking at some papers connected with her work when I went in, my right arm behind my back. She left whatever she was doing, moved away from her desk, and hurried toward me to give me a hug and a kiss. I embraced her with my left arm and, as we separated, gave her my present—the white rose I had bought for her. She took it from me and kissed me again, then quickly went back to her desk. She reached over toward a glass vase, in which stood . . . a red rose. Luda put the white rose in the vase, picked it up, and came toward me, smelling each rose separately, and repeating, "Mmm, krasivo, spasibo, tovarishch Walid, i spasibo, dorogoi Jamil!" As I watched reality cancel out our secrets, she thanked both of us, said that both our roses were beautiful, called me comrade, and called him dear. Then she put the vase back on her desk, turned to me with a neutral smile on her face, and said:

"Your rose is as white as your heart, Walid. You're a true friend."

Luda's message reached me clearly—as clearly as the truthfulness of my feelings. I realized that what was between her and Jamil was more than that between her and me. I felt alone in my defeat at that moment, but to reassure myself I told myself that I'd been right to buy a white rose. I'd had my doubts, but I'd done well. I wondered what would have happened had I brought Luda a red rose like Jamil; would we have been plunged into a "War of the Roses," in which we shed, if not blood, at least our emotions for her sake.

I went up to Luda and kissed her on both cheeks. "Jamil's rose is worthy of a lover like you, Ludichka," I said, without a trace of hesitation or stuttering. "Keep our mutual friend, and look after him." Then I left her room in the library, abandoning my fleeting dreams of Luda's love. I took my defeat and left. And from that time, I had retained a strong friendship with both of them.

I recalled these incidents from our late adolescence as I listened to Jamil recounting the details of the year we had spent together in Moscow.

Suddenly, Jamil turned toward me and asked, "Do you remember the two roses, Walid?"

Before I could recover my composure, he hastened to explain. "The ones we bought from Leningrad and hid from each other?"

"Of course I remember!"

"Bozhe moi, oh my God!" Luda said.

"You still use Russian exclamations, Ludichka moya?" I retorted.

"Yes, when I feel emotional—because I've still got the two roses."

"Bozhe moi!" I exclaimed in turn in Russian, not believing what she had said.

"Ever since Luda came to the country, she's kept those two roses in a glass jar," commented Jamil.

"Of course, because Walid's is a rose of friendship and Jamil's is a rose of love."

Finally, Julie, who had been struggling to eavesdrop all this time without saying anything, interrupted. "I don't understand anything, you sometimes speak Arabic and sometimes Russian. Look, I can say it as well: Bozhe moi!"

I explained the story to her, for she knew nothing about it, except for my friendship with Jamil. She wasn't surprised or given pause by the past of three adolescents who had one day met in the same place.

In this way, our drive of more than an hour and a half passed, as we looked at the scenery and recalled warm memories. Whenever something caught the attention of one of us, he would exclaim in Russian "Bozhe moi!," until Haifa opened its arms to us and we threw ourselves into its clutches.

3

Jerusalem

THE DAY HAD BEGUN TO make way for a pleasant evening when we awoke from a well-deserved siesta. Soon, Julie and I were to go with Salman and Aida to the Nafura Restaurant in Jerusalem at the invitation of Dr. Fahmy al-Khatib and his wife Nada. And despite the short distance, we were to go in Salman's Mercedes (a car that was much more sporty than he was himself).

I pulled back the curtain from the only window in our room and threw curious glances from lazy eyes over what lay outside, but I didn't find the Jerusalem I'd dreamed of visiting all my life. Just modern buildings scattered all over the place—the sort of thing you could see in any European town, as if we were not in Jerusalem at all. As if Jerusalem was somewhere else.

Night fell, and we left the hotel in Salman's car. He didn't seem to know the city well. He commented like a tourist guide who hadn't taken lessons in his profession or walked about the streets before. He would point out to us a corner or a landmark whose details were hard to absorb. He would show us little things he had generally only heard about. We looked and were astonished, each in their own way.

We parked near the Jaffa Gate, left the car, and crossed Omar ibn al-Khattab Square, then turned left, and entered Latin Patriarchate Street. We reached the Nafura Restaurant, which looked just like the other establishments around it, with their mostly blue old doors, and went in, one after the other. Once inside, we looked in more detail at the place where we would spend our evening, while the owner greeted us with traditional expressions of affection. Fahmy would later explain that it was his favorite restaurant, and that its owner was also a friend of his. The two men—who hadn't met for a considerable time, so he would later inform us—embraced and chided each other, exchanging the excuses that people habitually use—"You know how busy things are . . . by God, I swear . . . ," then, as he steams ahead with the rest of the usual formula, the other interrupts him, and says, "Don't swear, man . . . I'll divorce my wife . . . ," and the first won't let him finish for fear of him having to divorce his absent wife for the sake of a white lie.

Inside, the restaurant was a work of art. Tables covered with clean, neat cloths, with flowerpots between them holding roses that hid both pots and customers, and an enormous fountain in the middle, like those in old Damascus houses. The mezzes and grills were not much different from those served in other Levantine cities, but our being in Jerusalem gave everything the fragrance of the city. When the restaurant owner said that the wall directly facing me formed part of the Wall of Jerusalem (like the others, I had already taken my place around the table), a lot inside me changed, and I couldn't stop reading what the stones said the whole time we were eating supper. After finishing our first course, Salman laid out the essence of Ivana's instructions, along with our wish that Fahmy and Nada would help us carry them out.

The doctor seemed to understand the situation. He wasn't shocked that Ivana's body had been cremated after her death, though this was contrary to religious custom. "Why not?" he said. "In the end, every body turns to dust. Ivana, may God rest her soul, has merely taken a short cut."

Nada rolled her lips uncertainly, suggesting a temporary disquiet. But she kept her disquiet to herself and did not translate it into words. That encouraged Julie to say in English, with her eyes on Nada, "We've brought her ashes in a beautiful container."

"Did I understand from Salman that it's a glass vessel?" asked Nada.

"No, it's porcelain, in the shape of a woman's body, with the figure of my mother in her youth," replied Julie.

I cut in, to arouse Nada's curiosity, "You'll see tomorrow. Then you can choose whether to help us or not."

There was a silence like the moments that precede a decision.

Finally, we thanked our hosts and said goodbye, in the hope of visiting them the following day in their house in the Sheikh Jarrah suburb of Jerusalem. Then we left, to search for other details of the city. The car took us to the top of the French Hill district in the northeast of the city, its houses scattered along the line of our silent glances. Since 1971, the hill had been given a new Israeli name: Giv'at Shapira.

"They can call it what they like," said Salman, "we'll go on calling it 'French Hill.'" Meanwhile, all eyes were roving over the illuminated houses in the settlement amid the sleepy forest trees. Close to the settlement, lights were shining in the Hadassah Medical Center, and in the Hebrew University, some of whose students lived in the settlement, where they formed part of the total of seven thousand residents, in addition to a number of doctors and nurses of both sexes who worked in the hospital nearby.

"This is the highest point in Jerusalem," said Salman. Without waiting for anyone to comment, he went on, "I did a Google search on it yesterday. I don't know what brought it to mind. Someone—a female estate agent, I think—wrote about how she'd come with a client who wanted to buy an apartment on an upper floor in the settlement. The woman brought him here and took him to the building, showed him the apartment, then stood him on the balcony, and told him to look. The man turned to where she was pointing and saw a view to blow the mind. He couldn't believe he'd found an apartment in Jerusalem on a hill eight hundred and thirty meters above sea level!

"'Adoni,' she said to him, 'you see the road over there?'

"He turned to where she was pointing.

"'That road goes from Jerusalem to the Dead Sea.'

"'Beseder, okay, I like the view a lot. But the price you're asking is too much.'

"Laughing, she told him, 'The 400,000 US dollars that you'll pay is for the view in front of you. We'll give you the apartment for nothing. What do you say?'"

Aida, who lisped a little, gave a start and said, "It's not just the hill, Salman, my dear—the Jews have taken the whole of Jerusalem for free."

I didn't make any comment. Nor did Julie, who was concentrating hard on the discussion going on around her. But I whispered to her, "We've become like the rest of the Arabs, and like the prophets of the city: we just look at these places as they bury Jerusalem under them, settlement after settlement. We see new features piling up over the existing ones, and new names tramping on the old ones."

The night went on, loitering with us in the streets. Most of the evening had passed, and darkness covered the greater part of the city. Jerusalem appeared decorated with necklaces of stars, as the earth turned into sky. Eventually, Salman stopped his car.

"This is the American Colony Hotel."

We all turned toward the hotel. It was a beautiful building, constructed of the white limestone that is used a lot in the country. In front of it were six bougainvillea shrubs, whose flower-covered branches hung over the front wall. We used to call them the 'madwoman.' They reminded me of my mother Amina, who loved them a lot, and would wait for the summer to welcome them. As they crept up the wall of our house, she would watch them the whole time. She'd said that they were strong, and that it was their madness that pushed them toward the trellis on the walls and made them climb it. One summer, I'd asked her, "The madwoman that's on our wall, Mother, is she mad or sane?"

She'd turned to me with tears in her eyes, and said, "After Sharon's tanks destroyed our house, my dear, there were no more walls for the madwoman to climb up!"

I loved the madwoman as well. Like my mother, I loved her flowery madness. Sometimes, I would talk to the madwoman. I would tell her what my mother said about her: "There's no tree stronger than this one. She climbs up the walls like a thief. She's got a shameless eye, which makes amorous glances at anyone who's coming or going in the street, and talks with them." And I would laugh.

I started to laugh again now, as I looked at the flowers climbing up the entrance to the American Colony Hotel. I looked at them, silent on a silent evening, but I recalled that their flowers were the only ones in the whole of nature that smiled with three lips. I saw them smile at the very moment Salman snatched them from me.

"Hey, I'm going to surprise you. Look over to your right. What do you see? That's Orient House at the end of the street."

Without asking their permission, I put my mother and the madwoman out of my mind, and thought, *Orient House, Orient House, Faisal Husseini. I remember the day he died in Kuwait. The last day of May 2001. He went to deliver a letter to the Kuwaitis from the PLO, after the rupture that developed between them following the Iraqi occupation of Kuwait, and he died. It's as if the rupture, which had eluded repair, brought about his end.*

I contemplated the place from a distance of a few meters. I looked at the house, which had disturbed Israel for years. Israel only found peace and contentment in 1997 after it officially closed it and raised the Israeli flag over it, having already restricted, banned, and shut down its institutions one after the other. Faisal Husseini was known as Abul Abd—after his father, the martyred leader Abd al-Qadir al-Husseini, the hero of the battle of al-Qastal in 1948—and his family had inherited the house, which was built in 1897. When his turn came to manage it, Abul Abd had turned it into a headquarters for the PLO in Jerusalem, and had set up a number of media and academic research institutes, which he accommodated there. We'd thought we had a temporary site for the Palestinian capital.

"The Palestinians lost Abul Abd once, but Jerusalem lost him twice," I said. "Abul Abd was the crown on the head of the city. From the day of his death, Jerusalem has either been headless or sometimes had a hundred heads."

Salman prayed for Abul Abd, and the rest of us prayed with him: "May God have mercy on his soul!"

Salman's car moved on, turning right and following the road. After driving a short distance, Salman said, "We're near Salah al-Din Street. Let's get some sesame cake. Everyone who comes to Jerusalem has to sample its cakes."

I recalled the main commercial market in Jerusalem even before it came into sight, and the famous strike in the street when traders had opened the gates of Jerusalem to the First Intifada, which broke out in December 1987.

Suddenly, Salman stopped at the junction of two streets. He peered to his right, and started to debate with himself: "We're in Shabbat Square! I'm afraid I've got in a right mess. Now where will you go, Salman? Where will you go? This way or that way? We're in a right mess!"

"What sort of mess?" the other three of us asked.

I turned to where Salman was looking. There was a small blue sign with the name of the quarter written on it in white: Mea Shearim.

"If you're afraid of the monkey, he's bound to appear," I said.

I realized the disaster we'd landed ourselves in. The red traffic light had stopped us at the entrance to the Jewish quarter's main street, which announced its strict religious code in three languages. Directly above the sign bearing the name of the quarter were two posters in Hebrew and English, their texts lit up by the traffic light. With some difficulty, I read what was written in English on the poster: 'To women and girls: please do not walk in this suburb in immodest clothes!'

"Is there a problem?" asked Julie.

Salman answered her tensely, in his own broken Arabic. "Of course there's a problem. Big problem! The problem is that today is Saturday, and if the Orthodox Jews don't kill us, they'll at least smash the car. God, I just want the light to change so we can move on before we get into real trouble."

The light changed to green, but we were still exposed. As another green light appeared in the distance, Salman pursued it with his wishes: "God willing, we'll be able to get past it before it turns to red and we're in trouble again!"

But his wishes were apparently in need of renewal and reinforcement, for suddenly, at a distance of no more than fifty meters, two groups of youths appeared, loafing around in defense of their religion. If we stopped, they might surround the car, or they might confront us in the middle of the road and force us to stop. Then they might attack us. The road was completely deserted except for the youths, and the next traffic light—with all the fears that brought—and the light from some faint candles in a few houses that were staying up late for the Sabbath.

Salman quickly drove the car forward, trying to outstrip our fears. We passed between the shouts and curses that the two groups of youths all inevitably hurled at us, and passed the traffic light—which provided a few seconds of safety for us, after which it changed. We passed Mea Shearim, the quarter of the strict Orthodox Jews, who came from Eastern Europe before the Holocaust to form a unique community in the country. I don't know how we got back to Salah al-Din

Street, where we discovered a different world, unconnected to the rituals of the quarter we had just left.

We crossed Salah al-Din Street to Sultan Suleiman Street. Salman stopped the car opposite a bakery. There were several carts in front of it, and the voices of the sellers drew pedestrians along the street to where they could satisfy their appetites. We opened the windows and breathed in the distinctive Arab smell of cakes.

"Stay in the car," Salman told us. He got out and walked toward the market, pursued by our expectations. After a little while, he came back with some cakes. The three of us smiled at their smell, and our breasts filled with desire.

We all ate a portion of the famous Jerusalem confectionary, and then went back to the Ramada Renaissance Hotel, the smell of the cakes wafting from us—a smell foreign to the hotel where our rooms were, and to the area where we were staying.

4

Haifa

"Do you like Haifa?" Umm Jamil, Jamil's mother, asked me. "They say that any Palestinian who visits Haifa loses his mind and comes away mad." The expression on her face as she said it was one of anticipation.

Jamil's car took us up Mount Carmel from al-Jabal Street (which had become Zionut Avenue), and on to Wadi al-Nisnas, where the House of the Vine (Beit Hagefen) cultural center was situated, which still smelled of Emil Habibi and the *al-Ittihad* newspaper that we loved.

I remembered The Remainer in Jinin's novel, and his 'comradely' arguments in the offices of the Communist Party (Rakah) newspaper. I also remembered how Emil Habibi had abandoned his atheism and had asked God's forgiveness for that late morning when The Remainer had come into his office, and for every morning or evening that the two comrades had met before or would meet in the future. Now we were crossing al-Khury Street, where Haifa's rich lived, and passing in front of the Protestant school and church, as Jamil explained to us. Heavens, so this was Wadi al-Nisnas! An orange notice directed us to it. The quarter had lurked there since 1948, like a lion guarding what we still had in Haifa. It had remained Palestinian, even when Hezbollah's rockets had fallen on it in the 2006 war, destroying some offices of the *al-Ittihad* newspaper and killing two Palestinians near the school. The quarter was happy—overjoyed, even—at the death that had descended on it. Some residents congratulated each other and said, "We've been visited by Arab missiles—hello and welcome to our Lebanese guests!"

The car took us up to al-Isfahani Hill, borne on the shoulders of the Najla falafel restaurant. There, past the restaurant, under that tree in the corner to the left, the poet Ahmad Dahbur was born. Here was the vegetable market, and further up the headquarters of the Communist Party, then Shujeirat Hill. This was the street of the great historian, Emil Toma. Muhammad Mi'ari, former member of the Knesset and one of the founders of the 'Progressive List for Peace' in 1984, had lived near the corner over there. The poet Mahmoud Darwish had also lived here, as well as the lawyer and researcher Sabri Jiryis, originally from Fasuta in Upper Galilee.

To the left was al-Wad Street, where the *al-Ittihad* newspaper had once had its press. It had become the entrance to a bakery. On the left was Qaysariya Street, formerly the house of Tawfiq Tuba, who spent ninety years, his whole life, in Haifa, and had never lived anywhere else.

From al-Khury Street, we went up toward al-Hadar, Hadar HaCarmel, then al-Mahakim Street, and Hasan Shukri Street.

"Ah, what a cuckold!" sighed Jamil, shaking his head like someone wary of revenge, before going on to explain: "Hasan Shukri, my friend" (he directed his words at me, as if the women would not be interested), "was head of the council for a time. In 1927, the first municipal elections, in the true sense of the word, were held. Various parties took part in them. People say that we disagree with each other these days, but we've had our differences since back then. We've *never* been united. The Jews supported the candidate Hasan Shukri, because he cooperated with them and sold them land, as well as acting as a broker here and there. Then he won the elections, and the Arabs started to chant the slogan 'Hasan Bey, you cuckold, you sold the land for money!'"

We went down a hill, as tragic as the way up had been. Most of the houses here were deserted. Beautiful houses, all built of Arab stone—not an Israeli stone used in their building. The houses were advertised as being for sale, and could be bought from the Israeli Amidar housing company. Why shouldn't the Arabs buy them and return to them? Yes, indeed, why shouldn't the Arabs buy them? I almost shouted this to myself, and the others must also have been saying it to themselves. When the car took us down toward Wadi Salib, the way the Israelis had intervened to change the landscape began to be visible. They didn't hide what they had done. There was a slogan written on the wall of a house to the left, still clinging to the stones despite the fact that it had been written a long time ago. It acknowledged the crimes involved in driving the Arab residents out, and brazenly stated 'Pesha' meshtalim'—meaning 'These crimes befit us' or 'represent a gain for us.'

"Now I really have gone mad, Umm Jamil!" I told her. "It's the madness of Haifa!"

"A person living here in Haifa will stay sane, my boy," she replied. "It's the one who leaves his country and runs away that goes mad."

"Your words are golden!" said Jamil, praising what his mother had said—as indeed her words deserved. Then he leaned over me and said a few words in my ear, meant for me alone: "Thank the Lord, my mother's hard disk isn't faulty today."

Earlier, Jamil had warned me: "Later, you'll be sitting with Mother on the veranda, and listening to her talking in a normal way about normal things. But if her hard disk stops working, she'll start telling you about the jinni Marghodosh, who used to be her friend. She'll say he comes at half-past nine. I tell her, 'Mother, watch what you're doing with Marghodosh, you might not be performing all your duties toward him.' Every day, she gets up in the morning, turns on the tap, and talks to sprites, telling them, 'My brothers, I won't harm you, and don't harm me!'"

We both laughed. I told him that the deterioration of the hard disk containing the memories of old people was very widespread these days. I passed on the story of Zuhdiya, the wife of my late uncle, Muhammad. When I'd met her some years before, her three sons had drawn my attention to the fact that she had a fault in her hard disk. After she'd given me a hug to welcome me back to the country after a long absence, she had conveyed to me peace and greetings from my dead uncle, and I'd realized then that her mind really was affected.

"Where's my uncle, now, Auntie, what's his news?" I'd asked her.

"They say he's in Egypt," she'd replied, "and he's married an Egyptian. But I don't believe it. All his life, Muhammad's always loved me. But I know he can marry; he's a man and it's his right. I basically don't matter any more."

She'd paused for a moment, like someone who feels lost, before recovering a brief moment of consciousness and saying, "God have mercy on your uncle, he died a long time ago."

Then she'd stared at me and said, "You're not Walid! Walid lives abroad in exile. He hasn't come to Gaza for ages. What would bring him here?"

"Okay, who am I, then, Auntie?" I'd asked her.

She let out a shrill shriek of joy.

"What's this about, Auntie?" I'd asked her. "Who are you screeching for?"

"Hasn't Walid returned from exile?" she'd replied, and everyone in Abu Hatim's house had laughed.

When we got back to Jamil's house, his mother began to tell her favorite story, which Jamil said she told only to favored guests. It was a true story, which no defect in the hard disk could confuse or influence the details of.

"When I still lived in the house that the Jews took in '48, Izz ad-Din al-Qassam used to pray among the people. It was he who taught the neighbors to pray, he taught us all. He would stand in front, and we would be behind. We, the women, were always at the back. He taught them to pray. I was in the Islamic school. I saw his daughter Maymana at school. I was five or six years old. Once she was wearing black. I asked her, 'Maymana, why are you wearing black?' She said to me, 'Say: *I wish the Jews were dead.*' So I repeated, 'I wish the Jews were dead.' 'Say: *I wish the British were dead.*' 'I wish the British were dead,' I replied. I repeated whatever she said. I was young. Whatever she said to me, I would say as well. Later, I asked her, 'Why did you say, *I wish the Jews and British were dead*?' She was a strong girl. 'Because they killed my father,' she told me, without a single tear falling from her eyes."

Umm Jamil fell silent and wiped the tears from her eyes with the edge of her white kerchief. Jamil continued with the story of Maymana—the daughter of Sheikh al-Qassam—as she grew older, and her name grew with her: 'daughter of the Martyr al-Qassam.' He told how, with extraordinary bravery, she had stood up in the first Arab women's conference to be held for Palestine in 1938. She was the women's delegations' spokeswoman. She praised her heroic father, and with her head raised to the heavens said, "Praise be to God, not once but twice, who has honored me with the martyrdom of my father, strengthened me through his death, and not shamed me through the humiliation of my homeland and the surrender of my nation."

Umm Jamil picked up the thread again:

"It was dreadful, they killed him and took him away in a karra, a cart pulled by a donkey. They took him right away and buried him. They killed him, al-Qassam, in Haifa. I saw his body with my own eyes, laid out on the cart. The whole of Haifa got drunk then."

At the end of our evening—which lasted until just before midnight—Julie and I retired to the bedroom that our hosts had allocated us. Umm Jamil's stories had helped keep us awake, and now I couldn't sleep, for I remembered our appointment with Jinin in Jaffa. I took Jinin's pages out of my little bag, sat down at a table in the room, and started to read a new chapter of *Filastini Tays*, to the whisper of the waves in the sea nearby. Julie, who was exhausted from our travels, was unable to stay awake and dozed off instantly.

That morning in Gaza, Mahmoud Dahman rested his head on the edge of his mother's grave, which he had found after a long absence. He stretched his legs out in front of him. He looked at the dewdrops gathering on the edge of the grave, and on the leaves of the fig tree his grandfather had planted long before Mahmoud's father had planted him in his mother's belly. He and his siblings had called their grandfather's tree Mas'ud. It had an enormous trunk, twisted like his grandfather's emaciated body in his last days, when he was scarcely alive.

After he had asked seven times for God's mercy on him, and his sons and their mother had done the same, Mahmoud's father had described his own father and enumerated his virtues, saying:

"He prayed the dawn prayer under the fig tree so as to be close to heaven, only separated from it by the twigs and branches of a blessed tree mentioned in the Noble Quran. When he had finished his last prostration, and bowed down, and repeated his salaams—'Peace be upon you and the mercy of God . . . Peace be upon you and the mercy of God'—he got up, with the remains of prayer in his mouth, and his lips drew near to the fruit on the tree. He ate like someone eating figs in heaven. He used to water his tree with olive oil and manure it with thyme. He would smell their scents in the green figs, whose color was bright as the summer dawn, and his chest would open wide as the gate of divine mercy. 'Thyme is blessed, my children!' he would say. And anyone who heard him would repeat after him, 'Praise be to God, who has made for us in this world figs, and olives, and thyme.' And I would add to the prayer: 'And bread from the oven, father.' And my father would laugh."

*

Mahmoud wiped his face with his hands, steeped in dew and memories. He recited the Fatiha for his mother's soul, his head still resting on the side of her grave. His lifelong dream had been to rest his head on her shoulder, strong as the concrete of her tomb, but he had been too afraid. He had loved her a lot, but had been scared of her, too. Safiya had been strong. She'd had black eyes, hawk-like and angry for no reason by day, while in the darkness of the night they'd been like owl's eyes as they watched everyone sleeping. She'd had a Roman nose, like the noses of the ancient statues of that empire.

In their youth, Mahmoud and his brother Awni were often rude about their mother in her absence. They often agreed that she wasn't like other women, and wondered how she could have borne them. But they didn't find it strange that their father, known as Sheikh Ibrahim, had been stubborn enough to marry her.

"You do know, Mahmoud, that mother's a man?" Awni would say to Mahmoud, with an inherited astonishment that, like the stubborn gene, distinguished the Dahmans and governed their emotions.

Mahmoud would respond wickedly, "Of course, look how our father—tall and broad as he is—trembles when he stands and talks to her!"

The young males of the family called her Hajja Safiya, despite the fact that she was not a hajja and died still hoping to perform the pilgrimage. When she heard herself called Hajja Safiya for the first time, she searched in every direction, looking for who it might be. And she was right to, for she had not yet reached the age when people look for some means of cleansing their consciences and ridding themselves of their sins. Most likely, everyone called her Hajja because she was the wife of Sheikh Ibrahim, and she had a pure heart, white as his was, clean as a piece of calico cloth, or so people thought. A clean conscience, purer than that of many who had performed their religious duties and had hurried to shake off the mountains of sins that had piled up in their lives like dust piling up on an old carpet.

The Dahmans gave Safiya the title 'Hajja' without her having to shake any piled-up sins from her body. She clung to her hopes as the dew clings to the end of summer or to the fruits of the fig tree, and said, "God willing, He will grant us a pilgrimage, us and all Muslims." And then one day she found herself bearing the honorary title of 'Hajja' without even having tried to visit Mecca.

Hajja Safiya was not pleased by her elder son Awni's marriage to Aisha al-Faq'awi from Gaza, and only accepted it at the time under duress. She gathered together the fuel of her hatred for Aisha and lit a fire in the heart of her son.

The day Hajja Safiya had been waiting for came two months after the birth of her grandson Saeed, Awni's second son. For Saeed wasn't happy, as his name implied he should be. He emerged from the womb to a rumor that had accompanied his mother's pregnancy, and which became a fact talked about by everyone: "Saeed's not his father's son. Aisha's had a secret lover." The whole camp said it: "The boy's definitely not a bit like his father." Even people who'd never seen him said it. The view was that, after so many years of his wife not becoming pregnant, Awni was no longer able to father children to add to the son he'd already been blessed with. Within a couple of months, this opinion had become stronger than a fatwa from Sheikh Amin, the imam of the camp mosque. Hajja Safiya was delighted by the rumor, and confirmed it: "Aisha has never been faithful! From the day she married Awni, she's never loved him, never been able to stand him."

So Awni divorced her, and Aisha left the marital home that had held them together for more than fifteen years, took the 'rumor child' with her, and disappeared.

In Khan Younis, where Mahmoud Dahman went to repair the familial links that had been broken since the nakba, he found the old story of his brother Awni waiting for him.

His brother Rajab, who was three years younger than him, told him that Awni had gone mad and divorced his wife, but after no more than a month he had regretted what he had done. Whenever he recalled Aisha's name, he would beat his head with clenched fists and sometimes slap his cheeks with his hands like a woman who had lost a child. One dark morning, Awni got up early and went out, leaving his four-year-old son Fayiz asleep in his grandmother's bed. He took a taxi to Gaza, and went straight away to the Shuja'iyya quarter, where he made for the house of his father-in-law.

To calm himself, he told himself that he was ready to grovel on his knees in front of his father-in-law to get back his divorced wife. He would ask his Lord for mercy, and say to Aisha, "I have brought you back to my authority as your husband." And his father-in-law would say to him, "Take your wife, Awni, my son, and return home. May God guide you both." Then he would take her hand, which would tremble with her desire. He would take their child, Saeed, in his arms—a child cleansed by his words, and by his rejection of divorce, from the rumor that had clung to him all his life. Then he would take them both back to Khan Younis.

He passed the butcher's shop belonging to Bashir al-Fahmawi (Abu Umar). He greeted him and asked him to lend him a knife, which he said was to slaughter a sacrificial sheep. Abu Umar lent him the knife, but when he reached his father-in-law's house, Awni didn't ask his wife to gather her clothes, pick up the child, and come back to their house in Khan Younis. Instead, he stabbed her and killed the child in a way that even the police who arrived later had never come across before. The details of the crime were too horrific to be released. Awni was arrested, and a medical examination showed that he was insane, so a week later he was sent to the Khanka Psychiatric Hospital in Qalyubia in Egypt.

That incident had remained a powerful marker in Mahmoud's life. The tragedy of his nephew Fayiz never left him—a young boy who grew up with a dead mother, an insane father, and a brother killed by his father because of a rumor.

The Remainer had never imagined that his brother Awni would be the first Palestinian to honor the psychiatric hospital in Qalyubia with his presence. Indeed, he would become something of an ambassador in the hospital, anticipating the appointment of the first Palestinian ambassador in Cairo by decades.

At any rate, Awni wouldn't be there to receive Mahmoud in Gaza, to rejoice at his return, embrace him, and cry on his shoulders as he used to when his father beat him as a miserable young boy.

Mahmoud himself had sometimes had cause to beat his own son, Filastin, who had inherited his features, habits, and nature from him, as well as a lot of his stubbornness—indeed, he surpassed him in it.

Filastin often told the story of a particular incident which reminded him of his superiority:

One morning, I had an argument with Adil, our neighbors' son, over who should captain the Taba team in the quarter, and we came to blows. Adil insulted me in a way that was a slur on my father. "Why should you be our captain, you son of a laundryman?" he asked me, looking at me in a provocative way before running off. My blood boiled, and I could feel it almost bursting my veins. I picked up some stones from the ground, threw them, and hit him on the forehead. He started bleeding at once, and I could see blood flowing from between his eyes as his screaming grew louder. I was afraid he'd collect the whole quarter together around me, Jews and Arabs alike, so I fled toward Lydda station and didn't go back home until after sunset.

My father found out what had happened, and when I got back he shouted angrily in my face, "Are you mad or just stubborn, to hit the lad on the head with a stone and draw blood? It's a good thing you didn't kill him and get us into real trouble!"

"I'm not crazy or weak-minded, father," I replied. "You've told me a thousand times not to put up with anyone who insults you—and if anyone lifts a finger against me, then break it. And once you even said to cut it off! Well, Adil insulted us both."

"You idiot, I just meant that if someone crosses you, you shouldn't put up with it. Insult him, curse him, call him names, damn all his ancestors. You can slap him in the face, punch him in the chest, spit in his face, humiliate him, and wipe the ground with him—but don't put a hole in his head!"

"What have I done wrong? Do you want me to get beaten up by the children of the quarter?"

"Get out, you idiot! I don't want to see your face, you donkey!"

I ran away into our quarter, which was now half in darkness. From there I slipped into my maternal grandmother's house, which was near Lydda station. I spent the night there and told her everything.

In the morning, my grandmother prayed that I would find guidance, and advised me to go back home and apologize to my father, but I put off going until just before noon; I was lucky, for I didn't find anyone at home. I stole some money from my mother's drawer and took a taxi to Gaza, where I spent two days with Fayiz, my cousin.

Finally, I went back to Ramla, weighed down by a mountain of fears inside me. I was afraid of my father's reaction—he would certainly never forgive me. I crept into the house like a thief, one step at a time, with Fayiz creeping behind me, adding his fear to mine. I stopped and asked him to lead the way.

My father swallowed hard when his eyes fell on Fayiz. He smiled as wide as his lips would go. I followed Fayiz in and shut the door behind me. You're in luck, Abu Fils, *I said to myself. Yes, I really was in luck, for Fayiz's unexpected appearance on the scene changed my father so much that he was like a different person; Fayiz made up for my father not seeing his brother, uncle Awni. Fayiz was a miniature reproduction of his father, and he made my own father forget our neighbors' son Adil, his open head, the wound that hadn't healed yet, and the way I had left the house and stolen money from my mother.*

I smiled at this outcome. It was I who had brought Fayiz to see his uncle, who was delighted. He sniffed at him, searching for the smell of his brother in him. Here was my opportunity.

"Look, I've brought you my cousin Fayiz, in the flesh!" I said to my father, with considerable pride and satisfaction.

My father hugged and sniffed Fayiz again and again, until I called out in jest, "That's enough, father, Fayiz really smells horrible! Leave him, let his mother heat some water for him to wash."

My father's tear-filled eyes blinked, as he replied to me with an affectionate threat, "Go inside, you scoundrel, and watch you don't do it again or you'll break up the family. I'll forgive you this time for the sake of your cousin, but next time I'll hang you from the ceiling by your ankles if you wound another child. Understood?"

Then he looked again at Fayiz, searching in his face for his brother, who had been destroyed by my grandmother Safiya and the slander of the quarter.

Tired now, I put the pages to one side, and went to sleep thinking about Jinin's stories, The Remainer, and Jaffa, which we would visit the next morning.

5

Jerusalem

In the early afternoon, crowds of people poured onto Sultan Suleiman Street from all the side roads, alone or in groups, distributing themselves among their destinations and livelihoods. Some surged like waves of the faithful as they poured toward the Damascus Gate. I saw Jerusalem celebrating the noise of the cars, and the carts of the street sellers as they marketed their wares with their traditional musical cries, and the shouts of the drivers' assistants as they gathered passengers from the doors of wide, spacious depots, herding them into the buses that would take them to the cities and villages they wanted to go to.

We crept forward. We passed a frail man who relied on his faith to compensate for his size. He was sitting under an olive tree, which was not enough to protect him from the advancing afternoon sun. He shouted at Julie and told her off: "Cover your head, woman!" But Julie didn't understand what he'd said, and took no notice. If she had understood, she would simply have said something that the frail man wouldn't have understood: "That's funny, what's it got to do with him?" When Julie didn't turn toward him or pay any attention to his rebuke, however, the man supposed that Julie was ignoring him, so he repeated his shouts and his reproaches: "Curse the man who brought you up, and the one who keeps you in his house!"

When Julie and I caught up with Salman and Aida, who had already gone down the few steps in front of the Damascus

Gate and had almost reached the gate itself, the Jerusalem I remembered had deserted me, remaining only in the school books that had introduced it to me. I stood like the others, astonished, in front of the great gate, ready to enter the heart of the city amid the glances of three Israeli soldiers and the watchful protection of their weapons.

I thought back to our arrival at the foot of the Mount of Olives. After parking, we had left the place together and moved a little away, leaving our two wives to finish a private conversation they hadn't had time for on the drive from the Ramada Renaissance Hotel. Salman had turned to me, his finger pointing off to the side.

"This is the tomb of the prophet Zechariah, peace be upon him."

"Peace be upon him," I repeated, then asked him about the olives, whose name the hill bore. But Salman didn't answer. I looked around for the sacred trees, but I could find nothing but hundreds of Jewish graves, which it seemed had swallowed up the olives of the mountain.

I looked again at where Salman had pointed a few moments before. There were actually two tombs. I had read about them in the course of my intensive studies on Jerusalem in the weeks before Julie and I had come to the country: one belonged to the prophet Hizr and dated from the second century BC, the time of the Second Temple (though no one has yet discovered the first Temple). It sat in a massive face of rock, with three Greek-style pillars at the front of it, and no place for a body—though it was big enough for people to believe it was a tomb. According to Christian belief, it was the place where the Messiah appeared to his disciple, Saint James.

The second tomb, the one that Salman had pointed at, was that of the prophet Zechariah. "Peace be upon you, Prophet!" I repeated again as I contemplated the tomb: a monument carved from the solid rock, topped with a pyramid. I climbed the three steps that led up to it. Its outer edges were decorated with pharaonic designs. As for the pillars, I was struck by the cocktail of history and civilizations that I saw there, and would see in most of the buildings and streets in the Old City: Greek, Byzantine, Roman, Egyptian pharaonic, Arab, and Islamic.

But that was all ancient history, and in the clear light of the present, the soldiers of the Occupation drew my focus. I saw no more prophets in the city. I had come back hoping to find answers in the City of Peace, to find out what they had done for it from the time they had settled there to the time they had left, but they were long gone.

At the entrance to the Khan al-Zeit market, we were met by some peasant women from the villages around Hebron. As usual, they had come surreptitiously by the back roads, away from the Israeli military roadblocks. They'd smuggled themselves in, with their smells of mint, thyme, and other greenery, away from the eyes and noses of the soldiers, and now scattered their wares wherever they went in the city. As we crossed it, the market appeared to be decorated with peasant women, who were in turn decorated with their clothes, and their clothes with local silk. Women who looked like my mother squatted in cramped spaces in front of bundles of vegetables and soon became a familiar part of the attractive scene.

We passed by the women. We were joined by several other smells, which wandered with us along a street in which there was more scope for wonder than for visitors' feet. As I tried to take in the details of the place, Salman busied himself explaining the things that held my attention. Julie and Aida were absorbed in contemplating the nuts, herbs, and spices, discussing which were best, what they were all used for, and what Julie could take back with her to London.

"This is Jaafar's, my friend!" Salman told me. "Didn't I tell you to remind me we should eat kunafa there? Of course, you've forgotten!" he went on, pouring scorn on my weak memory. We all slipped in between the crowds of bodies and the sound of the kunafa knife touching the bottom of the large tray in a succession of beats, as it counted the number of customers.

"How many trays of kunafa do you make a day, my friend?" I asked the swarthy young man, his muscles taut from using the knife.

"On a Friday like today, a couple of hundred. People finish praying, have a bite or two to eat, then come to us to enjoy the kunafa," he answered between the knife-beats, which only stopped when one tray was exchanged for another.

"You know, Abul Silm," I whispered in Salman's ear, "Israel could go through a thousand right-wing or left-wing governments, sane or crazy, and Jerusalem would still smell of sesame cake, kunafa, and thyme. And it would still be decorated with peasant women. God knows, the Jews have only been a short time in this city!"

"Shut up, or the poet Munir Tabrani may hear you. The other day I read an article saying that he'd been at an evening with the novelist Rabai al-Madhoun—the writer we were talking about on the way from the airport—in the Abu Salma Hall in Nazareth. Our friend al-Madhoun, it seems, had finished off two plates of hummus, followed by two plates of kunafa, drank a jug of water, then got excited, and started to make a speech: 'We've got hummus, we've got kunafa from its home in Nablus. We've got our clothes, we've got the stitching of the decorations and the silk, and the rainbows on the chests of the peasant women. We have the whole of Jerusalem, and the souls of the prophets who left their sites on the Rock for people to fight over. So long as the women of our sacred countryside continue to bring their vegetables, their thyme, their basil, and their smells for us to savor in Khan al-Zeit and the ancient alleys, nothing will remain but our own history, our history that is ours . . .'

"Munir stood up in the middle of the hall and shouted at al-Madhoun, 'Forget your hummus, forget your kunafa, the

Jews have taken the whole country, and you're talking to me about hummus and thyme. Give us a break, man!'"

We laughed together. "You know," Salman went on, "Jerusalem would be nothing without Abu Shakir's and Abu Hasan's hummus. What would Jerusalem be worth without Salah al-Din Street and Bab al-Wad, and the Jaffa Gate, and all the gates that take people to their places of faith? If it didn't have all this, it wouldn't have the al-Aqsa mosque or the Dome of the Rock, the Christian quarter, the Church of the Resurrection, the Western Wall, the Khan al-Zeit Market, al-Khallaya, or the clever merchants who came to Jerusalem in bygone times and preserved its markets and commerce. That's without getting into politics and mentioning Orient House, the National Hotel, or the al-Hakawati Theater. Could Jerusalem be Jerusalem if it wasn't for all this, man—and above all, its mountains, its history, its walls, wars, and peace? Although, between ourselves, the City of Peace has never known peace!"

After saying all this, he drank a little water from his glass, at the same time swallowing the remains of his speech. One sentence, though, remained on his tongue: "Don't forget our appointment with Dr. Fahmy al-Khatib, like you forgot to remind me of Jaafar's kunafa!"

"We've still got two hours," I replied.

"Don't forget, either," exclaimed Julie, "that we have to see the Church of the Resurrection, to say a prayer and for me to buy some incense."

"Yes, dear, to say a prayer and buy some incense," echoed Salman, imitating Julie's accent. So we all left, and made for the Church of the Resurrection.

The four of us wandered along the ancient alleyways, accompanied by the past—like friends across a long period of history—until we reached one of Jerusalem's great landmarks: the Church of the Resurrection. We stopped in the courtyard in front of it, before a place that brings together Christians from all over the world—though as soon as they get inside it, they divide it up.

Julie made the sign of the cross over her chest and wept. She started her prayers for Ivana's soul before she'd even crossed the threshold into the purity of the church.

Salman said that he and Aida had visited the church many times, and they went off to wander around the neighborhood. I started to contemplate the church, the key to which had been entrusted to a Muslim Palestinian family, as the various Christian sects could not agree among themselves. Wajih Nusseibeh opened and closed the doors of the church every day. Muslims had also guarded it in a tradition handed down since AD 638, when the caliph Omar ibn al-Khattab had entrusted the key to Abdallah ibn Nusseibeh al-Maziniya, after receiving it from the Patriarch Sophronius, together with the keys to the city of Jerusalem itself. The Christian sects agreed to leave this task in the hands of two Muslim families, the Judahs and the Nusseibehs. The first kept the key to the church secure, and the second opened the door. This wise arrangement solved the problems that arose between the sects—as in the summer of 2002, when a Coptic priest had moved his seat from the agreed place, into the shade. The Ethiopians regarded this as a hostile act of aggression, and a fight broke out, which resulted in eleven people being injured.

Julie walked toward the church entrance and disappeared inside. I remained alone, looking at the groups entering devoutly and emerging even more devoutly. When she reappeared, she was so exhausted by her emotions that she expressed a wish to leave the place quickly. I didn't pursue it, but asked instead about the holy incense, and she confirmed that she had bought some. Then we turned around, to find Salman and Aida waiting for us at the corner.

We all walked together in silence until we left by the Damascus Gate.

*

Salman stopped his car halfway up the hill. "This is Dr. Fahmy's house. And there they are."

It was an odd scene. Fahmy and his wife were sitting at a large rectangular table set in the middle of a leafy terrace, like two people sitting on the edge of a public road. There was no sign of any house or building. In a side area were two cars which must have belonged to the couple. Salman drove his car in, parked it behind one of the other two cars, then got out. We followed him, Julie with a large bunch of roses we had bought on the way to the house, and I with the porcelain statue in my hands. We had already taken the statue out of the box it had traveled in—surrounded by pieces of sponge to protect it from breaking—and wrapped it in pretty colored paper.

After everyone had finished shaking hands and exchanging kisses, the first thing I said was, "Where's the house, doctor?"

He gave a deep laugh and replied, "Underneath us, man! Surely Salman must have told you . . . ." He gestured.

The house was perched on a slope at the bottom of the mountain. The garage was on top, and not at the bottom as usual. Residents went in through the terrace above the third floor, and then down into the body of the house.

Nada accepted the flowers with a smile as rosy as the flowers themselves. I put the statue to one side. As we were taking our places around the table, which had been laid with bottles of wine and light nibbles, I noticed that Nada had a look of satisfaction on her face, which made her look different from the woman we'd met at supper the previous day. I felt relieved, and put out of my mind the cross look I'd seen in her eyes when Salman had broached the subject of Ivana's ashes. I turned to Julie and saw a look of relief on her face that mirrored the relief I felt inside me.

We made some general conversation. As we talked, we took some wine, and this and that from the nibbles. Then Julie got up from her chair and I realized that the moment was upon us, that what had been just preliminaries were now the real thing, and that Julie had decided to commence the third and final ritual for saying farewell to Ivana, following the cremating of her body and the scattering of half her ashes over the River Thames.

Julie took her glass and asked the others to raise theirs. I looked at her, and I saw my mother-in-law in front of me: the same confident stance; the humble pride of a resident of Acre; the gaze that took in the others. I heard words that fondly recalled the rhythm of her mother's words: "Friends, let us drink to the health of a woman who wanted to return home—even if only half the ashes of her body, and half a sinful spirit. We say farewell to her, ask God's mercy upon her, and beg forgiveness for her."

As the expressions of mercy humbly made their way from her lips to the open air like a prayer, Julie took out a stick of incense and lit it with a match. I moved my glass and some of the plates from the table in front of me, and Nada hurried to help me. I took the statue and put it on the table. Then, like someone peeling a fruit, I slowly tore the paper in which it had been wrapped. As Ivana's porcelain body started to emerge in front of us, Nada's eyes grew larger, filled with a look of amazement.

"Incredible!" she exclaimed. "Amazing, a real gem!" Then she asked to hug the statue to her breast. When I had finished removing the paper and the whole statue could be seen, I passed it to our hostess, who stood up and took it, then hugged it, and kissed it with her lips and tear-filled eyes. Nada gestured to Julie to come over to her, which she did, and the two women stood together, Nada with the statue held up between her hands, and Julie holding the lighted incense stick, which had begun to send out clouds of holy smoke. As the smell of the incense filled our chests, I went up to Fahmy without thinking, and we took positions together behind the women, while Salman and Aida stood behind us.

Nada now addressed us all: "Come on, let's go down one step at a time to the sitting room on the third floor. We can pray for her soul and put the statue in the middle of the room, so that everyone who visits us can see it and hear the story from me or Fahmy, or even from our children, to whom we'll tell everything—they'll come back home this evening . . . ." As the others listened, I was searching for the Fairuz song 'Flower of Cities' and loading it on my cellphone. As soon as Nada finished talking, she moved away, followed by everyone else, to the rhythm of Fairuz's voice:

> For you, City of Prayer, I pray,
> For you, most splendid of dwellings, Flower of Cities . . .
> Oh, Jerusalem, Jerusalem, City of Prayer, I pray!

We left the terrace, and turned, still in the line we had spontaneously created, Nada and Julie at the front. As we descended the house's outside marble staircase, a beautiful panorama appeared in front of us: three- and four-story buildings climbing a wide hill, and olive trees racing each other in pursuit of them. Below stretched a valley, an extension of the Wadi Joz, from which smoke from burning car tires was rising up somewhere in front of us. A few meters away, there was a small gathering of people (a little later, when we went down to the garden—which clung to the bottom of the mountain—Nada would tell us, "Those are groups of Palestinian and Jewish leftists, some of whom still gather here. They're protesting against a government plan to annex a piece of land in the valley").

We went down the stairs one after another, enveloped in small clouds of holy incense, to the accompaniment of Fairuz's voice and the solemn rhythm of our feet. We reached the third floor, and our small funeral procession went in through the door of the guest room. Nada stopped, so we all stopped. She gave the statue to Julie and asked her to place it herself in a corner of the room. When she had done so, and without any prior arrangement, we paused for a moment of proper silence, after which Julie received final condolences for the soul of Ivana, which I felt—and no doubt, the others felt the same—must now be hovering over the heads of the protestors, before it began its final journey over the Flower of Cities.

We went down to the garden and Nada brought out tea. Then we listened to Fahmy telling the story of his family. He concluded by saying bitterly, "And here is our latest loss. Do you see the house over there? Just above my left hand?" Everyone turned to where he was pointing. "That's the house of my younger brother Mustafa," he went on. "He emigrated to America a year ago. He said he couldn't stand the situation at home. Every morning, I would be drinking my coffee here in the garden, and I would wave at him or he would call out to me, to say good morning to each other. May God have mercy on him, he didn't listen to my advice—he quit the house and emigrated with his family. Anyway, some months ago, I was standing in the morning with a cup of coffee in my hand as usual, probably thinking of Mustafa, when I turned toward the house and saw a Jew who'd planted a chair by the door and was sitting as though he was in his ancestral home. I went crazy, hysterical—I contacted the police, and submitted a complaint. Months have gone by, but the wretch won't leave the house. He ripped the door off, he's taken up residence there, and the police aren't willing to take any steps against him or get him out. We're waiting for a decision from the courts. And I'm afraid it'll be the same for Mustafa as it's been for thousands of Palestinians who've quit their homes and taken the keys with them."

Next morning, Julie and Aida decided to go back to the Khan al-Zeit Market to buy herbs and spices. Aida said Julie was insisting, and that she really liked Abd al-Mun'im Qasim's shops. Salman agreed to go with them and spare me the trouble of waiting for the two women to explore the huge variety of produce on offer. He said he would call in at a number of Jerusalem bookshops and seek out some new publications. That gave me a chance to visit the Temple Mount and the Dome of the Rock on my own.

The four of us passed the Damascus Gate amid a crowd watched by three armed Israeli soldiers. We walked on down the few steps in front of where al-Wad Street intersects with the Khan al-Zeit market, where we became part of the crowds vying for their share of the delights of the city. Julie and Aida didn't need a guide, or even Salman's help, to take them to the Suq al-Attarin inside, for the smells of the superb Palestinian herbs and spices were enough to draw them by the nose to such shops as were left in the market, though many of them had closed because of the taxes and other irritations, as well as continuing Israeli intimidation.

When the smells reached my nostrils, I left the others and headed toward the Dome of the Rock through the Cotton Suq, after agreeing that the other three would visit the Temple Mount and Dome of the Rock later while I went on my own to the Holocaust victims' museum known as Yad Vashem. We would all meet in the Ramada Renaissance Hotel in the evening.

I was now in the Suq al-Qattanin, the Cotton Suq, the most beautiful market in Jerusalem, built by Sayf al-Din Tunkuz al-Nasiri, the governor of al-Sham in the reign of Sultan al-Nasir Muhammad Qalawun in 1336. I looked at its colored stones, and its half-barreled roof, supported on pointed arches. I walked slowly under the eight openings through which the light and air penetrated, allowing the suq, which was crowded with people, to be ventilated. Like millions of other people, I sang to myself and to the city I loved:

For you, City of Prayer, I pray,
For you, most splendid of dwellings, Flower of Cities . . .
Oh, Jerusalem, Jerusalem, City of Prayer, I pray!

I sang, and whenever I came to a bit I couldn't remember, I re-sang what I could. When I reached the end of the road, still singing, I went up the first steps that eventually lead to the mosque of the Dome of the Rock, where an Israeli policeman stopped chatting to his female colleague (whose face looked Ethiopian) and indicated that I should stop. I did so, and my singing trailed off at "For you, City of Prayer, I pray."

"Hey, you, where are you going?" he asked.

"To the mosque," I replied.

"It's forbidden."

"Why?"

"Because it's forbidden. Don't you understand?"

"That's odd. Can you explain why it's forbidden?"

He blocked my way with his M16 rifle.

"I told you it's forbidden."

"I wish you'd had the same courage to say that in front of my mother. Do you know, if your government had tried to stop my mother from visiting the holy places, she'd have slapped you in the face and shouted, 'Go away! Is there anyone in the world that stops God's servants from visiting God's houses except your Occupation that's as filthy as you are?'"

"But it's forbidden."

"But you haven't told me *why* it's forbidden."

"Where are you from?"

"From this country. A Palestinian, if you like."

"Do you have ID?"

"I'm a British Palestinian."

I raised my head, and my eye caught sight of an Arab man sitting to the side of the people going up to the mosque. I was about to put my foot on the next step up again, when the policeman pushed his rifle forward until it touched my chest and surprised me by demanding that I recite the Fatiha.

"Why? Has someone died? I'll recite it for sure after I've entered the mosque, praise be to God for my visit there."

"If you don't recite the Fatiha, I won't let you past."

I was taken aback, and growing increasingly angry. This stranger wanted me to prove my Islam to him. Did they teach the Israeli police the Fatiha for this purpose?

At this point, the strange man I'd noticed sitting on the edge of a low stone wall at the side of the steps interrupted. "It's no problem, sir. Recite the sura of the Fatiha. You won't lose anything; in fact, it will bring you rewards in heaven."

That's a religious detective, a voice whispered inside me. *He's waiting to pass judgment and inform on me.*

I recited the Fatiha with a calm that was almost like contemplation.

"Please go in," said the policeman, who had stepped back a little.

I climbed what remained of the eleven steps, passing the policeman's rifle. Then I stopped directly in front of the religious detective, and gave him a disapproving look. The man, who was in his fifties, smiled, and spoke to me calmly:

"Sir, I'm a delegate of the Islamic awqaf department. It's we who are asking these questions."

"Pleased to meet you, sir, but why do you have to ask? Suppose I were a Christian and wanted to visit al-Aqsa, or even an atheist. Since when has it been forbidden to visit the holy places?"

"No, sir, don't misunderstand me; we're just afraid of settlers and Jewish fundamentalists slipping in. You know the situation. Every day or two, they try to storm the place."

I sat on the wide side staircase which leads up to the Dome of the Rock, and phoned my mother.

"You seem happier this time. There's laughter in your voice. Ha!"

"Is there anyone in the world who could be in Jerusalem, Mother, and not be happy?"

"Heh! It's a gift from God. They won't give me a permit to visit Jerusalem. So my son visits it, and I visit through him."

"Of course, Mother, consider it as your visit, and a sanctification of your pilgrimage to Mecca. I'm going to the Dome of the Rock in a bit—I'll pray two rak'as for you, and another two rak'as in the Haram al-Sharif. Okay?"

"Okay, and you . . . do you want me to pray two rak'as for you to reward you in God's sight?"

"Don't worry about it, Mother. Are you happy?"

"I'm okay. And Jala . . . Julu . . . I mean, Julie. May my tongue be cut out, I keep forgetting. Ah, that's right, she's a Christian. By God, you're both as bad as one another! I'll leave it to God to judge between you."

I stood inside the Dome of the Rock, not far from the door I had entered through, propped up by my emotions. I took off my shoes and put them on a wooden stand near the entrance. I walked like someone walking between two ages, holding on to neither of them—not even the present in which I found myself—toward a corner at the side, where I prayed two rak'as. When I had finished, and recited two salaams—"Peace be upon you, and the mercy of God. Peace be upon you, and the mercy of God"—I stayed sitting there for a few minutes, contemplating the Golden Dome from the inside, and the verses of the Quran that decorated it. I looked in the direction of the Rock, which I couldn't make out completely because of the repairs to the roof being undertaken by a team of Jordanian specialists. I got up and walked nearer. The Rock was irregularly shaped and a meter and a half high at its maximum. Under it was a small cave, with an area of 25.5 square meters at most, making the Rock appear to be suspended, which has given rise to all sorts of legends and fantasies about it. These legends have enabled anyone who hasn't visited it to mix myth with religion and fantasy with reality, producing tales and stories about it that are widespread throughout the country.

"There's a story, Amina, that the Rock flew and caught up with the Prophet (on whom be blessings and the best of peace) on the night of his ascension into heaven. The Prophet (blessings and the best of peace be upon him) chided it. 'Have some manners!' he said. So it stopped where it was . . . and it stayed suspended in the air."

My uncle's wife had told this story to my mother, taking advantage of her ignorance and my aunt's superiority to her in studying up to the sixth elementary grade. When my mother did not comment, and seemed to doubt what she had heard, my aunt continued:

"Did you know, Amina, that if a pregnant woman goes under the Rock, she'll have a miscarriage?"

"Oh! I seek refuge with God, the Almighty One. Lord, protect us!"

My mother believed what she had heard, and commented on the words of her sister-in-law with a naiveté that I had not previously been aware of (I was a child at this time). "Do you know, Umm Hatim, that if God gives me life and I visit Jerusalem, I won't visit it when I'm pregnant? I'm afraid for what is in my belly."

I praised God when I heard that. My unborn sibling would be safe!

I left the Dome of the Rock, borne along on my amazement at the design of the unique building and its interior decorations, and of the Dome itself, which lifts the person looking at it to new heights of pleasure in artistic contemplation. I headed toward the Haram in a southeasterly direction, went into the mosque and performed two rak'as, then emerged, my spirit soaring on an ethereal sense of repose born of the two visits.

On my way back to the Suq al-Qattanin, I detoured in a westerly direction to the Western Wall. A strange curiosity led me to make acquaintance with the place, which had now become known as the Wailing Wall, visited by fundamentalist Jews lamenting the loss of the temple. But my curiosity could not overcome the fact that the visit would not bring me any advantage or hold out the prospect of any particular pleasure. Indeed, it offered the visitor a strategic national obstacle course, beginning with the electronic security barrier guarded by a group of armed soldiers at the entrance, and ending with the Wall, which had imposed on us the Judaization of most of Jerusalem and the feverish efforts to impose a fundamentalist religious stamp on the state as a whole.

I continued walking in the opposite direction across al-Wad Street, and left the area via the Damascus Gate for the taxi stand, from which a driver took me to the museum for the victims of the Nazi Holocaust, or Yad Vashem as they call it.

6

Haifa

JAMIL HAMDAN DROVE US IN his small Fiat to the Merkaz HaShmona station, then went back to his work in the Ministry of Education. I bought return tickets for Julie and myself to Merkaz Savidor station in Tel Aviv. At 9:11 am, train number 107 arrived at the station, its final destination being the town of Beersheba in the Negev. The train was odd but nice, like a string of the famous red double-decker buses in London, each one attached to the next, though like a lot of trains it was actually pale silver. We got on together, and took two seats opposite each other beside a window.

Julie and I had traveled on a train like it in Paris a couple of years ago. We had spent two days tracing with our feet the maps and landmarks of the city. On the evening of the third day, we had gotten lost, swallowed up by a foolish murky evening stroll. We'd been forced to abandon what was left of the evening and look for a nearby Metro station to get back to Montparnasse, where we were staying in a hotel. Our feet had led us on—with no knowledge on either our or their part—to a station like an ancient castle. We went in by the main entrance, to be swallowed up in a maze of tunnels and internal corridors that circled around themselves and us. As they turned, we turned with them, until we ended up dizzy in front of a notice stuck on a wall, which displayed a map of the train routes for passengers' use. With no pity for us or the situation we were in, it informed us that we were somewhere in an outlying suburb, not served by the Metro, and the only help the map could give us was to provide details of the trains that passed through the station and connected with a Metro station, so that we could board the Metro and complete our unconventional journey back to the hotel.

The gloomy double-decker train had finally arrived. I said to myself at the time that it looked fit to transport inmates to some prison—prisoners who were forced to hew rocks for which there was no need at all, except to fulfill the sentences of hard labor issued against them—but not to convey two people like ourselves. This called to mind the Bastille, and 14 July 1789—when the first sparks of the French Revolution had appeared, the prison was stormed, and the date had become a national day of celebration.

The Haifa train was smart, and promised a quiet journey. It was clean inside. The seats were a dark blue, the color of the deep sea, and each of them was wide enough for two passengers. Between our seats was a table, suggesting an invitation to a lunch for four. By the window was an electric socket for people wanting to use a computer or charge their cellphones during the journey.

Julie sat with her back to the train's direction of travel, paying no attention to it. I sat opposite her, watching, through a wide rectangular glass window, scenes from the country introducing themselves to me for the first time, presenting features that I'd previously only studied in books and maps.

I explained to Julie that we would be getting off at Merkaz Savidor station in Tel Aviv, which had been built on the ruins of the villages of Sheikh Mu'nis, Manshiya, and Karm al-Jabali. The land belonged to Jaffa. We would leave the station and hire a taxi, which would take us to Dina's Café, at 34 Yehuda Hayamit Street, Jaffa. It used to be called King Feisal Street. There were still many Arab residents in the city who used the old names and refused to recognize the Israeli names attached to the official signs that had been put up at street corners. We were to meet Jinin there at 10:30 for a cup of coffee, as she had suggested, and from there continue in accordance with the program she had drawn up for us. I believed she would be taking us for a tour in her car, after which we'd go to the port, then on to the Old Citadel for a short tour there before she took us back to her house. We might also meet Basim, if he was there.

"Why wouldn't he be there?" asked Julie.

"I don't know. Jinin's been very quiet about him in her latest emails to me."

The train passed Haifa Bat Galim station, then stopped for a few minutes at Haifa Hof HaKarmel before resuming its journey. At Atlit station—which brought to mind the graphic stories about its notorious prison (one of the ugliest in Israel) and some of the worst instances of man's persecution of man that I could recall—a young conscript got onto the train, holding a copy of *Israel Hayom*, the most widely distributed right-wing free paper. A medium-sized rifle was slung over his shoulder.

The conscript chose to sit beside me. He lowered his weapon from his shoulder, and stretched it over his thighs, its base pointing toward me and touching my left hip. I didn't dare ask him to move it away, but reluctantly accepted the situation, while he proceeded to leaf through the pages of the paper with interest.

Outside the train, the window didn't offer us much: some agricultural land, some uncultivated land, villages in the distance, and stations that all looked the same.

The time passed uneventfully. It was a routine journey in an air-conditioned train, though the weather outside was mild. Despite our chatter, which was also routine, my wife and I tried to listen carefully to the train's loudspeaker whenever the name of a station was announced.

The train passed Tel Aviv University and Tel Aviv HaHaganah stations without our hearing the name Merkaz Savidor, or reading it on any sign—though my eyes were polluted by all the names I hated: Haganah, Stern, Lehi, and all the others, old and new, that represented the worst falsification of history and geography in the present age. At those moments, I felt the steel wheels of the train grinding the bones of the dead in the three Palestinian villages buried under Tel Aviv, and my own feelings were equally crushed.

"We've been traveling more than an hour, darling," said my wife. "Are you sure we haven't passed our station?"

The Israeli conscript snatched away my chance to reply to my wife's question without asking permission, like Israel confiscating a piece of land in East Jerusalem. "Where are you going?" he asked in a Palestinian accent.

"To Merkaz Savidor," replied Julie.

"You passed it some time ago, and now you're on your way to Lydda," he said, in a tone of gratuitous regret and slight censure. "You need to get off at the next station and head back the other way."

"But we didn't hear the name of the station or see any sign for it," I replied.

"Well, it went past a little while ago. Come on, I'll show you."

He got up, and I followed him in the direction of a train route map hanging in the space between our carriage and the one before it. Of course, he would know more than me: he was a local, while I was a foreigner, a tourist lost in the country. The soldier showed me the last station we had passed, then put his finger on the name of the station we were supposed to have gotten off at. We went back together to our seats, though I could still not understand how we'd missed our stop.

"You speak Arabic better than I do. Are you Palestinian?" I asked him cautiously before we arrived back at our shared seat.

"No, I'm Israeli," he replied, with a decisiveness free of any emotion. His confidence disturbed me. I swallowed as hard as I could, and sat down in silence. The conscript took his place and continued reading his newspaper.

At this point, Julie engaged him in conversation in the worst possible way. "Why are you carrying a weapon?" she enquired of the conscript, in her usual broken Arabic. My foot moved under the table, as I tried to signal her to stop talking. The young man hesitated to answer. Julie went on: "It's a lovely day, the weather's really nice, the train's quiet, and wherever we go people are living normally. So why are you carrying a weapon?"

Once again my foot issued a warning beneath the table, this time more forcefully, as if to say, *Why are you making problems with an Israeli soldier and creating a headache for us?*

"Of course, the weapon's necessary, essential. Otherwise . . . ," the soldier replied.

All my attempts to stop Julie's questions—to which she already knew the answers—failed. Despite my kicking her harder with my foot, Julie insisted on getting a clear and direct answer from the soldier himself. "Okay, why is the weapon essential? There's no war here, there aren't any problems!"

"But there might be trouble at any moment. We don't know. We need to be ready."

This answer silenced her questions like a blow. For my part, I tried to place his accent. Suddenly, I realized what I should have realized from the beginning: this Israeli army conscript was a Palestinian from the Galilee region, most likely a Druze, whose young men had been obliged to serve in the Israeli army (along with some of the Bedouin) ever since a number of traditionalist sheikhs of the sect had agreed on their behalf to the compulsory conscription decree.

As his rifle bumped my hip again, raising in me a shudder of disgust, I thought, *Why didn't you do as the writer Salman al-Natur's hero did, and scream, "Why have you killed us, Sheikh?" like an eternal condemnation, as he did in the face of Sheikh Fahd al-Faris? Al-Natur gathered together the voices of those who had refused or resisted conscription, demanded that the sect be relieved of subjection to his laws, and threw them in the face of al-Faris: "You're the killer, Sheikh!" Why didn't you refuse to serve, go to prison, and come out of it freed from the Sheikh's signature?*

Meanwhile, Julie was busily examining the map of the land that the train window was flashing past. She seemed to have dismissed the conscript. I made a mental note to share the soldier's paradoxical nature with her later.

Would this young man recall his colleague Samir Saad? Would he have even heard of him? Ought I to remind him? Samir had been a member of his sect, killed by Palestinians like himself. They had thought he was an Israeli—and they were right, since there was nothing Palestinian about him except his name and his origin. He was no different from a real Israeli—even though there's no such thing as a 'real' Israeli. A resident of the village of Beit Jinn (which since 1983 had been under the control of the Democratic Front for the Liberation of Palestine, one of the groups making up the PLO), Samir had served in the Occupation's Army of Defense. The sheikhs of the Druze religion had canceled his Palestinian birth certificate, and he had been silent and had accepted its cancellation. And in turn, he had been 'canceled' by true Palestinians on the Lebanese front.

On 13 September 1991, Israel received Samir's body in exchange for Israel permitting the return of the trade unionist Ali Abdallah Abu Hilal, originally from Abu Dis. Abu Hilal was a member of the DFLP expelled by Israel in 1986. At that time, the deal was clear: one Palestinian in exchange for one Israeli, and the Arabic name or sectarian affiliation didn't enter into the calculation of the deal. The family welcomed the return of the corpse, but they would have rejoiced over him as a martyr if he had respected his Palestinian identity. But he hadn't. He'd stood on the other side of the front. He was exactly like the man sitting next to me now, an Israeli who either delighted in his Israeli identity or was forced to delight in it.

*

The train reached Lydda station and stopped. We were now running about half an hour late. After wasting another five minutes looking for the exit, we left the station and found ourselves beside a taxi rank, where a group of drivers were already waiting, smoking and arguing among themselves so noisily that all one could make out was a jumble of colorful expressions.

I asked the nearest of the disputants about the possibility of taking us to Jaffa. This reduced the sound level of the conversation, and he pointed to the right, to a kiosk with a rectangular window, from which a man in his fifties with a religious appearance was looking out; he shouted to his other colleagues to let my enquiry get through to him. When he had grasped what I was saying, he asked for eighty Israeli shekels and the address we wanted to go to, then pointed to a driver of medium height, with a light brown complexion and North African features, who took us to an old, worn-out car, which looked like it had spent most of the years of its life in a garage for special care. As a result, the ride cost us a delay of another ten minutes, for the car didn't manage the road well, and we were unable to communicate with the driver, who only spoke Hebrew. Repair work to the drains in the area added a further five minutes, and we ourselves took another five minutes to get to the café by a roundabout route once we'd been dropped off, so by the time we arrived we owed Jinin an apology for a delay of around forty minutes.

When we reached her, on the agreed-upon street corner, we were met by the sound of a digger sinking its teeth into the body of the road.

7

Jerusalem

THERE WERE FOUR OF THEM, hovering in hopes of finding a passenger who'd finished his visit to the museum. They were chattering in Arabic. As I approached them, I became their prey, their hoped-for passenger, despite the fact that I'd come from the opposite direction—the direction of people making their way *to* the museum. Two of them got up from their plastic chairs and greeted me with a single question, preceded by two smiles designed to ensnare me:

"Wanting a taxi, Hajj?"

I ignored the question, and asked them, "Excuse me, where's Deir Yassin?"

My question disappointed them. One of them muttered in a disinterested tone, which I heard, "This guy looks like he's just run away from Deir Yassin, and yet he's come to ask about it!"

The same man then addressed me directly. "My friend, you can't see anything of it from here. The fact is, there's nothing left of it except for a few stones. If you like, I can take you to Giv'at Shaul B, just by the Hospital for Psychiatric Disorders—the loony bin, that is, if you'll pardon the expression—which is very near to it."

When he received no reply from me, he continued like someone retracting his offer. "Anyway, Deir Yassin is in that direction." He pointed to the south wing of the museum. "Go past the building. Look to your right, though you won't see anything. The village is more than three kilometers away."

Okay, I said to myself, *if it's like that, I'll postpone the sightseeing I dreamed about, and wander around for a bit inside the Yad Vashem Museum. That was part of my trip, anyway.*

Once again, I wondered about the value of a visit like this. Had I been truthful when I'd told Salman that I wanted to explore how the victims I'd be honoring stood in relation to their own victims? Did bombing Gaza help to keep the memory of the Nazi destruction alive, for example? And what was the difference between being burned in gas ovens and being burned by Apache rockets? Then again, what would *I* gain by counting the names of Jews on whom the most hideous crimes had been committed?

At the entrance, my speculations fell away from me and I paid them no more attention. I passed a small glass office, where a young man in civilian clothes was sitting, reading a newspaper. He didn't ask me anything and hardly registered my presence as I walked past him. I entered the museum through a long covered corridor and into halls designed in the most beautiful and artistic way. I passed through most of these rooms, both big and small, and stopped in front of several tables providing information, either in the form of pamphlets or else on computer screens. The Hall of Names made me pause and captured my feelings. I studied the names, and examined the features of the victims—who continued to scrutinize me as I looked at their faces—and tried to gauge their feelings at the moment the pictures had been taken. Moments that would no longer be there for people who had been reduced to skeletons or whose corpses had disappeared entirely. I lifted my head to follow the names upward until my gaze reached the hall's circular extremity, open to the sky. At that moment, I felt like the faces of thousands of Palestinians—some of whom I knew, but most of whom I did not—gazed down on me. They were pushing and shoving, as if they wanted to come down into the halls of the museum, spread through them, and take their places as victims. I felt sorrow for those from both groups, and

I cried for those who were crowded together in the sky, looking for a place to assemble their names.

I woke from my reverie and whispered to myself, as if someone was chiding or punishing me: "In the name of the people remembered here, the Israelis have lit in our country many fires, which may in the end themselves become a new holocaust."

I fell silent.

I finally left the main building, preoccupied and dejected. I turned to the right and walked on in the direction the Palestinian driver had shown me. The semicircular path took me to the back of the building, where I found myself close to a tree-lined strip of ground, no more than a few meters wide, which ran parallel to the building and ended in woods, which stretched for a considerable distance—perhaps three kilometers, as the driver had surmised. The whole length of the tree-lined strip had been planted with small signboards. I went up to one of them, and saw that it contained the names of more Jews who had been among the victims of the Nazi slaughterers. Underneath each name had been written the date of death, though some were missing. There were boards that bore the names of Jewish families that had been exterminated in their entirety. The victims' names were displayed in a different way further along: there was a small hut made of stones, with a twisted, roughly circular ceiling topped by a circular opening like a large hole. I stood for some minutes inside the hut, contemplating a work of art that aroused in me a mixture of emotions—admiration for the idea, and for the suffering that had inspired it. On the walls of the hut, which had no definite shape, identity cards and documents had been scattered. There were also scraps of paper of varying shapes and sizes, with phrases written on them like instructions, and the names of victims, some in handwriting, which grew closer to each other and more tightly packed the nearer they came to the ceiling. I found myself continuing to read them one by one with a strange curiosity, until finally I was gazing at a distant blue sky whose shape and size were defined by the opening in the ceiling. Artistically, the message had reached me. And as a human being, I understood it. I had to remember these victims, and their last, smuggled words. I asked God to have mercy on them twice: once as victims of the Nazis, and a second time as people used by those who traded on their tragedy.

I turned a little to the right. The scene revealed groups of people waiting in two small queues in front of two iron gates. I went up to a lady with an expression of worried anticipation on her face, and asked her in Hebrew, "Sliha, gvirti, excuse me, madam, why are these people gathering here?"

She looked at me, astonishment now written all over her face, making me feel that I had come from another age. Despite that, she answered me with cheerfulness: "They want to visit the other museum, on the other side over there." And she pointed to an area in the distance, situated on some mountain slopes whose features were difficult to distinguish. I didn't interrupt her as she explained to me what she meant. "Listen, sir, you're a stranger—in fact, it looks as though you must be a complete stranger! These people are waiting their turn to visit the Zikhron ha-Filastinim museum, it's a museum of Palestinian memories. It was built recently following the historic peace agreement that was signed just two years ago between the two peoples of the country, and which ended the bloody struggle that had lasted more than a hundred years. There are brand new electric cable cars like buses—you'll see them when you get nearer, they call them the 'tele-buses.' They're each large enough to hold twenty passengers, and take visitors to and fro along cables that stretch for three kilometers or more. Isn't that wonderful?"

Before I could reply, her cellphone began to ring. She apologized to me and looked at the device, then started to mutter happily: "That's my granddaughter Abigail, she's apologizing, she was going to come with me on my visit to the other museum, but she's changed her mind—she's inside here, wandering around with some friends of hers. Perhaps she didn't find the prospect of my company very attractive. She's right, my company is never very amusing for young people like her, but it might appeal to you, mightn't it?"

"Appeal to *me*?" I asked.

"Why not? Her electronic ticket's already paid for, anyway . . ."

She interrupted herself to show me her cellphone, saying, "As you can see, there are two sets of numbers, each containing five digits. They open the entrance gate, and then you board the tele-bus. Then the numbers are wiped from the phone's memory. Perhaps you'd like to accompany me, Mr.—?"

"Walid Dahman," I said, quickly filling the gap, as I welcomed her invitation and thanked her for it.

"Tala. Tala Rabinovitch," she responded.

We postponed any further conversation and headed for the assembly point, from where we arrived at one of the two doors. It was fitted with a small numerical screen. Tala looked at her phone, touched somewhere on the screen, and the entrance gate opened. I passed through the cross-shaped barrier, which closed behind me, and waited for Tala to pass through.

We found ourselves beside some doors that opened electronically just by approaching them. We went through, and soon found the tele-bus. A large number of other visitors had already boarded before us. In less than two minutes, the vehicle, which was like a cable car, had moved off.

The view from above was stunning and took the breath away. As the area opposite slowly drew closer to us, allowing us to see it more clearly, Tala explained to me, pointing to what I assumed was our destination, "Some years ago, that was the Giv'at Shaul B settlement. Now we call it 'Ir shel Slihanut,' which means 'City of Tolerance.' No one uses the name of the settlement any more—it reminds us of the period of struggle, which no one wants to remember. Now there are Palestinian

Arabs living in the city as well. By the way, Mr. Walid, any citizen of the new state can reside anywhere in the country. They're classed as a resident of the city they live in, though they remain registered on the electoral roll of the region where they were born, or where their name was registered after the general census that was carried out a few months after the two peoples of the country had been unified."

That was extremely interesting. I felt the value of my visit to Yad Vashem. The visitors to the Palestinian museum that we were heading for would doubtless also feel at peace after their visit to Yad Vashem—a peace that would prepare them for their visit to the other museum opposite. *Truly, the rights of the dead become equal when the rights of the living are equal*, I thought.

Then I turned to Tala and said, "At last, this has become a homeland for everyone, hasn't it?"

"Exactly. Albeit with a certain amount of acceptable and welcome differentiation with regard to national rights and the expression of identity with all its subtleties, including language. Arabic has become an official language of the country, and everyone here speaks two languages. We have become like the Swiss, with two languages, only ours are Arabic and Hebrew."

"But you haven't tried speaking Arabic with me," I pointed out.

"Because I only speak it a little. I'm from a previous generation, from the generation of the struggle, as we're called by those from the generation of the historic peace agreement—or the 'peacemakers,' as the intellectuals among them like to style themselves. But if you spoke Arabic to any schoolboy, he would answer in proper Arabic."

The tele-bus approached the terminus, then slid smoothly and gracefully onto the ground-level platform inside a clean room that had been built of white Palestinian stone.

We left the platform together and made for a large building containing several wings and offices. As I walked, I carried with me the question that I had put to the four taxi drivers without receiving any clear answer: *Where is Deir Yassin?* I put the question to Tala, who pursed her lips, lips worn out by chatter. This woman, who had just been speaking to me about a state for all and equal rights, didn't want to talk about the village of Deir Yassin, and gave the impression she had never even heard of it. Was it because she belonged to a generation for whom the history of the country began with the proclamation of the establishment of the state of Israel on 15 May 1948, the start of the Palestinian nakba, and considered anything before that date to be a void, a black hole that gobbled up everything in existence?

I pressed her: "Tala, if you don't understand what happened at Deir Yassin and remember its lesson well, the 'others' won't understand what happened to those victims at Yad Vashem."

At that moment, a woman came up to me from behind and asked me with a peasant's stutter, "Do you want Deir Yassin, Hajj?"

"Yes, madam. Do you know where it is?"

"I come from Deir Yassin myself, sir, from the Darwish family. My name is Widad. But my mother is from the Zahran family. Her entire family perished in the massacre. The Jews killed them and piled them up on top of one another, children on top of grown-ups, women on top of men. There's no trace of Deir Yassin now, not because the Jews destroyed it all that time ago, but because the site has become the memorial museum that we're going to now. You'll see it in a minute. I work there."

I looked around for Tala. I hadn't heard her voice since the woman from Deir Yassin had appeared, and I couldn't find her. She had disappeared as if she'd passed by in a dream, from which I was woken by Widad saying, "Here's the memorial, sir. The museum's behind it. That's the side of it, you can see it from here."

I lifted my head, to be met with a sight that linked earth and sky as this world is linked to the next. I found myself facing a large memorial, whose base covered almost sixteen square meters, and which was about a meter and a half high. It had been designed in the shape of a four-sided rocket, which grew narrower the higher it went, until it turned into a thin line that disappeared into the sky. Starting from the body of the rocket, a moving beam of light rose up, showing, inside a rectangle of light, the name of a Palestinian martyr, which shone for a few seconds, then moved up, for its place to be taken by another name. And underneath each name appeared the date of birth and date of martyrdom.

I continued to follow the names as they shone and rose upward. They had been arranged at random, reflecting the wish of the designers that everyone should be equal, with no distinction between those who had been martyred sixty years ago and those who had fallen victim to the latest Israeli raids on Gaza.

The names followed one another, lighting up in my eyes and awakening my memory before ascending: Fatima Jumaa Zahran, Safiya Jumaa, ...

Suddenly, Widad cried out, "These are all my relatives!" And she proceeded to repeat the names and to weep: "Fathi Jumaa Zahran, Fathiya Jumaa, Yusri, Fatima, Samiha, Nazmi, ..."

A few moments later, Widad collected herself and said: "Don't blame me, sir. Although I work here every day. . . . I don't know why today in particular all my grief has exploded."

I helped Widad with a couple of tears, and spoke to her kindly with words that matched her feelings. Then we walked away from the memorial together. In front of us, a short distance away, an enormous building could be seen, exuding power and splendor. It occupied the greater part of the hill opposite, the remainder of which was covered in thick forest. This was the museum, built to a sloping design on the edge of Mount Scopus, which rises to 780 meters above sea level. Its roof followed the shape of the slope itself, allowing anyone passing by the memorial to see its octagonal design and the eight Palestinian flags that fluttered over each of the corners.

I asked Widad, "Since you're from Deir Yassin, and work in the museum, can you tell me what your family said about the massacre? I know everything that's in the books and on television, but I'd like to hear more."

We walked together along a long path, paved with red bricks, flanked by two stone walls about a meter high, on which had been placed equally spaced flowerpots with various sorts of roses growing in them. Parallel with the walls on both sides were rows of olive trees, spread out at intervals, which led up to the edge of the nearby hills to the east and west. The walls continued to rise up with the hill toward the enormous building, with twists apparently dictated by the natural environment—or perhaps whoever planned it had wanted to say that it had taken a lot of effort and required the sacrifice of hundreds of thousands of Palestinians to get to the stage of allowing the establishment of a memorial museum for the Palestinians. I noticed that there were names and dates carved on the flowerpots. It was clear that these belonged to Palestinians who had fallen on the way to the contemporary Palestinian revolution at various times in a variety of places, either resisting the Occupation inside Palestine or during the various stages when the Resistance was dispersed.

Before I could continue formulating my own explanations and commentaries on everything I saw, Widad said she would tell me everything she had heard, and that everything she would tell me was third-hand via her mother.

"Honestly," she said. "I don't remember what happened. I wasn't yet born. Anyway, this is what my mother told me, and she got it from her own mother, for she was only little herself. She said that after numerous clashes and quarrels, the people of Deir Yassin and the residents of the Giv'at Shaul settlement signed a non-aggression pact. The residents of Deir Yassin were gullible and acquiesced in the agreement, but it didn't last long. The settlement that they had the pact with was the one from which the attack on them was launched on the morning of 9 April in the year of the nakba. A band of Irgun fighters led by Menachem Begin (may God send him to hell in his grave, wherever he's buried) came down from the settlement and attacked the village . . . ."

I interrupted her: "But God didn't spare Begin, Widad. Aliza, his wife, died, and he was overcome with grief, which consumed him for ten years of his life before he died in 1993. They buried him near here, opposite the village which he and his group were responsible for destroying."

Widad went on. "My mother said that when my grandmother Zaynab left Deir Yassin, she was twenty years old, and my mother was only just four. They were all collected together in a family house. 'Either we live together or we die together,' they said. My mother heard from her mother that the massacre happened between 3:30 and 4 a.m. As the people fled in the direction of Ein Kerem, the attackers came down from above, from the hill, and a gang of Palmach fighters slaughtered twenty-seven people from the Zahran family—my husband's family—immediately. They piled them up in front of the door to the house. My husband's grandfather died with them. My husband's father was a young boy, who was brought up in an orphanage in Jerusalem. My mother had two maternal aunts who also died, the sisters of my own grandmother, may God have mercy on them."

I told Widad that what she had said reminded me of The Remainer, and the novel to be published shortly, entitled *Filastini Tays*, by my relative Jinin Dahman. I recounted how The Remainer used to go to Old Jerusalem every Friday, reaching it an hour or two before the noon prayer. He would then walk in the streets and stroll in the bazaars until the time for the Friday prayer arrived, when he would head for the Haram al-Sharif (the Temple Mount). He would then catch a taxi to take him to the Giv'at Shaul B settlement. From there, he would walk in the direction of the ruins of Deir Yassin, passing the carob and almond trees, and stopping for a while at the cypress tree that remained there. He liked that particular tree. Whenever he reached it, he would embrace its trunk and kiss it, before going to pick up a large white piece of limestone, which he would take back beneath the tree. Then he would write on the stone in black paint the name of one of the victims of the massacre of Deir Yassin, and tell himself one of the terrible stories about it that he said had opened the way to the nakba, because everyone who heard what happened in Deir Yassin at that time left his home and fled. The Remainer did that regularly every Friday until he had written the names of more than a hundred and sixty victims, each name on a piece of stone, which still exist in the form of a small pyramid near the cypress tree."

"That's a fabulous man, sir. There should be more like him. But didn't they take the tree away some time ago while The Remainer was still alive?" she asked.

"You mean, in the novel? I don't know. I haven't finished reading it all yet. But I have the impression that Jinin, if she leaves him alive, will plan a really fabulous ending for him, because he really is fabulous, as you said."

I woke, to find myself contemplating the opposite area, where the driver said that Deir Yassin was situated, but I could see only forests and a distant settlement — perhaps the Giv'at Shaul B they were talking about, or some other nearby settlement in the area. Immigration was creeping forward and swallowing things up everywhere, and the Palestinians were no longer able to keep up with or remember the names of the settlements. The settlers' advance had no end.

I turned right again, and finished my route by winding around, until I came back from the other direction to where the four drivers had been sitting. I remembered their eagerness for a passenger like me—a "Hajj," as they had called me. I could only find one of them, so I asked him to take me to the Ramada Renaissance hotel, and he welcomed me as his four colleagues had done.

8

Jaffa

As she embraced and kissed her on both cheeks, Julie told Jinin that she was more beautiful than in the novel I had introduced her to, with all its characters and events.

"Of course. I'm the one who created Jinin," replied Jinin, who was clearly pleased. "I can't allow her to please the readers more than I do."

As the digger resumed its work, I interrupted to suggest a change of scenery, telling Julie and Jinin that I didn't think a cup of coffee in Dina's was worth this noise. They both agreed with me. Jinin suggested that she should take us in her car—which she had left near the street corner—on a tour to acquaint us with the principal sights in Jaffa, then take us to the fishing port. After that, we would go to the Citadel, where we would visit her house, before going to sample a Jaffa fish lunch—"which won't yet have come out of the sea when we arrive," as she put it—at the Old Man and the Sea restaurant.

Our tour around the streets of the city didn't last long, for there was not much to stop at, apart from Clock Square, the crowded flea market, the Abulafia restaurant (which had become one of the city's main attractions, its fame overshadowing nearby Tel Aviv), and the al-Bahr mosque. We also stopped for a little while at the fishing port, before wandering through the lanes of the Citadel, many of whose houses and inside alleys appeared to have undergone restoration.

At the end of a stone staircase, we came to a blue iron gate, which shut off an area no more than a meter wide, while forcing a man of medium height to stoop. "We've arrived!" exclaimed Jinin when we reached it. Julie and I looked at where we'd come to.

A tall man with a pale complexion, apparently in his forties, who had retained much of his youthful handsomeness and agility—like the smile that he at once put on his lips—welcomed us from behind the blue gate. Jinin addressed him by name: "This is Mark Rosenblum, a Jewish millionaire. He bought this small complex, and wrote on the gate 'Private Property.'"

He opened the iron gate and welcomed us. "Welcome, guys," he said in English.

We shook hands with Mark, who introduced himself as being an artist and a sculptor, as well as a novelist. He led us to a small courtyard, the details of which seemed slightly familiar to me. A stone floor, of no particular geometrical shape and crooked edges, surrounded by a number of old two-story houses. Mark pointed to one of them and said, "Come, I'll show you my little house inside. Come on, come on, it's wonderful, you'll like it a lot."

I went up to Jinin. "And where's your own house?" I asked her.

"Not so fast, cousin," she replied. "I'll take you there in a while."

Mark pointed to some apartments on the upper floor and others downstairs. He said that painters, sculptors, and other artists lived there, that the place was his, and that he had turned it into a residential area for creative artists.

It looks as if these people have carved up the Jaffa Citadel among themselves, I said to myself, anticipating some imminent disaster.

"This is a residential area, in fact," Mark continued, "with families living in it, one here," he pointed to an upstairs apartment, "and another family there. This unit is used as a gallery, a small exhibition space. Anyone who wants to live here has to be an artist. It's an artists' colony," he explained, using the English expression.

"You mean it's a settlement?" I interrupted.

"I'm sorry," he corrected himself. "I meant to say 'artists' community.'"

"And, of course, they're all Jewish? Could someone like me live in a small apartment in this community? Or would I have to be a millionaire to get one?"

"You don't need to be a millionaire to live here," he replied.

The three of us wandered around with Mark. The place seemed quite extraordinary, and twice made Julie gasp in admiration. We then went over to his own apartment, on which he'd fixed a beautiful old door. He said he'd spent several years searching for one with its artistic specifications, until he'd come across one on a trip to India and brought it back from there.

Inside the apartment, Mark had distributed a number of his extraordinary artistic works: a metal chandelier, sculptures, and other curiosities. Some large, rusty old keys had been thrown with an artistic touch on the edge of a stone seat beside the bed. As our eyes wandered over the things exhibited in the room, Mark gave us several pieces of information about the place and its contents.

I examined the whole place, accompanied by the same strange feeling that I'd had ever since we'd crossed the small courtyard below. I felt sure that I'd already visited this house and wandered around it. My God, was I going mad? Had I really visited this place? Was I dreaming?

The courtyard was just like the courtyard that Jinin described in *Filastini Tays*, where the elderly neighbor, Bat Tzion, painted. And here, in the house that Mark said was *his* house, was a bed in the same position as the couple's bed.

And that was the corridor leading to the kitchen. And there was the window that looked out to sea . . . .

I turned excitedly toward Jinin and looked hard at her. I was by now convinced that there had been a deception on her part, which she had covered up. "Jinin, I've seen this house before!" I said confidently, straight out.

"Isn't it a surprise?" she replied. "This really is Mark's house, Walid. I live in a different city, which we'll visit if we still have time. Honestly, I borrowed the house to let Jinin and Basim live in it."

I followed where she was looking, and recalled Basim throwing his clothes onto the bed. I could see her enjoying his legs, hoping for a 'take away,' a light love feast, and not getting it. I smiled to myself, as she continued, "And this is my desk. How many times my head's fallen on it from tiredness when I've been up late writing the novel!"

"I got to know Jinin about two years ago," Mark explained. "I met her by chance as she was wandering around the Citadel, and invited her to my house. She liked it a lot. She visited it three times after that, and remembered all its details."

"It helped me to find a suitable place to locate my characters," Jinin added. "It suits everything I imagined about Basim and Jinin's life together."

I felt at that moment that I was in the novel, and I liked what I felt. I walked toward the little window, sat on the chair next to it, and started looking at the little boats bobbing in the port, the gentle Jaffa waves behind them. I heard Mark say, "Would you like to move here? If you want to, I'll help you with that."

Is this an actual offer or a provocation? I asked myself.

He repeated the question. "Would you like to live here?"

"Mark, first and foremost, the matter depends on the Israeli authorities. My being of Palestinian origin makes my getting the right to residence complicated. And my having British citizenship doesn't make things much easier."

"I'm not going to solve the Israel–Palestine problem; I'm Mark and I'm asking you: do you want to move here to live in Jaffa? To sit here, watch the sea, and write—to do in reality what Jinin did in her novel?"

When I didn't give him an answer, he continued, "You won't buy or own the house, but you'll be able to secure the right to live there as long as you're an artist. The house belongs to the church, and the church can't expel you from it, either. You can buy the right to live in it for ninety-nine years. In fact, none of us owns any of these houses."

I thanked Mark for hosting us, and for his offer, and then we left.

On the way to the famous fish restaurant The Old Man and the Sea, I asked Jinin for news of the two Basims: the Basim of the novel, and the real Basim. She told me that the Basim of the novel would leave Jinin, and return to the USA. His wife would accompany him to the airport to spend his last moments in the country with him. They would embrace for a long time, and would part slowly, allowing time for Basim's last words to her before he disappeared from her life forever: "Listen, my Junayna, I'll tell you, this society isn't ready for coexistence. It doesn't want us to go to it, and it certainly doesn't want to come to us. If you change your mind, you know where to find me."

Then he would turn and walk off, to be swallowed up by the airport.

As for her real husband Basim, she said—with some reluctant satisfaction—that he had been working for some time as a teacher in Birzeit University, and that he was in good shape. But he had refused to settle in Jaffa. Before moving to live in Ramallah, he told her that his love was in Jaffa, but his dreams were in Birzeit. And she told him that her love was in Birzeit, but her dreams were the dreams of a Jaffan.

She said nothing for a moment, but seemed unhappy with her silence, and quickly broke it to say, "Ever since Basim left here, our marriage has become a sort of 'transit': sometimes he comes to me, and sometimes I go to him. Our whole life has become a 'take away.'"

During lunch, I was busy removing a small, slender fishbone from my fish when the restaurant manager, Abu Zaki, came up to me, and whispered that he had left a table reserved in a nice corner of the restaurant, which he would not allow anyone to sit at. He said it was for an exiled Palestinian writer, a mutual friend on Facebook, and that it would stay waiting for him until he was able to come to the country and visit the restaurant. Abu Zaki had given instructions to all the restaurant staff to change the tablecloth every day, and to put a new bunch of roses on the table. I stopped what I was doing, and listened, astonished, to what the man was saying. He confirmed that the table would continue to wait for its rightful occupant until he and his staff saw him in the restaurant, sitting there and looking at the sea. Abu Zaki would then send a group of fishermen into the open sea, and prepare appetizers for him until the fishermen brought back fish worthy of his return.

Amid Julie and Jinin's astonished gasps, which could be heard through the whole restaurant, I showered him with sarcastic looks, and accused him jokingly of acting the fool. Abu Zaki grabbed me by the right arm and pulled me up. I left the table, and had hardly taken two paces when Julie caught up with me, followed by Jinin. The man led us to a table by the restaurant window, which looked over the merrily clashing waves. I stood with the two women beside Abu Zaki, looking incredulously at a table, in the middle of which was a vase holding a bunch of roses, with a white, pyramid-shaped piece of porcelain in front of it. With confused emotions, we read what was written on it in English, Arabic, and Hebrew: 'Reserved for the Palestinian writer Khaled Issa.'

I asked a waiter in the restaurant to take a group photo on my cellphone of us all around Khaled Issa's table, which he did. Then I quickly published it on my Facebook page, as we all returned to our table and finished our lunch. When we had finished eating, I cried in a voice that reached Khaled Issa in Sweden, but was heard by no one else.

I turned to Jinin, who was drinking her coffee, and asked her where she actually lived, having now discovered that the place in the old Jaffa Citadel was just a house for her in her novel, and that the real occupier was a foreigner called Mark Rosenblum. She said that she lived in a rented apartment in Jaffa Street, which she said was next to the sea. The apartment was a reasonable size, and got the sun most of the day, on its east side in the morning, and the west side in the evening. It had a balcony, which overlooked a back street, and was shaded by the leaves of an enormous tree. She said that because of this she had started to live in two streets and belong to two neighborhoods—she would watch the pedestrians in the morning from the window to the east, and spend happy evenings on the balcony overlooking the sea.

I had enough time left before our train back to Haifa for me to ask my postponed questions about *Filastini Tays*—especially the scene that left the reader in suspense, when The Remainer went out from his house carrying two signs on which he had stuck two pictures, one of the massacres at Deir Yassin, and the other of the massacres that the Jews had suffered in Kiev. At the time, he had told Husniya that he would be going to Rabin Square (formerly known as Kings of Israel Square, until the right-wing extremist Yigal Amir assassinated Yitzhak Rabin in 1995), which made his wife's heart quiver like the stalks of mulukhiyeh between her fingers, as Jinin had put it in her novel.

Jinin put her cup of coffee to one side, and began.

"I'll tell you first," she said, "about my father, Mahmoud Dahman, whose story has been with you since you were a small child, Walid, as you told me the first time we met in your house in London. Then we'll talk about the scene you referred to in the novel.

"Just two days before his death, I traveled to Amman to attend the wedding of Asdud, the daughter of my sister Bisan, and I brought back with me a video of the wedding for him to watch. He hadn't been able to travel to take part in it or celebrate the wedding of his granddaughter, because his illness had been getting worse. Despite being unable to sit on the sofa to watch the television for more than a quarter of an hour, he watched the whole video, which took a full hour to show. He smiled as he pointed at all the relatives who were at the wedding. Suddenly, he recalled Ghazza, and asked me, 'Why didn't Ghazza attend her niece's wedding? She went to visit Gaza, so she could have traveled from Dammam to Amman to attend the wedding!'

"'Ghazza didn't know the date of the wedding, Father,' I replied, 'because your granddaughter's fiancé postponed it twice. Then Ghazza went straight to Gaza, and she couldn't get out, either via the Rafah crossing or by the Beit Hanun crossing. Ghazza was lost in Gaza, Father.'

"He shook his head and said, with a sorrow that was to be the last sorrow of his life, 'I wish I hadn't left Ghazza in Gaza the year of the nakba. I wish I'd brought her out with me, her and her mother.' Then he asked me to take his hand and help him get up, then take him to his room so that he could lie down on his bed.

"His death was hard and painful for both him and me. All his children were scattered far away, inside and outside the country. Even Filastin, the eldest of us, missed the moment when our father passed from us. He'd been out since the morning, looking for work. Poor Filastin, he was in the same situation as my husband Basim, perhaps even more complicated. Whenever he found a job and submitted an application for it, he received a rejection because of his name. Once, the official told him quite openly and brazenly, 'Come back when you've changed your name, my friend!'"

Jinin wiped away the tears that had crept into her eyes, as Julie and I wiped away a cloud of sadness that had swept over our faces. Then Jinin put her hand into her bag and took out some papers. She selected one of them and said, "This is the last scene I sketched for The Remainer." But instead of reading from the page she'd taken out, she put it to one side and said, "Let me also wrap up part of another puzzle, Walid. It's important for my readers, in fact."

I listened to her without interrupting as she continued. "Do you recall when The Remainer took the two pictures, and was about to go out, but felt the heavy key in his pocket at the door, so he propped the two pictures up to one side, and went back into his room?"

When I assured her that I did remember, she went on. "Well, my father put the key in his desk drawer. After he'd died, I passed by the desk and found the drawer unlocked. I pulled it open and found in it a notebook of his memoirs. On top was a piece of paper on which was written: 'Let everyone read them.' I understood. I became preoccupied with publishing the memoirs of my real father. Your friend, Salman Jabir in Haifa, is going to publish them for me."

Then she turned to Julie to apologize to her, and said, "I shall have to read the scene relating to the end of the novel in Arabic, so I hope Walid can summarize it for you later in English." Julie nodded in agreement, and I did the same. So Jinin proceeded to read:

The Remainer went out, carrying the two signs, and headed in the direction of Rabin Square. When he reached it, he stood with the two signs held up in his hands, next to the speakers' platform. There were more than half a million Israelis in the square, holding a rally to celebrate the victory of an extremist right-wing party in the parliamentary elections. Then, in a clumsy challenge to a group of madmen, he started singing the Internationale.

Suddenly, a shot rang out. The demonstrators pushed each other, shouting in alarm: Aravim, Aravim! Shout was piled on shout as they rushed in all directions. At that moment, The Remainer fell to the ground, his blood covering two shattered wooden signs by his side.

Mahmoud Dahman died, the man who was my father and who played his own part in this novel. The cleverest man I knew in my life, and the stubbornest Palestinian in the book. A man who refused to leave the country in 1948, both in reality and in these pages, despite the fires, destruction, death, fear, and murder, which were as widespread as a reckless autumn storm come to harvest everything. He died under the feet of Israelis stampeding with fear, because of an illusion on which their parties and politicians, left and right alike, had been living. He died proclaiming to them, in sound and image, a humanity free from any blemishes that men themselves might attach to it.

But The Remainer didn't actually die. I rebelled against my closing scene of the novel you have read, a probable scene of death, in the light of the rise to power of the Israeli right, and the rapid drift of the country toward the extreme right and the hatred of everything Arab. The Remainer arose from his presumed death, picked up his two signs, and left the square, which had ended its celebration of an angry rightist inferno. He walked away from the torn placards that those taking part had left behind—together with their cigarette stubs, empty cartons, and shards of drinks bottles—in the biggest Israeli square in the country, and departed.

The Remainer walked back with his two signs that no one had looked at. He walked on, accompanied by a voice that repeated the *Internationale* with him and promised him that they would return together:

So, comrades, come rally,
And the last fight let us face,
The *Internationale* unites the human race!

"My God, Jinin, what a beautiful, fantastic ending!" I cried, and Julie, who had been watching the emotions cross my face, cheered along with me.

9

The Tenth Day

Walid and Julie completed their travel formalities in Ben Gurion Airport in Lydda. Before sitting down at a table in the spacious circular departure lounge, waiting to be called for boarding via Terminal 3, Gate C-9, Walid ordered two cups of coffee for himself and Julie, and the pair of them sat there sipping them, mulling over the events of the preceding nine days. The tenth and final day of their trip would be complete when they arrived in London in the evening.

Walid Ahmad Dahman

Against the background of the footsteps of the Ethiopian girls who worked in the airport, Walid came to himself, to ask Julie jokingly, "Shall we buy a piece of land in the Dahman quarter that was originally ours?" In his heart, he thought it unlikely that the Amidar Israel National Housing company would sell him land that most Jews considered a gift from a god they'd appointed as director of a company selling land and real estate that belonged to Palestinians in exile. But his heart also acknowledged that Julie's suggestion both disturbed him and aroused his curiosity, prompting him to pose several perplexing questions. Should he return after this visit as a tourist, to go from time to time to the Israeli Ministry of the Interior, the Misrad Hapnim—like his relative Jinin, who although she had an Israeli passport, had struggled for years on behalf of her husband, Basim, to secure a residence permit in his own country? Would Walid apply for residence permits for himself and his wife in his own country? Where would they live? In Acre, which was no more than some fragments of recollections of old facts that Julie had gathered from her mother's dreams and of present realities from their visit that they were now bringing to a close? Or in his birthplace of al-Majdal Asqalan, where he had opened his eyes after emerging from his mother's womb, then perforce had closed them again and not set eyes on the place again for sixty-two years—to find it just the fragments of a city that had five thousand years ago been the flower of the cities of the Canaanites? What about Haifa, the mere mention of whose name was enough to drive every Palestinian mad? Haifa, at whose waters Salman had gazed from the window of the Kalamaris Restaurant, suspended in the air, and had seen it reposing calmly in its bay, the waves of the sea washing the feet of Mount Carmel. Wasn't it Haifa that had made him madly shout its name, until the eyes of all those present were fixed on him and on us? "Woe, woe for this land, I don't know how we lost it!" And several people in the restaurant, men and women alike, replied with one voice, until the mountain shuddered, and cried with them: "Woe, woe, and a hundred woes!" Haifa, with the Baha'i gardens hanging over its chest like bunches of joy; with the Arab cafés and restaurants adorning the chest of Abu Nuwas Street in the German quarter, letting Fairuz, Umm Kulthum, Halim, Amr Diab, Nancy Ajram, and the lovers of the evening and Arab entertainment, old and new, wander among their midst; Haifa, which blew the mind, even when Hezbollah shelled it and one of their rockets hit the building of *al-Ittihad*, the Haifa newspaper, and another rocket killed four of its Palestinian sons.

Luda, Jamil, Aida, Salman, Julie, and Walid himself—Haifa really did drive everyone crazy!

10

Julie Littlehouse

As she sipped her coffee, she took herself to task for hiding the truth of what had happened in her grandfather Manuel Ardakian's house when she went to place the ashes of her mother there. She recalled the details of the bitter episode, and rehearsed to herself how she might relate them. She would need to decide whether to put it all in front of Walid as soon as the plane took off, or else deny it so that her heart would remain at peace forever.

"When I reached the tenth step on the iron staircase that led up to the house, I stopped. I looked behind me. Fatima was still there, waiting for me at the bottom of the staircase. I went up step by step to the sound of the church bells ringing a strange, funereal peal. I kept going up until I reached the final step. I stood directly opposite the front door. The church bells stopped ringing. I felt their silence strangling me. I heard my heartbeats. I was nervous and afraid. I turned around again and noticed Fatima hit the air with her fist, then walk away. I understood her gesture. I turned around and banged on the door with my fist.

"After a few seconds, the old, two-paneled door opened, and I found myself confronted by a woman, apparently in her fifties, blocking it with her arms. I explained to her briefly, in English, the purpose of my visit. She said something that I didn't understand in reply, though I could feel the impact of her sharp tone. Then a man appeared behind her, at least ten years older than her, wearing thick glasses. He said something to her that sounded like a question. I looked from one to the other, imploring either of them to let me understand something of what they were saying, but without success. For a few moments, I was overcome by embarrassment, fear, and tension. The woman let her arms fall from the two edges of the door and stepped back a little. The man moved forward. He took her place and asked me in broken English what I wanted. I explained to him the purpose of my visit. When he understood, he jerked back and said first in Hebrew, 'Lo, lo, lo, lo!,' then in English, 'No, no, no, no!' as he refused my request.

"'Please, sir, the soul of my mother will never disturb you,' I begged him. 'Listen to me. She is listening to us now.'

"'Lo, lo, lo, lo!'

"The man looked at the glass container like someone looking at an evil spirit that's emerged from the darkness, wanting to drive it away. 'We do not accept strangers in our house,' he shouted. 'Go on, go on, go away!'

"I didn't go away. My feet were nailed to the threshold of the door, almost against my will. The man rushed toward me, threw himself on me, and snatched the statue from my hands. He hurled it over my head and slammed the door hard in my face. The statue flew several meters up in the air, then fell. I heard the sound of it smashing on the staircase. I covered my mouth with my hands to stifle a scream from inside me as my body shook. The church bells started to sound again. I watched the ashes of my mother rise into space in small, scattered clouds, which disappeared in the city sky. I stared around me like a madwoman as I went down the steps, then went back up again, until I chanced upon the silver chain lying on one of the steps, half of it hanging over the edge, covered with my mother's ashes. I picked it up and quickly left."

Julie put down her empty coffee cup on the table. She closed her eyes for a few moments to listen to her inner voice, which was like a beating of her conscience. *What will I gain if I tell this story to Walid?* she wondered. *Ivana wanted part of her body to return after her death, whether it stayed in a beautiful porcelain statue that looked like her—as she had dreamed before she died—or was scattered in the air of the city, and dispersed in its various quarters, as actually happened. And after it left Usfur Square, it could well have turned into a cloud, carried along by a light breeze, which would take it to every part of the country. In the end, Ivana returned to Acre.*

That comforted her. She smiled to herself, then turned her smile to Walid, and asked him, "Did you think about my suggestion?"

Walid put his cup of coffee on the table. He looked into Julie's eyes for a few seconds, and was about to say something, but was interrupted by an announcement: Terminal 3, Gate C-9 was now open for passengers on British Airways flight number 559 to London.

The couple picked up their hand baggage, and held each other's hand. Walid turned to Julie and said, "I think it's a good idea."

"Wow!" exclaimed Julie.

"We'll talk about it when we get home," he added, as they continued their way to the gate.

Selected Hoopoe Titles

Embrace on Brooklyn Bridge
by Ezzedine C. Fishere, translated by John Peate

The Baghdad Eucharist
by Sinan Antoon, translated by Maia Tabet

Tales of Yusuf Tadrus
by Adel Esmat, translated by Mandy McClure

*

hoopoe is an imprint for engaged, open-minded readers hungry for outstanding fiction that challenges headlines, re-imagines histories, and celebrates original storytelling. Through elegant paperback and digital editions, **hoopoe** champions bold, contemporary writers from across the Middle East alongside some of the finest, groundbreaking authors of earlier generations.

At hoopoefiction.com, curious and adventurous readers from around the world will find new writing, interviews, and criticism from our authors, translators, and editors.